CLAIRE MORRIS IS COMPLETELY LOST

KRISTINA THORNTON

NORTHODOX PRESS

Northodox Press Ltd
Maiden Greve, Malton,
North Yorkshire, YO17 7BE

This edition 2024

1
First published in Great Britain by
Northodox Press Ltd 2024

ISBN: 978-1-915179-37-1

This book is set in Caslon Pro Std

For Rich. I was lost before I found you. Stop laughing!

In memory of my dad.

For Debra and Sonya. Purely for the excitement levels.

Chapter One

Claire has the strongest urge to twirl, so she does. Face pointing to the sky, while lifting her arms up, the falling snowflakes land on her closed eyelids and upturned palms. The end of the working week is always something to celebrate, but to scurry out of her high-rise London office building into surprise snow is worth the child-like rejoicing.

Maybe I could run home and get the sledge? Perfectly normal for a twenty-four-year-old, right? Have I even got a sledge?!

'Concentrate. You're going to be late,' she mutters.

She stops spinning, shakes her head, and immediately glares at a fancy-looking couple. They're walking arm in arm, staring, and whispering about her winter ballet recital. Claire flicks her curly, brown hair off her shoulders and down her back before shivering and buttoning up her coat. Stomping towards the tube station, she runs through the evening's itinerary in her head. Bending and hooking her petite frame into the wind to shelter from the icy conditions. The plan is to get the tube to Enfield, meet Dad from work, and go to that Italian restaurant he loves for a pre-Christmas father-daughter treat.

Claire glances at her watch: 5.36pm. It'll take at least half an hour to get there, without the walks either side. She's already running behind and already talking herself out of the evening. It's got nothing to do with her work buddies heading to the pub after work, she's sure of it. It's also got nothing to do with

1

the conversation she was planning to have with Dad.

The pub, the chat, both irrelevant.

She factors in the time, the weather, the fact she'll see him soon for Christmas dinner anyway, and saunters away from the tube towards the pub to see her friends. She flips her phone open and holds down number three.

'Daughter!'

'Hi, Dad.'

'I'm just finishing up. It wasn't looking good. Larry thought he'd broken one of the machines, but it turns out he hasn't—'

Shit, he sounds excited. She can picture him smiling and standing at his desk, looping the dangling, coiled phone cord around his finger. Claire can almost smell that slightly sweet, yeasty aroma. Sometimes, after school, Dad would take her to the bread factory, while he finished up work. She stapled documents and stared out of the window.

'Dad,' Claire interrupts, 'I'm sorry, I'm not going to be able to make it tonight.'

'Oh,' her dad says quietly. Silence hangs in the air for a few seconds. 'That's a shame,' he concludes.

'I've only just finished. It's been a hell of a day and it's snowing. I've got to get the tube over, which takes bloody ages. It's going to be cutting it fine,' Claire says hurriedly, twiddling her hair and repeatedly tucking it behind her ear. Her curls remain behind her phone-free ear, but she keeps smoothing and re-tucking.

'Okay, yeah, probably best not to travel and venture too far when it's snowing. Very sensible, Claire,' he shouts, his voice distorting with the crescendo of his sentence.

She can tell by the hurt hanging on each syllable that he's rubbing his bald head, backwards and forwards. A habit he's developed when he's thinking or stressed. When he had hair, he'd let her play hairdressers. She would weave bunched up strands into tiny plaits, tying each at the bottom with brightly coloured bobbles. That thick, brown bushiness is long gone.

'Sorry. I'll see you next weekend for the big day, anyway.' Claire grimaces and licks her teeth.

I could talk to him about Mum then. Get it done before the New Year. I'll just tell him that I'm thinking about trying to find her. What will he say? Her stomach flips and churns.

'That's true,' he's speaking softly again.

'What?' Claire is jolted back into the conversation she's having now. 'Yeah. Another time, yeah? Something to look forward to in January once Christmas is done?' *I will re-book the table. I'm not just saying it to make me feel better and get him off the phone. I'm not.*

Eating out still feels like pure luxury. They rarely went to restaurants when she lived at home. Dad taught her how to cook and as a teenager she would get his dinner ready for when he got home from work. Shepherd's pie was his favourite and still is, not that she's made it for years. She can't remember the last time she got out that cream dish with the flowers down the sides. Last Christmas, it was just the two of them, as usual. Present opening, piles and piles of food, then loads of chocolate, a mammoth game of Monopoly, capped off by crappy telly. As usual, he won. Always with stupid Mayfair and Park Lane. She had a strop, so he gave her a cuddle, and passed her the Quality Streets. It was pretty perfect.

But Claire wants more, more family. She needs to speak to Dad, but not yet, soon, but not yet.

'Yeah, that would be nice.' Wind blows into the phone. 'Where are you now?' Dad asks.

'Just walking to the station. Think I'll have an early night.' Claire clears her throat.

'Okay, stay safe. Bye, daughter. See you soon.'

'Bye, Dad.'

As Claire closes her phone, she arrives outside the pub. She puts her mobile back in her handbag and peeks through the steamed-up window to see Charlie, Helen, and Victoria inside.

She hops in and tries to push any thoughts of her dad away, but he's still there, niggling away. Serious chats can wait. He was young once. He gets it. It's fine.

The pub is bustling with Christmas cheer. Early evening on a chilly Friday night in December and everyone is already in the festive spirit. It's rowdy. People are laughing loudly and drinks are being spilled as arms gesture wildly. Claire orders a Pinot Grigio before joining her colleagues. They're surprised to see her. She tells them her dad cancelled their plans, so she's free for a few drinks. They talk about the office gossip, which mainly centres around the boss having an affair with the new lad. It's all anyone can talk about.

'What do you think about him, Claire?' Helen asks.

'Yeah, he's a bit of alright.' She isn't going to tell them she's already snogged him and she isn't going to tell them that the rumours are true. He told Claire a few weeks ago about sleeping with their much older, married, and rather uptight boss. Well, she must be in her forties and he's in his twenties. The best sex he's ever had. That's what he said. It seems the uptight boss is actually the adventurous boss. Claire's bursting to share, but sometimes it's best to keep your mouth shut.

'So you would then?' Charlie says.

'Yeah, wouldn't you?' Claire raises her eyebrows.

'I might have already,' Charlie says slowly.

Everyone gapes. Open mouths all round.

'What?' they all shout.

'Just a snog on a night out!' Charlie holds up her hands.

Bloody hell, he's been everywhere. Claire definitely isn't going to say anything now. After about twenty minutes of kiss details, conversation moves on to their Christmas plans, and whether everyone's finished their shopping. Claire sips her wine. Having a good gossip with her workmates is the release she needs at the end of another long, boring week. She isn't sure how much longer she can be an admin assistant for. It isn't her passion and never has been, but it's easy, pays the bills, and funds her nights out. She can't quite bring herself to try and make it as a journalist. Her training at uni already feels like a distant memory. It's so competitive. What if she tries, then fails? Quite frankly, it's easier not to try. A sip of alcohol and these thoughts always creep in. So, instead of being lost in her own career misery, Claire tries to focus on the conversation her friends are having. She's reclining on a booth sofa-thing, watching Charlie and Helen argue about how the office printer works, when her phone rings. It's a number she doesn't recognise. She frowns at the silver flip phone as it flashes and blares out *Toxic* by Britney Spears, before she hurries outside into the snow.

'Hello?' she answers, while gazing back through the pub window.

'Hello. Is that a… Claire Morris?'

'Yes, who is this?'

'My name's Doctor Hawkins at North Middlesex Hospital. What's your relationship to Alex Morris?'

'He's my dad.'

'We've got your dad here. He's been in an accident. Can you come down to the hospital?'

'Yes, I'll be there as soon as I can. What's happened?'

'We can tell you more when you get here. See you soon.'

'Bye,' Claire whispers. She closes her phone, slowly pushing against the hinge, while looking at her feet in the white stuff and then back through the window at her friends who are playfully arguing and laughing, before running to get a taxi.

In the back of the cab, Claire doesn't know what to think, what to do. She just needs to get to the hospital. Her head feels light, yet heavy. *An accident.* The doctor was very to the point while also being incredibly vague. *He didn't want to tell me details over the phone.* She's still holding her mobile. She hesitates for a second, gulps down the rising panic, and with shaky hands, calls Chris.

'Hello?' Chris says, the greeting dripping with aggravation.

Yes, I know we're no longer together, but I need you. 'Chris, it's

Claire.'

'Yeah, I know. I thought you were never going to speak to me again?' Chris laughs.

Music and general pub hum pour down the phone. He's out. As always. He's probably wearing his favourite burgundy shirt, his dark hair gelled to perfection, and aftershave seeping from every pore. *Yes, you cheating bastard; I was planning on having nothing to do with you.*

'Something's happened with my dad. I'm on my way to the hospital now. Can you meet me there?' her voice wobbles.

'Oh, right. I'm out,' he slurs.

'I know, I can hear that. I'm struggling here. Can we just forget about all the shit that's gone on for a second? I need... I need... some support.' Sobs burst out of Claire.

She's asking for help and not holding back. A common theme in their arguments was Chris thinking she wasn't fully invested. He often thought she wasn't bothered about him, but the opposite was true. She was obsessed with his cheeky smile, gregarious nature, and carefree spirit. Her coldness was about protection, not a lack of interest. Building trust takes time, especially for Claire. Then he did what he did.

'I'm sorry your dad's in hospital. But I'm not your boyfriend anymore. Can't you call Saskia or something?' It's suddenly eerily quiet. He must have stepped outside.

Claire snaps her mobile shut. She'll do this alone.

#

At the hospital, Claire can't find the right ward. She keeps receiving directions and then getting lost again. All the corridors look and feel the same with their cream walls, squeaky blue floors, and anti-septic mugginess. The flooring system doesn't make sense. There are numbers and letters, but 2B doesn't seem to come after 2A. It's excruciating. A nurse, a porter, and a barista give her directions and she tries to listen, but she can't focus through the tears, the glass of wine, and the worry.

She finally arrives and is asked to wait in the family room. It's nothing more than a tiny, boiling hot cupboard. There's one small window which is cracked open slightly. Claire's legs give way next to it and she crumbles into a chair before opening the pane of glass wider, to let the cold wind flow over her face, and push her tears away.

A couple of medical-looking people come in and take their seats. A man and a woman, both middle-aged and knackered. They introduce their perplexing titles and names; the woman speaks first and then the man. Claire is struck by their calm and deliberate delivery.

Their uniforms and serious faces seem to merge into one, until she hears something familiar. 'What did you say?' Claire says abruptly.

The man pauses. 'I'm Doctor Clive Hawkins. We spoke on the phone.' His eyes are steady and locked on her, his expression, unreadable.

'Yes,' Claire says quietly. She wants to shout and demand that he get on with telling her what's happened, but now she's here and is about to be told, she's not sure she wants to know.

'Your dad was in a car crash, along with his friend, Larry, who has minor injuries. Your dad. I'm sorry. He didn't make it. We believe Alex passed away almost immediately,' Doctor Hawkins says in a sombre tone.

He carries on speaking and giving more details. She lets the words and all the wretchedness they hold wash over her, as she tries to process their meaning.

It appears another car hit the passenger side – Dad's side of the car – at high speed.

The machines are keeping him alive, but he's gone.

His brain is dead.

They're sorry.

They did everything they could.

He was brought in by air ambulance.

He was given CPR at the scene by a witness and then by paramedics.

There hasn't been any brain activity since he arrived.

He's been gone since impact.

It probably all happened before he realised.

Her head is foggy, distant, and detached. She gazes out of the window, which looks out onto the hospital car park. It's full. People are coming and going. *Are some of them dealing with what I'm dealing with?* You'd never know. A man with a plaster cast on one leg hobbles on crutches, a woman hooked up to a drip is smoking a cigarette at the entrance, and another woman is shouting at her kids to stop running in a car park.

'Do you want to see him?' the woman sitting next to Doctor Hawkins asks. Her name badge says, "Tara Smith, Chief Nurse".

Claire refocuses on the room, and nods as she tries to take in the barrage of information.

No brain activity, air ambulance, machines.

She's in the room, she can hear what they're telling her, see their lips moving, and understands what is being said. But it feels like she's watching herself. She's one step removed from the atrocious sentences spilling from the mouths of these people in front of her. Her brain feels cloudy and in slow motion.

Is this really happening?

He must have got a lift with Larry after work, when I cancelled.

Should she be calling people now, to let them know? No, that can wait. She doesn't feel like talking to her dad's friends, not yet. His brother, she should call his brother, Uncle Arthur. That's his name. She will, but not yet. She could call Saskia to come and keep her company. Claire's sure her best friend would be here in an instant, ready to crack some jokes to try to lighten the mood, not that the mood can be lightened. No, the calls can wait.

'Take as much time as you need,' the nurse says before leaving.

Claire swallows and hovers at the end of the bed.

He looks like Dad.

There are a few tiny cuts on his face, but other than that, you wouldn't know he's hurt. Well, more than hurt. He could be sleeping. His eyes are half-shut/half-open. He sometimes does that in his sleep. She feels jittery, so she treads around to the side of the bed to hold his hand. After a few beats, she snatches her hand away and his drops onto the sheets. It feels so unnatural. When was the last time they held hands? She should tell him she loves him because she does. But when was the last time they said that to each other? *Had they ever?*

She drags a bright orange plastic chair to the bed, to sit and face him, to just stare and try to take it in. The bawling then stops, and she feels numb. This awful thing has happened, and all she wants to do is ask him how she should deal with his death. She needs to talk to him about this.

Claire can't take her eyes away from him. She observes and waits for him to twitch or move in some way, yet he's frozen. The life support is keeping him here, but he's already gone. The urge to bolt, to run, and keep running away from the horror in front of her is strong, but at the same time she never wants to leave, because then she would have to continue without him.

While gingerly stroking his arm, she watches the machines, and she watches him. 'I love you, Dad,' Claire whispers and tries holding his hand again, but it feels too strange, so she holds her own shaky hands in her lap. 'Thanks for always being there. What am I going to do without you, eh?'

There's a glimmer of hope he'll respond. For a split second, she waits for his reply, but there's nothing. How dare he?

It's truly shocking. She can't fathom it. It's beyond her.

He really is dead. They're not just saying it.

She scans the white room of wall and curtains. It's just the two of them, as always.

Claire pushes the chair back as she stands up, the legs scrape on the floor, seemingly shrieking her pain. She strokes the small cuts on his face while holding onto his arm. One hand is tender and loving, the other is tight and gripping, like a newborn's strong grasp.

'Daddy?' she whispers.

The tears flow and splash onto his forearm and drip onto the bed. The need to cuddle him takes over, and she throws her arms around his neck. He still smells like Dad. There's still a hint of him.

Claire breathes in his mango shampoo and kisses his cheek. 'Bye, Dad.'

Chapter Two

Five Months Later…

Sunday 6th May 2007

Claire is lost. Completely disorientated in the woods behind her new home. She's been living in the quiet Peak District village of Baliston for all of… one day. Tugging a leaf from a branch, she rubs it between her fingers, and rips it apart. Each tree looks like the last and the narrow, muddy path is never-ending. The dense wood sways in the wind, mocking her. Alone, she's isolated in beauty, nature becoming less beautiful by the second. The sky offers nothing. There are no clues to her whereabouts in the clouds.

Birds are tweeting away, like they do. She rubs her sweaty forehead. The pigeons coo-cooing sound oddly judgemental and Claire can't identify the other birds making a racket.

How do ordinary people know different bird calls?

She knows: pigeon. The end.

The rustling, squawking, and earthy bitterness remind her of trips to the countryside when she was a child. Claire manages a small smile. She once jumped straight into a huge cow pat, thinking it was a large shiny stone. Dad shouted at her for being so silly, before realising the ridiculousness of the situation, and started laughing hysterically to the point where he was unable to help her clean her shoe.

Hotness creeps up Claire's neck and reaches her cheeks at

her most recent rural mishap. The London city girl lost in the country on her first outing. Dad's deep yet quiet voice rattles around her head. *You should've looked at a map and planned your route.* Claire rolls her eyes. The map obsession started after they went for a holiday hike years ago – funnily enough in Derbyshire – and found themselves going round in circles. *We never did get to have that lovely pub lunch.*

Dad was fuming that day.

Hilarious.

A map would be advantageous right now, actually, not that Claire's exactly astute at reading them. How do you know where you are in relation to the map?

The heat prickles the back of Claire's neck. She stops walking and once again surveys her surroundings. The bushes, the trees, and the encompassing brambles all feel familiar, but she doesn't know if she's been here before or not. Everything blurs together, browns and greens, everywhere. She blasts out a long, piercing scream. It scratches her throat and shakes her chest, but liberates some of her anguish and frustration. A squirrel scurries away and birds flap off. Her high-pitched assault on the quiet hangs in the air. Claire squints into the bark, into the undergrowth, through the darkness within the bushes. Something is moving erratically, but she can't see what. She rubs her hands down her face before following the track towards the movement. *What am I doing?* This area looks different, it actually looks different. She's not been here before, she's sure of it; she isn't retracing her steps, she's stumbled upon an alternative route. Claire, released from the sea of leaves, finds herself in space, next to a field. A horse neighs loudly and aggressively, and it becomes clear what the thrashing was. The animal has managed to get his head stuck in the fence, which surrounds the grass. Captured between two wooden planks, he keeps trying to break free, but each time he moves, he scratches his nose on barbed wire.

She steadily approaches the large white and grey speckled horse.

'Hey, boy.' She strokes between his eyes, away from his injuries. He flinches at first, but her touch seems to calm him and he stops trying to pull his head through the gap. Deep cuts criss-cross his nose. 'The grass isn't always greener on the other side, hey boy?' she speaks in a quiet, singsongy tone. Claire pinches the barbed wire on the twisted flat part separating the spikes and pulls it down. 'Go on,' she says and gently pushes his nose.

The horse twists his head, and this time isn't scratched by the sharp metal and manages to free himself. He stands for a moment as still as a statue, and observes Claire, as if to show his gratitude and then gallops off. Claire beams. She can't help herself and find her way, but she can help a horse. Surely, she must be near a farm or stables or something, if somebody keeps horses here? While inspecting her new environment, she sees a red-tiled roof in the distance. She puts her hands over her mouth, in an effort to return her earlier scream, before jumping up in celebration of civilisation. Maybe someone heard her. Hopefully, she can ask for directions.

See, I can sort myself out. Well, she's not had much of a choice since Christmas. No Dad, and any plans to try to find Laura, her mum, abandoned. Now she's chosen to be even more alone in Baliston, but at least she's not going to have to "Bear Grylls it" in these woods. She'll be back to her cosy cottage in no time.

The roof belongs to one of several buildings, around a courtyard, which make up a farm. Next to towering crops, Claire's shoulders fall and she leans against one of the outbuildings, taking comfort from the bricks and mortar. Then she plods around to see if anyone is about.

Claire is standing in the middle of the courtyard when a man appears from the large Derbyshire stone farmhouse. He slams the door behind him, striding with purpose. Claire can see he's checking off a list of jobs in his head, his lips moving slightly, in between taking huge bites out of an apple. She watches him. He's about her age, maybe a little older. He's wearing a red and black checked shirt tucked into brown cords. His freshly washed, slicked back, strawberry blonde hair is starting to dry and fall into his eyes. The look is a modern take on the nineties "curtains" hair do, which every boy had at secondary school. He reminds Claire of a taller Leonardo DiCaprio in *Romeo and Juliet*. The outline of the man's muscly arms is visible through his shirt, the sleeves straining a tad at the top. As he passes her, head down, she notices the shirt is taut across his back as well, his broad shoulders trying to break free from the material.

Claire slides her lip balm laden lips together and clears her throat. 'Hi, excuse me…'

'Shit!' The man jumps out of his skin and turns around, his eyes wide and wild.

'Sorry… I was in the woods… and I'm a bit confused… about…' Claire trails off. She can feel her face reddening. She pushes her curls away from her forehead.

The man frowns, throws his finished apple into a bush, and sighs. 'The public footpath is down there.' He points to where Claire has just come from. 'There's no public access through the farm,' he says, almost shouting. He points at a green sign at the edge of the woods near the outbuildings, which does indeed say, "NO PUBLIC ACCESS". 'This is private land. You can't just go wandering around a farm unannounced. There's dangerous machinery. Trust me.' The man waves his arms around, gesturing towards some sort of robot tractor which is all shiny metal and blades. His voice is deep and monotone, he sounds bored, like he's given this speech before to unsuspecting walkers.

Claire marches off the courtyard, back to the edge of the woods. She can feel him watching her. It makes her very aware of each movement, as she puts one foot in front of the other, focusing on the slight sway of her hips. Claire tuts to herself, half expecting him to start shouting, "GET OFF MY LAND", already convinced the man is a walking, talking stereotype. She's now standing closer to him, but not in the courtyard.

As usual, Claire can feel the threat of tears, but she's refusing them. 'I was just hoping you could give me some directions. I've recently moved to Baliston, and I'm lost.'

'I didn't think you had the rambler look,' he says softly, with a definite Derbyshire twang to his words. He chuckles while giving her the once-over.

Claire looks down at her floaty summer dress and flip-flops. 'Quite,' she says.

'I'm Sebastian.' He walks towards her and reaches out to shake her hand, in a very business-like manner. She takes his hand in hers. His palm is quite soft, but his fingers are rough and scratchy.

'Claire.' She can't help but notice his eyes really are very blue. Stop-what-you're-doing-and-stare blue.

'So, you're lost, you say?' He folds his lips and puts his pointing finger over his mouth as if to ponder the situation.

'Yes, how do you get back to the village, please?' Claire says in a formal and overly polite way. She can feel him judging her. Bloody country bumpkin. There's a hint of a smirk behind his hand. She stares straight at him, her chin in the air, challenging him, daring him to take it further, and really take the piss. Claire then notices his eyes are tired and bloodshot. Fine red lines hide around the edges. They're clear to see once you get past the dazzling blue.

'The path continues, around the field, behind the farmhouse… if you follow it… you'll end up in the centre of Baliston near the shop,' Sebastian says.

'Thank you. I'll be off.' *I won't ask him if he works out. I won't.* 'By the way, what's it like being a farmer?' She wants to keep him chatting. It's to annoy the up-himself little shit and absolutely nothing to do with his arms.

'Don't know, really. I've only been doing it about a month. This place is my dad's.' Sebastian points with his thumb over his shoulder towards the farmhouse and surrounding fields.

'He's taking some time out,' his voice trembles ever so slightly on the word "out".

'Oh, right… I thought… sorry to assume…' She hangs her head. He's not what he seems. She stops inspecting the grass and their eyes meet. Claire recognises that look in his eye, she's been surprised by it, in the mirror.

'So, you've just moved here?' Sebastian says, before pulling out his phone from his trouser pocket. He starts jabbing at the Blackberry.

She instinctively reaches for her own phone in her dress pockets, but it's somewhere among the boxes back at the cottage. 'Yeah, I'm actually here because of my dad.' *Why did I say that? I don't need to tell him or anyone about what happened.* Claire adjusts the straps of her dress, then clasps her hands in front of her.

In her mind, she can see Larry at the funeral. He tried to explain what had happened that night, wanting to absolve himself. He said he wasn't speeding. He was concentrating on the road. The other car came out of nowhere.

Larry grabbed hold of her and sobbed. "I miss my best friend. I'm so sorry. I can't forgive myself".

Claire told him it wasn't his fault.

She pushes the memory away and another from last May appears. She took her dad to a charity darts event, and he absolutely loved it. He was so thankful to her for organising the night out. It wasn't her scene at all, but they donated, and her dad's excitement and enthusiasm was infectious. He knew everything about each famous player taking part. Claire listened and nodded, simply enjoying making him happy. What a difference a year makes.

'Lovely,' Sebastian mumbles. 'Will you be okay finding your way?' He starts striding towards one of the barns.

Claire frowns, then raises her eyebrows. He wasn't listening to her, anyway. Rude bastard. Sebastian didn't take in what she said at all, probably for the best. She watches him tramp away. *I guess that's my cue to go.* 'Yes, thank you for your help,' she shouts after him. Wait, the horse. 'Sebastian,' Claire shouts louder, 'before you go.'

Sebastian stops and walks back towards her. 'Yeah?'

'Do you own horses?'

'No, why?'

'There's a big white and grey horse in the field back there.' Claire thumb-points behind her, which she has literally never done. She's copying his mannerisms for some reason. She tries to disguise it by scratching her head. 'He'd managed to get his head stuck in the fence and every time he tried to get out, he kept scratching his nose on some barbed wire. I managed to free him, but his nose is injured. He was bleeding.'

'Oh, I know which horse you mean. I know the owner. I can let her know. I'm sure she'll want to get the vet out.' Sebastian pauses to study Claire, as if seeing her for the first time. 'Thank you. You said your name's Claire, right?'

'Yes,' she says, returning his stare.

'Thanks, Claire. Maybe I'll see you around the village.' He flashes her a winning smile and twitches his head to flick his hair out of his eyes.

'Maybe,' she says quietly to his back as he rushes off again. That hair flick really is quite something. *I bet he knows it as well.* Claire coughs.

Sebastian turns and waves before he disappears into the barn.

Claire follows the path back to her new village life.

Chapter Three

The next day, Claire decides to make a dent in her unpacking. The boxes have taken over her tiny cottage, making it almost impossible to move from one room to another. She had really wanted a thatched cottage to attain the perfect chocolate-box look. Here, there are tiles on the roof, but it's ideal in every other way. A nice little lounge with a wood burner. A teeny-tiny kitchen with traditional country cupboards, an Aga, and wooden beams on the ceiling. The beams are very important. They're a problem for anyone over six-feet, but for Claire the exposed timber provides the ultimate country feel, making her new home the quintessential cottage. There are two bedrooms upstairs, one for sleeping and one for all Claire's clothes and junk. At the moment, it doesn't look like a home but more of a storage facility. She unpacked the essential kitchen stuff on her first day, and now it's time to sort out all her clothes and fill the two rails in the spare room. A mind-numbing task which allows her mind to wander.

She's actually here, she's actually done it – quit her job and moved to the countryside on her own.

After organising her dad's funeral, attending the inquest, sorting probate and his will, selling the house, and tying up all his affairs, after doing an excellent impression of a tower of strength, she finally gave into that urge to crumble and run. When scrolling the internet one evening, she stumbled upon an advert for this delightful Peak District cottage, available to rent for six months. It wasn't long before she was handing in her notice on her flat and leaving her job and London behind.

Now she's here, unpacking, alone. Outside the back bedroom window, the leaves on the trees ripple in the wind. Those blasted maze-like woods. She feels clammy and her stomach does the *Macarena*. She winces as she thinks about yesterday and Sebastian. His muscly arms are quite distracting. Floppy, strawberry blonde hair, blue eyes, and freckles on a tall body make for a striking mix. Claire rips open a box with extreme vigour, while recalling Sebastian enjoying her misfortune and lecturing her about bloody land rights. Now, feeling annoyed that she's annoyed, she tries to focus on the task at hand and concentrates on straightening and hanging up clothes, finding peace in the repetition.

Why do you have so many clothes? His voice seems even more present at the moment. Claire shrugs. It's probably just the upheaval of the move. Her thoughts often turn to her dad, as if by default. They had been on many holidays to the countryside, often in Derbyshire. It was one of the reasons why her escape had been here. She'd hoped a change of scenery would mean he wouldn't be on her mind so much, but that hasn't happened yet.

A childhood memory strikes, of him pushing her on a swing. He'd refused to push anymore, insisting on her learning to make herself rock back and forth. Legs straight and forward, then tucked under to go backwards. She had understood what she'd needed to do, but she couldn't quite get it to work. She'd begged him to push, so she could enjoy herself, but he wouldn't budge. She had started to cry, before giving up and going to play on the roundabout instead.

A chocolate and magazine break is needed. She grabs her keys and puts on her shoes to walk to the village shop.

Clouds are gathering over Baliston, yet the village still belongs on the front of a postcard. Wonky and whimsical homes show their age, but are obviously cherished and cared for. Mature gardens and massive trees line the main road. There's a lot here for such a small place; a shop, a fish and chip shop, a pub, and a school. Claire scuttles along, head down. She passes neighbours talking over their dividing fence. Their voices boom and float through the air. She hears something about a knee operation being a success. A tractor rattles through, catching her attention. The driver waves at the two men.

It's like she's been dropped in another world.

Inside, Claire grabs the biggest bar of chocolate she can find. None of the magazines are catching her interest, so she picks up a copy of the local paper, *The North Derbyshire Chronicle*. The front page is about ongoing congestion around a school. As she scans the article, she cringes. The lady behind the counter glares at her, she's moments away from… "this isn't a library, you know", so Claire makes a big show of folding the paper in half and tucking it under her arm, clearly illustrating that she is in fact going to purchase the paper. Claire wanders around the shop before paying as an act of defiance, a rebellion against the establishment. She puts her nose in the air and saunters around, then feels immediately guilty for showing the smallest bit of attitude, realising she will see this woman again and again. The shop is cramped and has an oppressive feel. There're shelves stacked high, with dried pasta, tins of chopped tomatoes, and other stock cupboard stuff, but there's also crap hanging from the walls. A plastic children's cricket set, a bucket and spade (in the Midlands?!), then there're envelopes and birthday cards next to the dog biscuits. Claire surveys the dizzying mess.

You could probably get just about anything from here.

A noticeboard catches her eye. It's fascinating. A gardener is advertising, somebody needs a dog walker, someone else is trying to sell a rather old and dirty pram. One notice really stands out, on light pink paper, in exquisite, loopy writing, in thick, black ink…

HELP WITH ODD JOBS NEEDED
Cleaning, shopping, simple DIY
Around five hours a week.
Contact Hazel.

That's all it says. No telephone number or address. Just contact Hazel. Does everyone know everybody here? Claire's interested. It's surprising. It would be good to busy herself and get out of the house and stop wallowing. The money from selling Dad's house means she doesn't need a job, not for months yet, but having no job and no real purpose is already proving tough, just a few days in. Even though the plan was not to work and to process everything that's happened.

'Just these please.' Claire hands the chocolate and paper to the woman behind the counter.

The shop worker smiles. 'Do you need a bag?'

'Yes, please.' Claire gazes around the shop. 'I was looking at the notices. I was interested in one. Who's Hazel? Do you know?'

'What's your name?' the woman behind the counter answers Claire's questions with a question.

'Claire. Sorry, I should have introduced myself. I've just moved here. I'm renting a cottage up the road.'

'Ah yes, Bramble Cottage. I'm Susan, I own this place, have done for twenty years.'

'Nice to meet you.' Claire glances around again and starts studying some tiny monster toys hanging on the far wall.

'Hazel lives in the village. She didn't want to put her phone number on the advert in case of weirdos.' Susan widens her eyes at Claire to labour the point. 'You seem okay though; she lives at 5 Crampton Road. She'd prefer you to call round than ring.'

'Brilliant, thank you,' Claire says, while handing over her money and taking the shopping bag.

Susan hands Claire her change. 'What do you think of

Baliston, then?'

'Beautiful, but I'm still getting to know the place. I've only been here a few days.'

'It really is a wonderful place, but more so because of the people,' Susan says wistfully.

Claire tries to muster a smile and leaves. She hasn't come here for the people. There's too many of them in London. Always asking how she is, checking in on her.

Is there actually less anonymity in a small community?

This hadn't occurred to Claire until now. She'd imagined being surrounded by calm, no one knowing who she is. She'd spent hours reading about how trees reduce the stress-related hormones, cortisol and adrenaline. The plan is six months of solitude to reset, and then figure out what the hell she's going to do with the rest of her life. Isolation in the Peak District, the place which Dad loved, and where they'd taken many holidays. The shop woman, Susie or whatever, already knows where she's living. She didn't even need to tell her. She's only been in Baliston for all of two seconds.

It's raining. The sky is the colour of the pavement. There isn't a break in the clouds. She shoves the chocolate bar in her pocket and holds the newspaper over her head to form a makeshift umbrella. It doesn't do much, other than ruin the paper, so she rolls it up and stuffs it under her arm before marching up the main road back towards home. Back to the beautiful cottage, where no one waits for her. She sighs, the weight of everything pushing her to the ground.

A black cat shoots out of a privet hedge, dancing to avoid the rain. The sopping moggy stops her in her tracks. When the cat spots Claire, it meows and rubs its body against her legs, its tail in the air, using her as a stroking post and shelter from the rain.

'Okay, kitty... move,' Claire shout-whispers, lifting her legs up, as the slinky pet entwines itself, looping in and out. She clenches her teeth together, pressing until her jaw hurts, and looks around the street. The cat continues scraping and weaving. There's no one around, it's just her and the furry animal. 'Go!' she bellows and motions wildly with her hands. It peers up at her. They connect for a second, then it darts off, jumps up a wall and disappears into a nearby back garden.

Claire bends down to rub any fur off the bottom of her legs. There isn't really any, but she keeps brushing and picking at bits of dust on her jeans. Her hair drips into her eyes, and her mascara stings. The newspaper is becoming slippery, water falls from the front page, and the print begins to smudge.

I can't catch my breath.

She crumples into a ball, crouching on the pavement, her bottom hovering above the ground, cuddling her knees tight. Claire hugging her mum's legs when she was small flashes up in her mind. The memory makes her flinch.

The newspaper slips from her grasp and falls into a puddle. The ink bleeds, the words blur, then the tidy columns flee their boundaries.

Her eyes hurt as the tears escape.

What if someone sees me like this? A crunched up watery mess.

Claire lifts her head. She's eye level with what is supposed to be a cheeky little chap, perched on the edge of someone's front garden. The gnome has the widest smile. It's not endearing though, judgement oozes from him. One hand is nonchalantly in his dungarees pocket and the other is holding a red spade, which matches his long, red, pointy hat. His eyes bore into Claire, his cheeriness infuriating.

Who has these stupid things?

She feels pathetic, breaking down in the street in the rain, wanting to run from people, but hating feeling desperately alone. Now this gnome is laughing at her.

Laughing at her for cancelling on her dad and then never seeing him alive again.

Laughing at her for not comprehending Dad was enough.

Laughing at her for not treasuring him in the final months of his life, and instead stressing about looking for her mum, who left when Claire was three, never to be seen again.

While glaring at the ridiculous tiny pot man, Claire stands up.

She'll never get to ask Dad about Mum. She'll never be able to get his opinion on tracking her down or on anything ever again. It had always been Claire and her dad facing the world together. She struggles to recall her mum ever really being there. There are flickers of memory, snatches of a mother. Like a dream, she's not sure if they're really recollections of Laura or something she's conjured up to fill the mum gaps. Claire can remember her blonde hair and loud laugh. She remembers Laura splashing with her in the paddling pool. At least she thinks she can. The ghost of a mum who disappeared with another man.

The rain pounds on Claire's head and shoulders. Her breathing is ragged, and her heart is loud. Claire maintains her scowl at the idiotic garden ornament and clenches her fists, nails digging into her palms, just like they did when the doctor turned off dad's life support.

Dad was left to muddle through and raise Claire on his own. As she got older, he tried to date. She'll never forget the look on his face when he returned home early one night. His blind date had stood him up. He flopped onto the sofa and reached for the remote. They snuggled up together and watched his favourite programme, *Star Trek*. Dad's arm around her shoulders and balled up body. Claire listening to the rhythm in his chest. His brow furrowed.

Claire's head feels too full, and the pointy-hatted one continues to sneer at her.

She boots it.

She kicks the gnome.

It skids along the grass, then the driveway, and smashes into a wall. It shatters, loudly. Claire can't quite believe what she's done.

Shit, shit, shit.

She's sweating.

She speed-walks up the main road towards home, her body hunched against the wind and rain, her paper still in the puddle, forgotten. As she gets further away, she hears quick footsteps behind her. Claire peeks over her shoulder.

'Hello again,' Sebastian says, raising his eyebrows. He's holding a large umbrella. He stands close to Claire, but far enough away so that she remains in the monsoon.

'Hi.' *Him again.* His strong aftershave finds her nostrils. Oaky, expensive, and overwhelming. She brushes her wet hair out of her face. No harm in being more presentable.

'You're drenched.' Sebastian shivers. 'Are you okay? I saw you squatting.'

'Yes, all fine, thank you.' Claire gives a small, flat grin.

'Well, I'll let you go.'

Claire nods. 'Bye.'

They both turn to walk in opposite directions, but Sebastian turns back around to face Claire. 'Sod it,' he mumbles, 'I saw what you did.'

Claire swivels around to face him. She rolls her shoulders back, like a boxer in the ring, their entrance music still blasting out. 'What do you mean?' She arranges her face into the picture of innocence.

'You kicked and broke a gnome back there.'

'Um... no, must have been someone else.' Claire fixes her eyes on his. 'Anyway...' She shuffles to the edge of the pavement and glances left and right. 'Nice to see you again.' Claire steps down off the kerb.

Sebastian jumps in front of her. They're both now standing in the road, at the edge. 'Wait,' Sebastian says, his voice getting louder, shouting above the rain and the cars whooshing by, each one creating small landlocked waves especially designed to soak pedestrians. 'Jesus.' He brushes the water off his trousers with one hand while clutching onto his oversized brolly with the other.

'What?'

'What are you doing smashing up garden decorations? Simon will be upset. He loves his gnomes,' Sebastian says. 'These things mean a lot to some people.' He glares back at the scattered, broken pieces. While balancing the umbrella on his shoulder and holding it in place with the underside of his forearm, he rocks the strap of his silver watch, as if to check it's secure on his wrist, and then strokes the face with his thumb. Sebastian's eyes flit between the watch and the shattered gnome in the distance.

'Oh, mind your own business,' Claire elongates each word, hanging on them.

'I saw you do it. If you go back, knock on Simon's door, explain, and apologise, I'm sure he'll understand. You need to go back. You can't just leave it.'

It's the honest and honourable thing to do. He is right. Claire can admit this to herself, but not to him. He's so self-righteous and definitely one for the rules. A strong moral compass, it seems. 'I don't need another lecture,' Claire says, raising her voice. 'Wait, were you watching me?'

'I was on the other side of the road. I was only looking because you were crouched down. It's not every day you see someone almost sitting on the floor in the rain.'

'I suppose.' She shrugs like a sulky teenager.

'Are you going to do the right thing?' Sebastian asks, his voice softer.

Claire flinches. If only she had done the right thing months ago. She swallows. *I'm not going to cry again. I'm so sick of crying.*

'Come on, I'll go with you.' Sebastian takes her hand in his, in a bid to lead her back towards Simon's garden. As he looks down, Claire looks up through her eyelashes. She's aware of his soft yet firm touch, her newspaper-print-covered fingertips against his skin, her quickened breathing, and his deafening umbrella.

Claire snatches her hand away from Sebastian. 'I'm not going to tell some random man I kicked and smashed up his gnome. He won't understand and he'll think I'm insane.' She takes a deep breath. 'Look, I can't. I've got a lot going on right now. Simon will get over it.'

'We've all got a lot going on.' They contemplate each other for a few moments, both standing still, the rain dripping from Claire's nose. Sebastian's is dry, protected by the umbrella. 'Maybe I'll tell him then,' Sebastian continues.

'Oh god, will you just fuck off and get your own life!' Claire screams.

Sebastian rests his open brolly on the ground. 'Well, fuck you too.' He pumps the inner sides of his fists together, twice, in quick succession. A clear *Friends* reference, the secret fuck off gesture used by two characters, siblings, Ross and Monica when they were children. Claire can feel a smirk fighting to spread across her lips. She refuses to let it out, instead she releases a drawn-out exhale through her nose as she watches Sebastian pick up his umbrella and walk away.

What just happened? Maybe she should have gone with him and seen this Simon guy. It's all too much. Everything. She shakes her head. Her eyes sting, not only from dripping mascara. She runs back to Bramble Cottage; the deluge slapping her in the face.

Chapter Four

Two weeks pass before Claire plucks up the courage to knock on Hazel's door. It's chunky, light green, and the knocker is in the shape of a smile. The house is a small two-up two-down terrace, with wisteria climbing up the exterior. The tiny front garden is immaculate. Each flower is an equal distance apart. There are no fallen leaves, and it looks like the small patch of lawn has been cut meticulously blade by blade with scissors.

A woman answers the door. She's elderly, but her age isn't clear. She could be sixty-five or eighty-five. She's as put together as the front garden. Her grey hair is in neat curls which frame her fully made-up face. Claire's eyes are drawn to her bright red lipstick. The woman is wearing a flowery dress, with a brown belt around her waist, cinching her in to create an hourglass. Lots of bangles jingle-jangle from both of her wrists. They look like they're from around the world and each has a story. She's beautiful and really quite striking.

'Hi, my name's Claire Morris, are you Hazel?' The woman stares at her. 'I've been speaking to Susan at the shop. I wanted to apply for your job.'

The woman's face softens. 'Oh, great. Yes, I'm Hazel, and yes, I need someone around here. Do you live in the village?' Hazel says, each word is fully enunciated and posh sounding.

'Yes, I'm new. I've been here a couple of weeks.'

'Where were you before?'

'London.' Claire smiles.

'Bit different in Baliston.' Hazel tips her head back and

laughs. 'Come in, let's have a chat.' Hazel steps aside to allow Claire into her hall. She indicates for Claire to take a left just before the stairs into the lounge.

No kidding, it's a bit different. Claire hovers in the front room, waiting for Hazel to enter after shutting and locking the front door. Baliston is so different to what she's used to. She thought, before she moved here, that the quiet would enable her to process her thoughts in a more ordered way, but in reality, the silence is deafening. How is she supposed to think when she can hear... nothing? There is no background hum, just the occasional car or tweeting bird. It's unnerving.

'Sit down, I'll put the kettle on. Tea?'

'Yes please, white, no sugar.'

'I suppose you should be making it to test your skills.'

Claire can't tell from Hazel's expression whether she's joking or not, so she starts to stand up.

'Sit down.' Hazel sniggers, then slowly makes her way to the kitchen.

This Hazel woman is something of a joker. Claire re-sits down in the big, green, velvety armchair, while mentally trying to restrain the blush which is threatening to creep up her neck. She does so by diverting her attention away from her uneasiness to the room before her. The walls are white, but it's hard to tell because they're weighed down by photos, paintings, and trinkets. There's a painting of a naked couple in a raunchy embrace next to a photo of a young boy and girl, sitting next to each other in school uniforms. Grandchildren? On the mantelpiece there's a black-and-white photo of what must be a young Hazel on a horse, jumping over a thick hedge. In another, she's holding a massive pumpkin and laughing hysterically. There's another, larger photograph of Hazel on her wedding day. She's wearing a simple white dress which ends at the knee. There's no lace, no fuss. She's holding a small bouquet of roses, and there are tears in her eyes. Her husband is smiling, but he isn't showing any teeth. It's a small, almost secret smile, as if there's a shared joke. He's tall, with dark hair and is wearing some sort of military uniform. Her arm is hooked into his, and he's clasping her hand, clinging onto her with pride. Claire strokes the arm of the chair. The green velvet is worn, revealing the brown material underneath. It's comfortable and homely. There are plates and a sword hanging on the far wall. A room full of life and so many stories. Claire tries to take it all in. She wants to immerse herself in it, to focus on someone else's life, to be free of her own. She wants to hear this old woman's stories, and she's got a feeling she will.

Hazel walks into the lounge with two cups of tea. 'So, why did you move here?' she asks.

Nope, this isn't where Claire wants the conversation to go. Every time someone asks this question, she gives a different answer. Somehow it always catches her off-guard, even though it's often the first thing people ask. 'Just some time out to write my novel,' she blurts out. This is a complete and utter lie, and is a new answer, which takes Claire by surprise. As she says it, she can't quite believe she's actually speaking the words, and by the end of the sentence her voice goes up like she's asking a question. *Where did that come from?* Maybe one day she'll tell Hazel the real story, but that moment isn't now.

Hazel studies her hands. 'Oh, lovely.' She doesn't ask any more, much to Claire's relief. 'So,' Hazel says before pausing for a moment, 'why do you want this job? There's no literary glamour here.'

'I'm missing having a job and when I saw your notice, I thought, I'll be good at that,' the truth comes more comfortably from Claire's mouth, 'and, I could do with earning some cash.' She offers a weak smile.

'I would want you to spend about three hours cleaning each week, then that would leave you with a couple of hours to do the food shopping and do any little jobs around the house.

Have you done this sort of work before?'

'Well, I had an admin job in London, so I'm used to organising. I worked at a fast-food restaurant when I was at uni, that involved lots of cleaning and of course I clean my own house,' Claire says.

'Okay, let's give this a try. I can pay you ten pounds an hour. I'll employ you for a two-week trial period and we'll review it at the end of the fortnight.'

'Brilliant, thank you.'

They then sit and chat for a bit and sip their cups of tea. Hazel is charming and very welcoming. Claire can feel herself warming to her. She can see Hazel is struggling with the fact that she needs some help. While she's sitting on the sofa, holding court, telling Claire all about Jean down the road, you would never think she needs any help with everyday life. But when she gets up and walks around, she's a little slow and a little stiff, although she tries to hide it.

Claire thinks she's hidden her inner turmoil and constant feelings of guilt and grief, and successfully come across as a happy-go-lucky twenty-five-year-old until she steps out of Hazel's green door into her quaint front garden.

'Tell me about that novel sometime, girl, yeah?' Hazel peers into Claire's eyes and gives her a wink and an arm squeeze.

Claire freezes. *She knows I'm lying. She's calling me out, calling my bluff.* No, that's ridiculous. How could she know? Claire's always been crap at lying. It's just exhausting telling people about Dad, and Baliston is supposed to be her time to grieve and sort her head out in private without others constantly checking on her and asking her to talk about her feelings. This is her time for herself. She doesn't need to feel guilty about not telling people her life story. It's none of their business, anyway. Guilt is already consuming her life. Claire's at sea trying to swim against the current, the strength of the water engulfing her, gradually dragging her further out. It's taking every fibre of her being just to keep swimming, to remain vaguely in the same place. Maybe one day it'll all become too much and she'll be dragged out, far away from land, far from the person she used to be.

As so often happens, she's running their last conversation over and over in her head. It's always there, it's become a default setting. In her dream mind she gets the tube, meets up with Dad, they walk to the Italian restaurant, then eat pasta, and chat. None of these things happened, though. Instead, she went to the pub and talked shit with her mates. Her dad got a lift with Larry and died. Would that have happened if she had met him, as planned? Usually he would be in his own car, but if they went out together, often he wouldn't drive, so he could have a drink, choosing to get a taxi at the end of the night. He asked Larry for a lift home when she cancelled, as Dad was at work without his car and his daughter had bailed on their plans. Would the crash have happened if they'd got a taxi after the restaurant? Surely, they would have been on a different route at a different time and he would still be alive now.

It's my fault. Claire knows it is. If only she'd stuck to the plan.

Hazel breaks the silence and asks another question, 'Can you start a week on Monday?'

Claire frowns.

'Just got a few things to sort before you start.'

'Things that I could help with?' Claire asks.

'Not really, I'll see you a week on Monday,' Hazel whispers, and with that, she shuts the front door.

Claire scratches her forehead and walks away, glancing back at the modest brick house. She wants to run home, slam the door, get under the covers, and cry until her head throbs, then have a bath. This seems to be her life now. She needs to escape that last phone call. It haunts her. The decisions she made that night haunt her. She's not sure if she's made the right choice going for this job, but she also knows she needs... something.

Chapter Five

'I need to get out of my comfort zone,' Claire mutters, as she wanders around her cottage. She's fed up of mooching around the house and needs adventure.

She asks the man next door to borrow his bike. They've previously only exchanged "mornings", but Claire's seen him riding it and he seems nice enough. It turns out his name is Gareth. He works from home, something to do with telephones or communications, he explains, but it still isn't clear. He's happy for Claire to have his bike and helmet for the afternoon as long as she returns it to him this evening. His willingness to help someone he doesn't know overwhelms Claire. The whole exchange is disconcerting yet joyful at the same time.

Asking for help is almost alien to her. It's not something she often does. Only growing up with a dad forced her to be self-sufficient. When she was eleven, her friend, Georgia, was the first in class to start her period. The stories of bleeding for a week freaked Claire out, so she asked Dad about it. He got all flustered and confused while trying to explain about tampons. The next day, after school, he handed her a book on puberty and periods, and that was it. Conversation over. Claire read the book and school and friends filled in the gaps. Sally said her mum took her out for dinner to celebrate her "becoming a woman". When the time came for Claire, she cried in the bathroom, alone.

Later in the afternoon, after lots of faffing, Claire heads out on the men's white mountain bike, ready to take on a challenge, even if it means wearing someone else's smelly and sweaty blue helmet. She heads north, further north than she already has, hoping to see the hills of the Peak District.

Claire is huffing and puffing. The snaking, curling country roads are mostly uphill and they're steep. Maybe she should have headed south and coasted downhill all the way back home to London. She shakes her head to get rid of the defeatist thought and carries on pedalling. She tucks herself tight to the hedges on her left, in case any cars come hurtling up the road, but there's only the odd one now and then. Claire can hear the birds; the sunshine is on her face and she can already sense her shoulders are no longer around her ears. The endorphins are starting to be released, and surprisingly, it's actually quite enjoyable. She relishes the exertion needed to get up each hill before stopping to catch her breath and take a swig of water. She's sweaty, and she knows her cheeks are bright red. She feels unfit, but it's positive to be doing something, to be leaving Baliston and exploring. She sticks to the same road, going straight and following it, so when she wants to go home, she will simply turn around and go back the way she came. The last thing she wants is to get lost again.

Her mind wanders to the last time she rode a bike. It's been years. She must have been about thirteen. She wanted to ride to her friend's house, but it was a good half an hour away and Dad wasn't sure. Claire can see him now, frowning, weighing up the pros and cons. He always struggled in those moments, hesitated with no one else to talk to and ask their opinion, no one to allay his worries, it was up to him, and he hated it. He ended up letting her go; she managed to talk him into it. She promised to be back at a certain time and to take a certain route and she kept her word. He allowed her more freedom after that. He could see she was ready for more independence. Dad rewarded her maturity.

Claire continues pedalling uphill, panting. Being outside and thinking about a happy memory is a welcome relief from crying while hiding in bed or in a bubbly, hot bath. She gets to the top of the latest hill and the view is breathtaking. It could be in *The Lord of the Rings*. The different greens are intense, the hills rippling, the clouds drifting above, almost touching the tips. It seems to go on forever, a never-ending patchwork of natural beauty. Claire is struck by the wildness that lays before her. She feels so far away from home, she could be in New Zealand. It's refreshing and daunting. Claire spots a bench next to a public footpath sign and parks up the bike, before collapsing into the wood and taking out her cheese sandwich and crisps. Not a great picnic, but all she could muster. She munches while fully experiencing the scene before her, breathing it in, trying to inhale the calm. This is why she moved.

The clouds become thicker and greyer, and Claire is chilly just sitting, so she finishes up, to continue riding, maybe a touch further before heading back. The next bit is actually downhill, a rare find! She'll be able to wizz down before climbing her next Everest. Helmet on, she climbs onto the bike, which is slightly too big for her, and takes a deep breath before going for it, child-style.

She sticks her legs out straight, as if doing the splits and shouts, 'Woo-hoo!'

Laughing, she keeps her legs spread-eagled as she descends, while her hands firmly grip the handlebars. The wind noisily rushes by her ears, becoming louder as she picks up speed. The hill is longer and steeper than she had anticipated. The bike bumps over the uneven road. Claire hits a large pothole, which throws her. She tumbles through the air, bracing for impact.

#

Claire wakes up with her face being tickled by green. It's grass, she landed in the grass, that's got to be a good thing?

Was she unconscious, by the side of the road?

It's raining now, the drops spitting at her. She gingerly sits up and surveys her body. All limbs intact. Her left arm is cut and bleeding, but doesn't look serious. Now, to try standing up, to see if that's an option. She wobbles upright, and screams in pain, her left ankle is not okay. Broken? No, maybe sprained. She sits back down and lifts up her joggers to inspect the damage. Her ankle is red and swollen, like it's trying to grow and escape her leg. The bike! She scans the ground. It's by the side of the road. She rolls onto her tummy and drags it by the wheel onto the grass. The back tyre is completely flat. She has no puncture repair kit and even if she did, she wouldn't know how to use it. Her ankle is throbbing, and the rain is dripping down her back, sneakily finding the little opening between her neck and jacket.

She decides to hop to the bench.

It's terrifying.

The grass has turned to slush; the mud taking on the sliposity of an ice rink, and who hops on an ice rink?

After some stop-start and tentative one-legged jumping, Claire reaches the bench and sits down to regroup. The hills have become foreboding, the crashing hill waves, no longer inviting and magnificent, but threatening and angry. She reaches for her phone in her jogging bottoms pocket and lets out a sigh of relief when it's still there and in one piece. She flips it open. No signal. Who would she call, anyway? Who would come running to help her? She lies down on the bench. It feels better to prop up her injured ankle. The rain starts to subside, now just tickling her. At least that's something.

Claire closes her eyes. She's cold, wet, bleeding, and injured and she doesn't actually know where she is. *I need one of those red flare things that shoot up into the sky, or maybe I should use pebbles to spell out SOS.* Her head hurts, a headache like no other, a deep, sharp pain.

#

'Claire?!'

Someone is shaking her. She opens her eyes; did she fall asleep? She feels the damp wood beneath her and realises where she is… on a bench in the middle of nowhere, injured with a useless broken bike. A shadow is standing over her, and there's a green 4x4 parked next to the bike on the floor. 'A-huh?' It's all she can manage in her confused state. She tries to focus. 'Chris?'

'No, it's Sebastian, are you okay?'

'No.' Claire blinks several times while studying Sebastian's face. Nope, definitely not cheating ex-boyfriend, Chris. Why does she still think of him when the panic starts? Fuck. How hard did she hit her head?

'Come on, I'll take you home. You do get yourself in some scrapes.'

Judgement, she can feel the judgement. 'Why are you here? Are you stalking me? Every time I turn around, you're there.' Claire bristles. This is so embarrassing. *He must think I'm a lunatic who can't look after herself.* Just some crazy city girl getting lost in the woods, kicking garden gnomes, and falling off random bikes. Urgh.

'You live in the countryside now. You see people you know. I live here too, remember?' Sebastian chuckles.

At first, Claire thinks he's laughing at her, but then realises he's trying to be good-natured despite her annoyance. She gulps. It's not his fault everything has gone to shit.

Sebastian runs a hand through his hair. 'Come on, we don't have to talk. I would help any cyclist dying by the side of the road.'

'I'm okay. I can sort myself out.' *I'm fine. I can do this on my own, like everything else.*

Sebastian surveys her like she's completely mad. 'What?'

'I'm sure I can hobble home or someone else will give me a lift.'

'Who?'

'None of your business. I'm fine.'

'You're hurt, your bike is bust. I'll take you home,' Sebastian's voice is louder but still calm. It's as though he's telling off a tantruming toddler, but in a controlled and measured way. He stares at her, then turns away to face the stunning view. Sebastian interlocks his fingers on the back of his neck, making his own headrest, his elbows pointing upwards. Some sort of grunting noise comes deep from his throat as he waits for Claire's reply.

'No.' She smiles calmly and firmly. 'Thank you.'

He spins around and releases his weaved fingers. 'You want me to leave you here?' Sebastian points his palm at the empty road and the never-ending hills.

She nods.

Sebastian observes Claire for a few beats. She can see him searching her face for answers. He starts to walk to his car, but stops. He opens and closes his mouth. He's turned into a glitchy goldfish. 'I could call someone else to get you?' Sebastian puts his hands in his pockets and shrugs. 'If that's the issue,' he mumbles.

'No signal.'

'I've got signal, you have to be on a certain network round here, which I'm guessing you're not on.'

'Just leave, I'm fine. Thanks for your concern, but I'll take it from here.' *The one person I want to call, I can't.*

Dad at her graduation randomly appears in Claire's mind. He was so proud of her. He must have taken about a hundred photos. There was a glow about him. Throughout the whole service, he never stopped smiling. He chit-chatted to her friends and got into a deep conversation about newspaper ownership with her lecturer. Dad soaked up every second. His genuine interest and support during that big moment made Claire feel loved and lucky. Her one and only guest in the audience. *I want to call Dad.*

Sebastian frowns at her. 'Okay, if you insist. I can't force you to accept my help.' He gradually walks back to his car, his head down, focusing on each step. He turns around to look at Claire before climbing inside, and goes to say something else then retreats into himself. Sebastian salutes, army style, before speeding off.

Claire watches the green 4x4 disappear and realises she's shaking. The sun is now shining and the clouds have buggered off, so hopefully she'll start to dry out. She hops over to the bike and picks it up. It makes a very fine walking frame. She can half lean on it and hop along. This is how she is going to get home. It will take a while, but she will get there.

How long was she riding for? An hour, maybe? So, what, three hours hopping? It'll be starting to get dark by then.

It'll be fine.

It will be fine.

Decision made, the only hero she needs is herself. Good old Morris grit and determination. You don't need anyone but yourself, especially not a judgemental, strangely handsome, and magnetic new farmer guy.

This is a stupid plan. Progress is slow. Forty minutes later, and she's hardly moved. She's alone and hurt. Maybe this is what she deserves. A parentless, gnome vandal deserves to die alone in a hostile, foreign environment. At least in London, there's always someone about.

A white Mini is driving towards her. 'Thank god,' she whispers. She waves and mouths, 'Help.'

The woman behind the wheel remains expressionless and pretends she doesn't see her and drives by. Well, that was a very London response. Maybe this place is more like home. Claire lets a single tear fall before wiping it away and continuing to hop.

Another car approaches. Claire will make this one stop. She is determined.

It's a green 4x4. He's come back. Relief floods her body. She will get home.

Sebastian pulls in, switches off the engine, and puts on his hazards before getting out. 'Will you let me take you home?'

'Yes, please,' is all Claire says.

'Drop the bike in the bush. I'll put it in the boot in a minute. Put your arm around my waist and I'll get you in the car.'

Claire silently does as she's told. She squeezes his body. It's hard, she can't find any flab. He puts his hand around her waist to steady her. His hand feels massive. It makes her feel tiny. She leans in on him. He smells outdoorsy yet expensive. He sits her in the passenger seat and puts her seatbelt on for her, leaning over to plug it in. The side of his face is centimetres away from hers. He's not shaved. The stubble outlines his square jaw. Orange freckles seem to dance around his face while his strawberry blonde hair falls into his eyes. This time his hair and overall look reminds her of Hugh Grant in *Bridget Jones's Diary*. Claire has the urge to kiss him on the cheek. She slides her hands under her thighs to stop herself from grabbing his sandpaper face. It's like he knows. He refuses to meet her eye and smiles to himself before shutting the door and retrieving the bike. Sebastian chucks it in the boot and stomps around to the driver's side. He climbs into his seat, starts the engine, and *Radio 1* blares out of the speakers. She raises her eyebrows and sticks out her bottom lip. Sebastian quickly shuts off the radio and reverses the car, turns around and heads in the direction of Baliston. Claire peeks back at the bench and the view. Now the sun is shining again. It's back to how it looked when she arrived, a thing of beauty, rolling hills beckoning her, rather than trying to swallow her as the rain encapsulates her.

'Quite some adventure for you,' Sebastian says, breaking the silence.

'You could say that.' Claire inspects her swollen ankle and muddy trousers. She takes a big breath. 'I'm sorry about before. Thank you for coming back for me. It's really kind.'

'Why wouldn't you get in the car the first time, instead of messing about? Why wouldn't you accept my help?'

Because I've always had to rely on myself, even more so now. 'Just trying to be independent, I suppose, and I don't really know you.' Claire doesn't know what else to say. She's hardly going to tell him about how this is the worst time of her life, about how everything fell apart in December, never to be the same again.

'I'm one of the good guys.' Sebastian glances away from the road and sparkles at Claire. His eyes are bright and full of humour.

'That's exactly what a bad guy would say.' Claire beams at him. Sebastian's good company, actually. Looking at his profile while he drives, she notices his nose isn't perfectly straight. There's a small bump in the middle. It adds character to his face. Claire picks at some mud on her jogging bottoms, then focuses back on him. 'Did you tell Simon about the gnome?'

'No.' Sebastian is concentrating on the road ahead. 'I'm still hoping you will.'

'Right, I see.'

'Apparently, Simon is concerned. He thinks there's now a crime issue in Baliston. Someone's shed was broken into the other week. He's linking the two and is going round calling it a "spate of incidents". Please speak to him and put his mind at rest.'

'Okay, I will.' Claire thinks she's telling the truth, but she's not quite sure. 'That's not me, not my usual behaviour, you know?' She doesn't want him to think badly of her. She isn't herself.

'I don't, but okay.'

Claire shrugs and stares out of the window. He really is quite sanctimonious. Gorgeous but holier-than-thou. Her head still hurts, and her ankle is throbbing. They're getting closer to Baliston and closer to her, having to explain to Gareth that his bike isn't exactly in the best shape.

For the rest of the journey, Sebastian concentrates on driving and Claire watches the hedges wizz by. It's not long before he's pulling up outside Bramble Cottage. He parks in front of the house and turns to her.

Claire meets his eye. 'Thank you.' She really means it.

'You're welcome. How's your leg?'

'Bit swollen, but nothing major.'

'And you've cut your arm, haven't you?' He strokes her right arm, searching for the cut.

'No, it's this one.' Claire turns to show her left arm.

'Oh,' Sebastian whispers. He gently inspects her arm.

The closeness is intoxicating. His breath smells of coffee. What does her breath smell of? It's probably horrible after being knocked out or fainting or whatever happened. Claire takes a deep breath, closes her mouth, and fixates on letting her nose do the work. Sebastian stops rubbing her arm, then rests his hand on the side of the passenger seat. He's withdrawn from her, but he hasn't. His little finger is ever so slightly touching the outside of her thigh, just brushing her. It's distracting and all she can focus on. The arm touching and the pinky brush are making her want him. Why is he having this effect on her? What would happen to her if they actually kissed or went further than that? She would probably melt. Not that any of that will happen because he thinks she's mad. It's just been a while since a man's touched her, months and months in fact. She can't help her body's response, it's involuntary.

'Do you think you should go to hospital?'

'No,' Claire lies. She probably should go – she lost consciousness – but she doesn't want to. She's not been in a hospital since the day everything changed. The thought sobers her up from her drunken Sebastian stupor. 'Thanks again,' she mumbles.

'No problem.' He purses his lips. 'The gnome thing was a one off, right? You don't make a habit of losing your temper and damaging other people's things?'

'No,' Claire says quickly.

'Good, so why did you?'

'I don't know. I've been having a bad, well awful time. I'm all over the place at the moment.'

'I know how that feels.'

Claire jerks her head to study Sebastian's face, but he's rubbing his forehead and she can't see his eyes. Is he having a terrible time too? She's thankful he doesn't ask her to clarify why she's all over the place. Claire's got a hunch it's probably because he doesn't want to talk about his circumstances either. 'I'd appreciate you keeping my disastrous first few weeks to yourself. I don't want to be the talk of the village,' she says with a little laugh.

'But you already are.' Sebastian pauses and gazes into Claire's eyes for a few long seconds. 'You look cute in your helmet.'

Claire reaches up and touches the curved, smooth plastic, before running her fingers along the chin strap and tugging at it. She'd forgotten she was wearing the helmet. *I won't blush.* 'Thanks.'

'And when you're annoyed, you wrinkle your nose… here.' He touches the bridge of his nose and beams. It's the most genuine and beautiful grin. Sebastian clears his throat and quickly mumbles, 'Anyway, I'll get your bike out, then you're on your own.'

Really? A compliment, I think? I can't tell through the mortification.
She hobbles to the front door, and he hands her the bike.
'Bye, Claire.'
'Bye, Sebastian.'
Claire hurries inside before Gareth sees her.

#

Gareth was actually okay about his bike, he said something about "accidents happen" and he wouldn't accept any money for repairs. Claire felt relieved, but she had a feeling that she wouldn't be borrowing his bike again.

After confessing to Gareth, Claire spends the next few days hiding out in the cottage, only going out for essentials and short walks. She can't face Sebastian or anyone else in the village. She's stressing about her far from perfect start to

Baliston life when her phone rings. It says Saskia in the small screen window, so Claire flips the mobile open.

'Well hello there, stranger,' Saskia shouts.

'Hi.'

'I'm coming to visit you. Expect me in a few hours. I'm getting the train.'

'I might be busy. It's Saturday.'

'You're not. I'm coming. You need to show me this dump you've run away to. Laters.'

She's coming then. It's the last thing Claire wants.

Chapter Six

Claire drums her fingers on the side of the sofa while she waits for Saskia to arrive. The TV is on, and the news has just started. Four-year-old Madeleine McCann is still missing after disappearing from her hotel room in Portugal. Claire stops drumming.

That poor girl. Is she lost and alone?

Saskia said she would be a few hours. It feels much longer. She did call again while she was on the train; the signal kept cutting out, but Claire managed to deduce that she'd imagined that she could get a train straight from London to Baliston, but that, of course, isn't the case. Saskia is, in fact, getting a train to Derby and then a taxi or bus to Baliston. She sounded frazzled, like she's regretting her decision to make the visit.

They've been friends for years, ever since they met in fresher's week at the University of Nottingham. Saskia had asked Claire if she could borrow her lipstick in the toilets of a grubby pub on an organised "Welcome to Uni" pub crawl. Claire had said she didn't have one, Saskia had been horrified, but then Claire had pointed out that Saskia also didn't have a lipstick and they collapsed into a pile of drunken giggles. It turned out they lived in apartments opposite each other in the on-campus halls of residence. From that moment on, they became firm drinking and shopping friends.

Nothing about what's happening with Saskia's journey surprises Claire. This is her best mate all over, spontaneous without much reasoning, planning, or thinking about how she's going to do the thing she wants to do. Claire hadn't wanted her to come when she called, but over the last few hours, she's come round to the idea. She absentmindedly hums their karaoke song, *Don't Go Breaking My Heart,* by Elton John and Kiki Dee. Claire is always Elton and Saskia always Kiki. Without fail, if there's karaoke, they're up and singing. That hadn't happened for ages, though. A once weekly event that's drifted into nothing.

Being alone is harder in reality, and the heaviness she felt in London hasn't disappeared in Baliston. At least she's starting with Hazel on Monday. Cleaning and talking to her will be a welcome distraction. Claire has been making a concerted effort to get out in the fresh air, her limp almost gone. She even ventured into the woods again and didn't get lost. There had been a few close shaves, and she'd ended up at Sebastian's farm again, but then she knew the way from there and safely navigated her way back to the village. She'd looked over at the courtyard, but there was no sign of Sebastian.

As she approached the farm, she'd whispered to herself, "Please don't be there, please don't be there". When he wasn't there, the sinking feeling – draining through her body – surprised her.

Claire hasn't seen him since he rescued her and gave her a lift home, but then she hasn't been out much either. Other than for walks, she's been in her cottage, hidden from the world. Languishing in bed, reading a book, watching telly, or flicking through old photo albums. The pictures are mostly of her doing different activities.

Claire, when she was three, building a sandcastle.

Claire, when she was seven, climbing a tree.

Claire, when she was sixteen, all dressed up for a school disco.

Her dad was always behind the camera, so there are very few photographs of him. The albums are quite depressing, showcasing an apparent lonely existence. They're full of her doing things alone, but in reality, he was there, but looking back, he isn't.

Claire rests her head in her hands and forces her attention on the TV. She flicks over the channel to a wildlife documentary. Two giraffes are having a fight, swinging their necks like giant, spotty lassos and whacking their heads into each other. Vicious.

She hears the unmistakable click, click, click of Saskia's heels on the pavement and the wheels turning on her suitcase as she drags it up the road. Sure enough, someone is now hammering on the front door. Saskia's knock is comparable to how she approaches life. Claire gets up and nonchalantly walks. She's in no rush, a smirk starting to creep up her face. She's ready to have the quiet smashed into smithereens.

Claire opens the door ajar and pokes her head out. 'Yes?' she says, pretending Saskia is a stranger.

Saskia glares at her. 'Let me in then, I've travelled to the fucking back of beyond. You can at least let me in.' Her bouncy curls wobble on her head as she waves her hands about, clearly not in the mood for Claire's idea of a jape.

And she's back. Claire's obnoxious, London-loving friend is back. She never thought she would be so pleased to see Saskia. A few weeks ago, she couldn't wait to escape her. 'Okay, I'll let you in, if I must.' Claire opens the door wide and throws herself at her friend. Jumping up to reach and embrace her. She swears she can smell the city smog in her faux fur.

'So, you've missed me?' Saskia is now smiling.

'Maybe, a bit. Come, welcome to my humble abode.' Claire stands to one side and dramatically swings her arm into her little cottage, to present her new home, like a butler welcoming guests.

'Very nice,' Saskia says, sounding unsure as she stumbles inside. 'It's hardly banging around here, is it? But I did see on my hike through the village that there is a pub. I will let you take me there this evening and buy me copious amounts of wine.'

'It's a deal,' Claire says.

'How are you doing?' Saskia's face has changed. She's giving

Claire "that look". It instantly makes her shudder, having successfully evaded it since leaving London. Within seconds of Saskia arriving, Claire knows she's done the right thing in coming to Baliston. She can't breathe when people look at her the way Saskia is looking at her now. She'd been questioning her decision, the loneliness suffocating, but that's nothing compared to this.

'Fine, have been unpacking and going for walks.' Claire can't quite meet Saskia's eye. 'And I went for a bike ride the other day... hurt my ankle a bit actually—'

'Are you fucking ninety? I think you're insane. Can we go to the pub yet?' Saskia interrupts.

'Okay, okay. Take your bag to my bedroom, then we'll go.'

Saskia dutifully stomps upstairs. Claire lets out a slow, long breath. It will be her first visit to the local. She hasn't felt like venturing in on her own. Her chest swells with gratitude. She's thankful her friend has come to visit her. Tears sting her eyes, but she blinks them away and instead peers into the hall mirror, grabs her eyeliner from her handbag and starts touching up her makeup. She can hear Saskia in the bathroom upstairs, probably doing the same. Claire traces the outline of her eyes, truly studying herself. She's tired, older. The only thing she can see is sadness.

Surely, that's not what other people see? Only she knows the true extent of what's happened and why she's here. You can't read someone's eyes that deeply. Can you? She's thought about talking to Saskia many times, but she can't quite find the words. Even months on, Claire still can't talk about what happened because then, it would be real. If she escapes and ignores, part of her hopes it won't be true.

Claire strokes her eyebrows into place and runs her fingers through her hair. 'You coming?' she shouts upstairs to Saskia.

'Yes, Mum,' is Saskia's response.

Claire waits outside on the street. A group of cyclists zoom by along the main road. They're talking to each other by shouting at the top of their voices. They're discussing where they can stop to take a break. *There's a nice bench about an hour's ride away.* Her ankle is nearly better, but it's still bothering her.

She can hear the faint hum of someone mowing their lawn. *I bet it's Jean.* Hazel did mention that she's obsessed with her grass. Apparently, Jean often mows her lawn on a summer's evening, that way her grass is the neatest in the morning. Claire never realised mowing could be a competitive sport. Despite having the most pristine front garden and lawn, Hazel says she doesn't participate in "lawn wars" as she puts it, although the evidence seems to suggest otherwise.

Claire gazes upwards, searching for shapes in the few scattered clouds in the darkening sky, while she thinks about Hazel. She would never have thought a year ago that this is where she would be. Living in a Derbyshire village, a job as a helper and that's the most exciting thing in her life? Madness. It's only been a few weeks, but it feels like forever. It's going to be a long six months, but Claire is determined to stick with her decision and see it through. She's got the rest of her life to live in London and pursue a career. She tuts to herself and grabs the face of her watch: 9.14pm. She's usually in bed by now. She won't tell Saskia that.

Looking every inch the part-time model and art teacher that she is, Saskia skips down the steep, old stairs and tips her head to one side when she sees Claire waiting for her outside. 'What are you doing there?' she says while checking herself out in the hall mirror before walking through the open front door.

Claire doesn't answer, and simply closes the door and locks it. 'Did you see what the pub was like when you walked past?'

'Have you not been in?'

'No, that's not what I'm here for.'

They walk in silence to The White Swan, which is on the other side of Baliston, which means a five-minute walk. They link arms out of habit, but they don't chat away like they usually do.

Having a quiet drink at the village local isn't their usual scene. Some of their best times at uni were when they were out all day and night. They'd sunbathe in Nottingham's Market Square before drinking pints at The Trip. The pub is nestled into the rock where Nottingham Castle stands and is apparently the oldest in England. They would find the perfect spot in one of the cosy yet chilly cave rooms and chat and drink, while encased by stone. The walls having witnessed and listened to many conversations over hundreds of years. Then it would be onto The Bell for jazz night. The drinks were cheap; the music was unique and the people inside were characters. Once, an old couple even got them to judge who was right in an argument. Naturally, Claire and Saskia sided with the lady. And if they didn't collapse and fall asleep from all day drinking, they'd end up dancing in a nightclub before stumbling to the nearest food place for cheesy chips.

Claire can make out the clanging and rumbling of farm machinery in the distance, and wonders if it's Sebastian. He keeps floating into her mind. She'll be thinking about something else and somehow her brain ends up back at him. Even though he's mostly been annoyed with her and she's found him annoying, she can feel he's kind, she can feel it in her bones.

'So, you don't talk anymore? Is this part of the new country Claire?' Saskia rolls her eyes.

'I was thinking about the uni days. The Trip... The Bell... dancing in Oceana.'

Saskia smiles. 'I think we're in for a different type of night, tonight.'

'Exactly.' Claire squeezes Saskia's arm. 'Who have you been going out with, then?'

'The usual crowd, except you, really. Jon, Daniel, and Cecelia.'

Now it's Claire's turn to roll her eyes. Saskia must be desperate to go out with that lot.

They fall into silence again as they listen to their heels tapping on the pavement.

'It really is quiet here, you can hear… nothing and the stars are so bright.' Saskia bends her neck back to study the sky, which has blackened even more. Claire does the same. A beautiful, dark blanket covered in twinkling diamonds. They stand still and admire the sky for a couple of minutes. Claire tightens her grip on Saskia, she feels like home. The realisation hits Claire that she does miss home, but she knows she can't be there right now.

They start walking again to the pub. A typical English pub. The outside is freshly painted white, but on closer inspection, the bricks are crumbling beneath. It must be hundreds of years old. There's a picture of a swan swimming above the words "The White Swan" on the front of the building. A signpost near the road, which has the same picture of the swan, is swaying and creaking in the wind. They're met with laughter as they enter through a big, black door. A busy Saturday night, the whole village could be in here. There's the lounge on one side and the bar on the other. Claire and Saskia waver in the entrance, not sure which way to go. They opt for the bar. There's more noise coming from that direction. They're hit by warmth, a fire blazes in the corner, dark wooden furniture fills the room, and cream walls lift the place. Saskia strides straight to the bar and orders a bottle of Pinot Grigio and two glasses, while Claire finds a table and sits down.

Saskia plonks the glasses and bottle on the table. 'You can get the next bottle.'

'It's going to be that kind of night, is it?' Claire says, but she's smiling. She could do with letting loose.

'I've been doing some more modelling,' Saskia announces.

'Really? It's taking over, isn't it?'

'Yeah, I'm still doing the art classes, but I'm not taking on any more. I haven't got time. I'm in the mix for a new campaign for a massive fashion brand.' Saskia raises her eyebrows.

'Who for?' Claire asks.

'Can't say, it's very hush-hush.'

'You can tell me, who am I going to tell?' Claire scouts the room. There's a group of four elderly women sitting in the corner talking about gardening, a couple of old blokes at the bar, and some rowdy twenty-somethings in the corner, laughing and joking about a game of darts.

'Fair point. But I'm still not saying. You'll find out soon enough.'

'I'm starting a new job on Monday.'

Saskia stops chugging her wine and stares at Claire. 'I thought the plan was NOT to work for six months.'

'It is. It's just doing odd jobs for this elderly woman in the village for a few hours a week. I need something to do.'

'You may as well come back to London.'

Claire sighs, and once again ignores her friend, and concentrates on sipping her wine. That's when she sees him. She's hiding behind her wine glass, trying to avoid Saskia's gaze, when she realises, he's in the pub too.

Sebastian.

He's among the loud darts playing group. She didn't notice him before. He must have been in the middle or something. He's laughing, crying-laughing, and holding his stomach in pain from chuckling to the extreme. Sebastian keeps trying to take deep breaths and calm down, but he thinks about the funny thing again and starts hysterically howling. He's relaxed and carefree.

On the farm, in the street, and in his car, he was serious and seemed older.

The cords and flannel shirt are gone. Now, he's dressed all in black. Black jeans and black top. Very plain, but obviously very expensive. Sebastian is younger, cheekier, and more dimply. His arms are on display in his T-shirt. She imagines those arms wrapped around her waist, drawing her towards him, wrapping her up. Claire would nuzzle in, disappear within him.

'What are you smirking at?' Saskia whispers and follows Claire's eyes to Sebastian, who is standing behind her. 'You know him?'

'I've bumped into him a few times. He's hot, right?' There is no way Claire is going to tell her any more than that.

Saskia glances over again, trying to be subtle but failing. 'He's very you, not very me.' She wrinkles her nose.

Sebastian turns around, probably sensing he's being ogled. He does a double take. Claire carries on staring, forgetting that he can actually see her; once she realises she starts studying her nails.

'He's walking over,' Saskia says out of the corner of her mouth.

He arrives at their table and peers down at them. 'Hi.'

'Hi,' Claire says.

'Remember me? I'm the guy who saved your life… twice.' He grins a smug grin.

Saskia quickly snaps her head away from Sebastian and glares wide-eyed at Claire.

'I wouldn't go that far.'

'I think you'd still be lying by the side of the road or maybe still be in the woods if it wasn't for me.' Sebastian chuckles but then gathers himself.

'Thank you for helping,' Claire says quietly.

'I'll stop now. Seriously, are you okay?' His blue eyes bore into her soul. He's genuinely concerned and genuinely gorgeous.

'I'm fine. Nothing a few wines won't cure.' *God, I sound like an alcoholic now. Why do I keep embarrassing myself in front of this guy?* Claire tries to take control of the situation. 'This is my friend Saskia, she's come to visit me for the weekend.'

'Hi, I'm Sebastian. Nice to meet you, Saskia.'

'And you,' Saskia says and leans forward on the table, her arms resting on the wood while also squishing her ample cleavage together. She really can't help herself. She just has to flirt with everyone.

Sebastian barely notices though; his attention is back on Claire. 'I think we've gotten off on the wrong foot. I could show you around the village if you like? It seems like you've had a rubbish start to village life. Let me show you the sights?'

Claire gazes up at him and raises her eyebrows. She's not

sure what to say. She wasn't expecting to be asked out. Claire knows she's been all over the place and Sebastian has seen that, but he still wants to get to know her. He's intriguing, and, sure, it helps that he's handsome.

'We could get a bite to eat here as well?' Sebastian asks.

Claire's stomach somersaults. 'Yeah, that would be nice. You can be my tour guide.'

'Nice one.' He grins at her and runs a hand through his hair.

Claire watches him, willing him to keep fiddling with his strawberry blonde hair, but he doesn't. 'Where shall we meet? I can meet you at the farm if you like? I'm sure I can find my way now,' Claire says. She sticks her chin out while tipping her head back and smiling up at him.

'No, that's okay.' Sebastian's brow creases, he's aged again. It's some transformation. What's worrying him? 'I'll pick you up. I know where you are.'

'Great.'

'It's nice to get some fresh blood around here.'

Saskia finally speaks. It's like she's been so shocked by the whole exchange she temporarily lost the power of speech. 'What are you? A vampire?' she asks.

Sebastian lets out a fake sounding laugh. 'No, it's just the average age here is about eighty-five.' He smiles. 'I'm not sure what day I'm free for lunch and a tour.' He does a little bow in Claire's direction. 'Can I text you to sort?'

They exchange numbers. Saskia makes a snide comment about Sebastian playing darts, before he returns to his friends.

'Did he ask you out and then back out and sort of cancel?'

'Don't know, I don't think so. He's working on his dad's farm, so maybe he has to check when he can take some time off.' Claire shrugs.

'Ohhh, he must have some money then!' Saskia rubs her hands together and takes another swig of Pinot. 'I can't believe he just asked you out. He didn't even really look at me.' Saskia fluffs her afro, straightens her back, and pushes out her chest.

'It was pretty direct. We've hardly even chatted before,' Claire says, 'just argued…' she says more quietly. Saskia doesn't ask about what happened in the woods or by the road with Sebastian. It's always all about her. She's right though. He didn't really notice Saskia, because he was completely focused on Claire, which makes for a pleasant change.

For the rest of the night, Claire sits on the edge of her seat, glugging wine and chatting away to Saskia, while every now and then glancing over at Sebastian. He does the same. It's an intoxicating evening.

As the two friends sway home at midnight, after many glasses of wine, Claire feels warm and fuzzy.

Chapter Seven

Saskia wakes up late the next day, then announces she needs to get back to London to go to the gym and prepare for a shoot.

'The Sunday trains will be atrocious, you'll be better off going Monday morning, if your shoot is later in the day,' Claire warns her.

'It'll be fine. I'd rather be back today, even if it takes a bit longer,' Saskia says as she rushes around the kitchen, making breakfast. A slice of toast is hanging out of her mouth when she runs upstairs to pack her things. It's a common theme – Saskia rushing in the morning. She never seems to sit down and eat, probably because she's usually late.

It was the same when they lived together in the final year of uni. Saskia would even sometimes eat a bowl of cereal on the way to lectures. She'd be shovelling cornflakes into her mouth on the walk, then she'd hide the bowl and spoon down an alleyway and pick them up on the way home. They had a flat, just the two of them. At the time, it felt grown up, compared to halls of residence. Saskia would make sure the kitchen was well stocked with the basics such as milk, bread, and pasta. Claire was absolutely skint, but Saskia had plenty of money, thanks to her family. It meant Claire never went hungry. It was an unspoken act of complete and utter friendship. This arrangement was never articulated, never spoken about, but Claire is forever grateful.

Claire hugs her best mate for longer than usual at the front door.

'You know if this place isn't working out, you know you can

come home. You don't have to stay for the full six months,' Saskia says, her eyes fixed on Claire, waiting for her reaction.

'I know. I'm going to stick it out. I think it's doing me good.'

'I knew you were going to say that. Have fun in Boring-ton,' Saskia says with a huge smile and a cheeky raise of the eyebrows.

Claire watches Saskia leave from the front window. It's like she's wilting away in the countryside and needs to return to the capital to regain her power. Claire chuckles as she sees Saskia turn the corner onto the main road where she's meeting her taxi. She's glad it turned out to be a flying visit. She hadn't planned on having any visitors to Bramble Cottage, and now alone again; she feels absolutely exhausted.

The rest of Sunday is spent sleeping and watching films, and when Claire isn't doing those two things, she's checking her phone.

He hasn't text her.

Maybe that's what she's finding draining.

The bloody anticipation.

She ends up putting her silver flip phone on top of the kitchen cupboards. It feels like a victory in the battle in her own head. Nestled in the dust, her mobile is face down and on silent, meaning she won't hear any beeps or see the rectangular front screen light up, or witness the lack of beeps or lighting up. But Claire keeps climbing onto the kitchen counter to sneak a glimpse, seeing there are no messages and climbing down again. *If he does message, I won't text him straight back anyway, so I don't need to keep checking. I don't. I'll make him wait a few hours for a response.* Not that she has anything to respond to.

Then on one of her kitchen counter climbs, autopilot takes over. She opens her mobile, holds down number three, and calls the one person she always wants to speak to. Her go-to person for when she needs to talk, needs help, needs to moan. He always answers, well, he did. Before the call connects to nothing, Claire hangs up and crumbles onto the floor. Her dad won't answer this time. She throws the phone in the kitchen bin and runs upstairs to bed.

#

Claire wakes early on Monday morning, having gone to bed at about 7pm the night before. She feels more buoyant after a decent night's sleep. Her eyes feel wretched. In the mirror she sees pissholes in the snow. Tiny, bloodshot eyes. Crying doesn't do anything for the beauty regime. She gets into the shower, wanting to wash everything away. She's in no mood to clean Hazel's house or do whatever she wants her to do, but she forces herself to get ready.

Claire manages a bright smile when Hazel answers the door and an enthusiastic voice when she's asked to clean the house from top to bottom. The monotonous scrubbing actually feels therapeutic and the bleach fumes, cleansing. Focusing on something small and mundane is strangely comforting, and she loses herself for the next couple of hours. She thinks of nothing else. Her thoughts revolve around wiping, scrubbing, vacuuming, and mopping. The relentless motion like being rocked into a relaxing state.

The bathroom is almost done, and she's polishing up the bath taps when she hears Hazel answer the door downstairs. There's now someone else in the house. She can hear his voice. It's deep, definitely a man. Claire carries on buffing the gold taps until she can see her reflection in them. She's scanning the bathroom, to check she's finished, when she senses the mood and conversation have changed downstairs.

Listening at the top of the stairs, she waits.

'It's fine, Andrew.'

'I'm only an hour away, half an hour when I'm at work. I could pop round after work and do whatever, it wouldn't be a problem,' what-must-be Andrew says.

'You're so busy, though, and you have your own family to think about. It's fine. It's sorted!' Hazel sounds aggravated and louder.

'But you don't need to pay a complete stranger. It's stupid when you have me.'

Hazel says something back, but Claire can't hear what she says. Should she go downstairs? They do seem to be talking about her. She can't linger on the landing forever, and she has actually finished the cleaning. Claire hesitates for a few more seconds before stomping her feet on each step and clattering the bottles in the cleaning basket as she descends.

They're standing near the front door. Andrew's coat is unbuttoned. He's wearing a suit and has coffee spilt down his tie. They both look up from their now whispered conversation when she reaches the bottom of the stairs.

'Hi, I'm Claire.' She does a mini wave, then immediately regrets it and starts to fiddle with the bleach lid in the basket she's holding.

'Hello, I'm Andrew, Hazel's son.' Andrew offers out his hand for a handshake. It's firm and sweaty.

'I heard a bit of what you were saying. I'm going to do a good job.' Claire flinches at her own directness.

'I'm sure you are,' Andrew says firmly. He nods, then turns to Hazel. 'I've got to be off, Mum. I've got a meeting. I'll call round one evening after work.' He kisses Hazel on the cheek, looks Claire up and down, then leaves. Andrew gets into a black BMW and speeds away.

Hazel is flushed and flustered. Claire continues to stand at the foot of the stairs, not sure what to say or do.

'As you've probably figured out, he isn't too happy about me hiring you. Well, furious might be a more accurate description.' Hazel touches her hair and straightens her belt.

'Why? If you don't mind me asking.'

'He wants to help me and thinks I don't need to hire someone to help. But he's busy with work and has lots going on. I'd rather do it this way.' Hazel points at the basket of cleaning bottles that Claire's clinging onto.

'I don't want to cause a problem.'

'You're not, don't worry. He's had his little tantrum now. He'll calm down. Why is it that as you get older, the children start thinking they're in charge? I'm still the mum.' She shakes her head and shrugs, signalling the end of the discussion.

Claire puts the cleaning products and vacuum cleaner away before checking the downstairs rooms for anything she's forgotten.

'You've done a fab job,' Hazel says as Claire packs away the mop. 'I've never seen the place so spick-and-span.' Hazel smiles at Claire, who only half smiles back. She's focusing on folding some cloths. 'Would you like a cup of tea? I think you definitely deserve a break. Well, you're done for today now, anyway.'

'Yes, a tea would be lovely,' Claire says.

'Good, good. Go and take a seat in the lounge, my lovely.'

Claire folds into the velvet, green chair, surrounded by happy faces. It's like the softness of the material and the love within the photos are cuddling and embracing her. She can hear the kettle boiling, and Hazel pottering about the kitchen, humming a tune which stops when she's stirring the drinks. The ting-ting of the spoon on the cups signals Hazel's imminent return to the room. Claire straightens her hair and crosses her legs. She's ready for bed again. Her eyes feel heavy and scratchy.

'There you go, nice and hot.' Hazel passes Claire her cup of tea. 'Could you do the food shop for me tomorrow morning?'

'Yes, of course. What time shall I come round?'

'Eleven?'

'Yeah, fine.' Claire sips her tea. It's too hot, so she cradles the mug in her hands. 'I love your wedding photo.'

'Me too. It's still my favourite photo of us and there are hundreds more of us together. That's my Jack.' Hazel's eyes fill, but they do not drop. 'He's no longer with us.'

'How long were you married?'

'Well, as far as I'm concerned, we still are. But to answer your question. Fifty-eight years.'

'Wow, that's a long time.'

'It didn't feel it.'

Claire tries to appear cheery, but instead, she bursts into tears.

'Oh, what's the matter? Is it Andrew? Don't worry about him. He's a fucking little shit sometimes.' Hazel's expression is earnest.

Claire starts giggling. The tears of pain turn into laughing tears.

Hazel's face scrunches into confusion.

After a few minutes Claire says, 'Sorry, I don't think I've ever heard someone, um, your age swear like that before.'

Hazel chuckles. 'I like a good swear. Jack would roll his eyes.' Hazel rolls her eyes. 'What is wrong?'

'I'm not coping.'

'What aren't you coping with?'

'My dad's death.'

#

They talk for hours. It's the first time, since the funeral, Claire has said out loud that her dad died. Only speaking about it in official settings when sorting out his affairs in the New Year and never since. It's the first time in months she's even acknowledged it's happened.

It had always been Claire and her dad. Well, her mum, Laura, had been there for the first few years of her life, but any memories are hazy. Flowery skirts, singing *Erasure,* shouting. Dad was everything. The one parent that was there for everything. He even made notes at parents' evening, for god's sake. He was the only one to do it. Claire could feel her face burning as the teachers spoke and Dad scribbled away. Other parents just listened. He said he didn't want to miss anything. Now she's only twenty-five, and he's gone; he left, not by choice, but taken suddenly, abruptly, bringing everything crashing down.

She doesn't tell Hazel what happened that day. She can't bring herself to go into the details. It's all she thinks about, but for her mouth to form the words and explain would be too horrifying. She would then have to go into the part she played, and how can she ever tell anyone that?

Instead, she tells Hazel about Alex Morris, the man who raised her on his own, the man she feels lost without. Dad lived in Enfield all his life, had always worked at the bread factory, and seemed to know everyone. They would go on walks together and chit-chat about nothing. He was a man of few words, and he didn't like to get emotional. When walking through Baliston, she feels closer to him. The village reminds her of childhood holidays in the countryside, of Dad wanting to show her a quieter, greener way of life. She could see him retiring in a place like Baliston, if he ever could've left his beloved Enfield. As she got older, Saturday afternoons were their time together to go and watch the footy and stuff pie and chips into their gobs. Claire couldn't care less about his precious Enfield Football Club. She was there to eat pure carbohydrates and watch with amusement as her dad, a reserved man, shouted at the top of his lungs at the players. Forget any movie, stand-up comedian, or play, Alex Morris provided the best entertainment when at the football on a Saturday afternoon.

'I understand your pain. I know it's different, but I did feel lost when my Jack died.'

Claire rubs her eyes. 'I'm sorry Hazel. I've been banging on about me. I've just never spoken about it.'

'Never?'

'Never.'

'You need to talk about things to work through them. It makes you feel better.'

'Not the Morris way, I'm afraid.' Claire's opened up just a fraction, but now she's keen to stop. She doesn't want to go anywhere near the guilt that's weighing her down. A change of subject is needed. 'Did Jack do your head in?' *I can't imagine being married for a lifetime.*

Hazel jerks her head up in surprise. 'People don't usually ask that!' There's a twinkle in Hazel's eye. She's pretending to be offended. 'Of course, he fucking did. I lived with the man for decades. People are annoying to live with.' She cackles like a witch. 'He was my best friend, but he was also the most irritating person ever. He would make a cup of tea and always leave the tea bags on the side. Just on the counter. Who does that? Well, Jack for one. He left his dirty clothes on the bedroom floor. He didn't know how to sit still, even if he tried, he'd be tapping his big toe on the floor or drumming his fingers. And another thing, his farts. So loud and stinky, I used to shout at him to go and stand in the garden and do it.' Hazel finishes her monologue, takes a deep breath, and smooths down the skirt of her dress. She gazes up at the wedding photo on the mantelpiece, before pursing her lips, and dabbing the corners of her eyes with the back of her hand. 'Thank you for asking that very random question. It's good to talk about the silly annoying things. It makes him feel real again, like a person. Rather than just singing his praises about what a good soldier he was, what a good dad, blah, blah, blah.'

'Was he those things?'

'Yes, the best. I should have complimented him more when he was here, rather than when he's not.'

'I bet he knew.' Claire reaches over and squeezes Hazel's hand.

'I'll tell you more about him another time.'

'I look forward to it,' Claire says while getting up and heading into the kitchen to put her mug in the dishwasher, grabbing Hazel's on the way. 'I wanted to ask you, actually,' Claire shouts from the kitchen as she opens the dishwasher door, 'do you know Sebastian? His family own one of the farms here.' Claire walks back into the lounge and hovers near the doorway.

'Yes, he grew up here. He doesn't live here now. He's just here for a bit for his dad.'

'Yeah.'

'Why do you ask?'

'He asked me on a date, well at least I think he did. I'm waiting for him to text.' Claire reaches into her jeans pocket to get her phone, before realising it's still in the bin at home.

'He's a lovely lad, handsome too.'

Claire doesn't know what to do with her hands. She scratches the side of her head, drags her fingers through her hair before opting to clasp them together behind her back. One palm gripping onto the back of the other. It feels odd, so she lets go and her arms swing, creating long skiing-like pendulums. 'Anyway, I better get going. I'll be back in the morning to do your food shopping.' Claire makes her way to the front door, collecting her coat from the bannister post on the way. 'Sorry, I've taken up your time telling you all that stuff. I hardly know you and you're my boss.'

Hazel slowly stands up and plods over. 'Don't be silly. I'm not your boss. You're just helping me out with a few things. Also, I love chatting and I did ask what was wrong. It's good to get these things out, rather than letting them rattle around your head.'

Claire agrees, but she isn't sure what to say, so she simply nods. She turns, opens the door, and as she's shutting it behind her, says, 'Bye.'

Claire walks back home, back to her dinky Baliston cottage, re-running the conversation with Hazel in her head. It's strange that she partly unburdened herself, it isn't very much like her, it just spilled out. It's been bubbling away under the surface, and she could no longer hold it in. Her heart still feels shattered, yet her step is a little lighter. She feels sick, and as usual, her eyes are red and stinging. As it begins to rain, she mutters, 'Some summer.' Before putting up her hood.

At home Claire surveys the clock on the mantelpiece: 5.15pm, it's after 5pm so she can have a glass of wine and not feel too guilty. She gets the opened Pinot Grigio bottle out of the fridge and pours it out into a large glass. The white wine glugs out of the neck, as each new wave of grapey goodness falls.

She leans against the kitchen counter and takes a sip, then jumps upright, sloshing her wine, as she remembers her phone in the bin. Digging through the black container, she gingerly moves egg shell, wet kitchen roll, and baked bean juice. Claire finds her phone and gives it a wipe with a tea towel. Phew. It's still working. That was a silly thing to do. She might actually want to contact the outside world again at some point.

He HAS text.

It's not exactly a poem or a sonnet, but it's straight to the point and does the job.

SEBASTIAN: Can u do Wednesday?

She hugs the phone to her chest and checks when he sent it: 9.22pm LAST NIGHT. *Wow, I really am playing it cool.*

She couldn't have asked for more, it couldn't have gone any better. Maybe putting her phone in the bin and not staring at it is the best thing ever. Claire sits down at the dining table and leans on the wooden surface, to give the message the full attention it deserves. "*Can u do Wednesday?*" Can she? Physically she can, she's not doing anything on Wednesday, unless Hazel asks for something, but she probably will have done this week's hours after the food shop tomorrow.

The excitement in her gut begins to fizzle down, settling into uneasiness. Sure, being asked out massages the ego, but does she actually want to go? Isn't she supposed to be alone right now? Isn't that the whole point of being here? What is she going to talk about with him? Cleaning Hazel's house? Staying in bed to cry? He seems nice though in a quiet, nosy – and attractive – way. She hasn't got the energy to make all the conversation.

CLAIRE: Yes.

Give as good as you get. He asked a question, and she's answered. She doesn't need to suggest something to do, or propose a meeting place or time, as she would then be asking him out, and he's supposed to be asking her out.

Her phone beeps.

He's messaged back straight away.

Does he know nothing?

SEBASTIAN: Wednesday it is. I'll pick u up at 12, quick tour of the village and then we can have lunch at the pub.

Again, straight to the point, does the job. He's taken the lead. Excellent. Claire shuts her phone. Her insides churn.

Chapter Eight

Tuesday. The day before her date, but first, food shopping for Hazel. It's just one excitement after another. Claire feels uneasy about going back to Hazel's. She can't quite believe she started crying and going on. The aim is to help Hazel, busy herself, and earn some money. That's it. It's not even like she really needs the money. After all, she's got her inheritance. Claire worked out she could have six months of no job to sort her head out before needing to find work. However, this extremely part-time helper job will provide some structure, distraction, and bring in some cash. She doesn't need a new friend or a counsellor. She'll let the old lady talk if she wants to, but that doesn't mean she then has to divulge her whole life story. Having made this decision, Claire marches with purpose through the village.

Claire knocks, and Hazel opens the door. 'Morning,' Claire singsongs.

'You're chipper, today.'

'Well, yes, I suppose I am. Sorry for getting all emotional yesterday.'

'No problem at all, you're only human. He's texted you, hasn't he?'

'That obvious, is it?' Claire stifles a grin and studies the swirly carpet.

'When's he taking you out?

'Tomorrow, for lunch.'

'Lovely. Oh, can you pick up my prescription from the chemist this afternoon then?'

'Sure, is that everything for this week after the food shop and the chemist?'

'Yep. Cleaning, food, and prescription. All done. I could get used to having you around.' Hazel holds onto Claire's arm to steady herself. It's as if her age suddenly shifts. When she's chatting away, she's the same age as Claire, but then her body betrays her and Hazel is reminded of her age. It's written on her face, her eyes are older, her wrinkles seem to deepen, and her light, bright energy turns heavy, decades of life pressing her down. 'Cup of tea before you go?'

'Go on then,' Claire says.

Again, they're sitting in the lounge, cradling hot cups. Claire is very aware that she doesn't want a repeat of yesterday. The thought stiffens her. 'There are a lot of children on your walls. How many have you got?' Claire peers at the frames, happy to have thought of something to say, happy to focus on Hazel.

'Four children. All grown up now, of course. Sarah, Elizabeth, Heather, and Andrew.' Hazel points at each school photo, showing which is which. Claire recognises Andrew. His face is now basically the same as years ago, just plumper and saggier. Hazel continues answering, 'Six grandchildren. None of them live here, but they're not too far away.'

'I can't imagine having four children.'

'It certainly was busy. Maybe one day when you have a husband, you will start to imagine it.'

'I can't imagine having a husband, either.' Suddenly, in her head, Claire's walking down the aisle. She's wearing a lace wedding gown and a flowing veil which completely covers her face. Underneath, she's sobbing. Walking alone to the faceless man at the top of the aisle, clutching her bouquet with both hands, she has no one to hang onto. He's not there. He won't be there. This thought, this image, this reality is new. It's never entered her mind before. Her dad won't walk her down the aisle.

She's never come close to getting engaged, so even with the hours spent in bed over the last few months, going over everything, this scenario had not been one of the many she'd screamed into her pillow about.

No mum to take his place, either. No one. She's truly alone.

I'm choosing to take time out, away from people, but if I wasn't, who would I be with, anyway? It had been them against the world. That's the danger of relying on one person. If they go, what do you have?

Claire realises Hazel is watching her. She chugs the hot tea. The liquid scolds her throat. 'Thanks for the tea. Have you got the list?'

'Yes, I'll get it.' Hazel puts her tea on the coffee table and shuffles into the kitchen.

Claire takes a deep breath and waits by the front door. Hazel passes the list to her, and she stuffs it in her pocket. 'Thanks,' Claire says as she walks out.

'See you soon,' Hazel shouts after her.

Claire turns around and waves back at the old woman. She's still standing at the door, her face full of questions. Claire knows she's acting strangely, like a different person to yesterday. She'd opened up a fraction and now once again she's tightly closed. Claire storms home. She needs to ring for a taxi and wait. Why has she taken on a job to run about for someone when she doesn't even have a car? She slams the front door of Bramble Cottage before digging her nails into her clenched hands.

It takes Claire hours to get a taxi, do the shopping, ring Hazel to ask which chemist she needs to go to, as she'd forgotten to ask in her haste to leave, get the prescription, and return to Hazel's. Claire and the taxi driver unload the plastic bags from the boot of the taxi. She thanks and pays him and he's on his way. Five bags are heaped together on the pavement. She knocks on Hazel's door.

'You're back,' Hazel says as she opens the door. 'I'll help get the bags in.'

'No, that's what I'm for.'

Hazel points her finger in the air and says, 'Right you are.'

Claire puts the food away in the fridge, freezer, and cupboards, before scrunching up the plastic bags and placing them under the sink.

She hands Hazel her medication.

'Thanks so much,' Hazel says.

'No worries. I'm going to go home. I'm pretty tired.'

'You know you can talk to me and it's fine to do so.' Hazel holds onto Claire, gently grabbing her by both arms.

'Thank you,' is all Claire can muster. Then she surprises herself, and says, 'I would like to talk more, eventually.'

Hazel hugs Claire. It takes every bit of strength for Claire not to crumble. Maybe the being alone in isolation plan is easier. She doesn't know anymore. Unsure what to think, what's for the best, or what she's supposed to do with herself. Grief and guilt seem to be winning at the moment.

'How old are you?' Claire asks, slicing the tender moment in half.

'What? Fucking hell! Where did that come from?' Hazel says between bursts of laughter and frowning.

'It was getting too sentimental, and it popped into my head.' Claire shrugs.

'I'm seventy-nine years old, hence needing you to do things that I just, well... normal things... that are a little tricky these days,' Hazel says while glowering down at her body with disgust, it's failing her, and she's fuming with it.

'I didn't think you were that old. It's weird you just feel like a very wise twenty-five-year-old.'

Hazel wells up. 'I think that is possibly the nicest thing anyone has ever said to me,' she says while pushing her shoulders back, appearing to grow taller. Hazel stands straighter and more upright, pushing her boobs out and brushing her hair away from her face.

'Well, it's true.' Claire folds her arms. 'Well, I better be—'

Hazel interrupts, 'Yes, yes, I know you're probably busy and you've got other things to be doing. But… why don't we have a glass of wine to celebrate? Oh, actually I might have a bottle of champagne knocking about somewhere.' Hazel directs well-practiced puppy-dog eyes at Claire.

'What are we celebrating?' *What's going on? I need to climb into bed and prepare for tomorrow.* Hazel has got a mischievous look in her eye.

'You saying that I'm like a twenty-five-year-old. That is music to these seventy-nine-year-old ears!' Hazel says before scurrying off. She starts pulling out things from the cupboard under the stairs. A very old and dusty golf bag and clubs, thick winter coats, and a decades-old vacuum cleaner.

'What are you doing?' Claire laughs. Her employer is a mad woman. *God, she's great. Totally not what I expected AND she's funny, funny without even realising.*

'I'm looking for the champs, of course. I'm sure I won a bottle at the summer fayre a couple of years ago…' Hazel continues to rummage. 'A-ha!' She holds up a bottle of champagne with a ball of wool hanging from it. 'It'll be warm, but who cares? Can you do the honours?' Hazel passes the bottle to Claire.

'Yes, I'll put it in the freezer, and it can chill for a few minutes while I put everything back in the cupboard. Maybe sorting this could be one of my jobs?' It really is a mess in there. She does need Claire's help.

'Mmm, maybe.' Hazel surveys the debris spilling into the lounge. 'This was Jack's domain. I've sorted it a bit, but not much.' She slides out one of the golf clubs from the bag and gets into a putting stance. Claire watches as Hazel grasps the golf club, swings it as if hitting an imaginary ball, and then jabs it back into the bag. 'We could sort all this stuff out together. There're some bits I would like to keep. This bag needs cleaning, but I need to keep it.'

Sitting with their glasses of fizz, Claire and Hazel smile at each other and clink their flutes.

'Day drinking? You're a rebel,' Claire says.

'Ha, always have been. It's you, you bring out the old me. Well, the young me, actually. People my age are often very boring. I don't know why because most of us still feel like twenty-five-year-olds in our heads, our bodies just let us down. Oh, wait until I tell Jean you said I'm "like a wise twenty-five-year-old", she'll go green.' Hazel takes a big gulp. 'I'm going to need a nap after this.'

'Hazel, you said I can talk to you—' Claire says quietly while stroking the bottom of her glass, her eyes fixed on watching the bubbles pop.

'Yes.'

'When did Jack die?' Claire now focuses on Hazel. 'If you don't mind me asking?'

'Oh.' Hazel puts her glass down and rests her hands on her knees. 'A couple of years ago now.'

'How are you so together? I feel like I'll never get there.' Claire rakes her hands through her hair but her fingers get caught in her tangled-up curls.

'You will. It takes time. And there are many moments when I don't have it together. But I just think about Jack and how he wouldn't want me moping about. He'd want me living my life.' Hazel gestures at the photos of her grandchildren, at the Tenerife magnet on the radiator, and the gardening gloves on the side.

'True, my dad would say the same.' Claire swears she can feel her heart aching. It feels like the sadness, the guilt, the loneliness, the grief, the anger are all gathering and crushing her most important organ, and yet it still beats.

'You'll get there. It will become more manageable. Spending time with my grandchildren re-energises me. There's something about being with someone who's brand new. They are curious about every single little thing. Things that you don't even notice anymore, things that you take for granted. The other day me and Asher, who's four, watched the bees in the garden for ages.

We got up close and really studied them. He was fascinated and had many questions.'

'I don't think the answer for me is having kids.' Claire suppresses a smile.

Hazel coughs and splutters. 'That's not what I was saying!' she shouts and then cackles. 'I've got chess club later, I better not have too much of this.' Hazel raises her glass and swallows the last few drops.

'Ha, down in one. So, you go to chess club?'

'Yeah, it's alright, I go for the gossip, really. Apparently, Gloria has been getting it on with Edward and he wants to propose, but he doesn't know she's also been hopping into bed with James. Good on her, I say.'

'Really? There's bed hopping amongst a group of pensioners?' Claire's mouth hangs open. She's flabbergasted. *I hope I'm still having sex in my seventies.*

'Well, yes. We're just people you know, not aliens. We still have needs.'

'What about you? Are you dating anyone?'

'No. Sometimes I like the idea of it. But I was with Jack my whole life. I don't want to be with anyone else. I might change my mind, but for now, no.' Hazel shakes her head and absent-mindedly rolls her wedding ring around her finger.

'Fair enough. Thank you for cheering me up. I was feeling a bit strange about talking to you about my dad and telling you so much. I don't usually get emotional and chatty like that.' It's the truth. Claire feels better being herself with Hazel rather than pretending to be cold and pushing her away. Pushing people away seems to have become a habit this year.

'Honestly, it's fine. What are friends for?'

'I wasn't looking for a friend,' Claire says softly. Hazel jerks her head towards Claire. 'But I'm glad I've found one, even if you do play chess.' Claire grins.

'Shh, or I'll make you play a game.' Hazel points her finger in a fake telling off.

Claire finishes her champagne. 'Well, I better actually be off now, hot date tomorrow and all that.'

'Ahh, yes, of course. Hope it goes well. He's a good one.'

Claire leaves and briefly Sebastian floats into her thoughts before she's back to the woman she's just left. There's something about Hazel which makes her want to open up and talk about things that she's never spoken to anyone about. She's disarming. The wall Claire has built up since the end of last year seems to be gradually falling away, brick by brick. She doesn't even really know her, but they connect.

Hazel seems to understand. With most things, she's been there and done that. The same weight is on her, pulling her down. There's a heaviness to it that lingers. Grief. She's sure Hazel doesn't have the regret and the guilt, though. Maybe that's the one thing Hazel can never understand. There's something about finally having an older woman to speak to. A deep longing remains buried in Claire for her mum, but any plans for trying to seek her out were shelved when Dad died. She shouldn't have been distracted by a parent who deserted her. Maybe if she had been more focused on Dad, he would still be here. *I hope Hazel is right and these feelings go away with time.* It's too hard.

What would Dad say ahead of a date? What would he say to her now? A teeny giggle escapes Claire's mouth as she makes her way back to Bramble Cottage, imagining her dad's reaction to finding out she currently lives in the countryside. 'Not expecting that, hey,' she mutters.

He would tell her to be herself, ask questions, find out about her date, and try to have fun. Dad feels close in this moment. Claire can almost touch him, she's sure of it, he just feels present. Maybe this is what happens when she opens up to Hazel. In that case, she decides to do it more. It's like she's getting a cuddle from her dad and that's all she really needs right now.

Chapter Nine

Claire stands in front of the wardrobe, wondering what the hell to wear. She only seems to own jeans, tops, and short party dresses. There's no happy medium. Her look is slob or "it girl". Well, there are options somewhere. She just can't bloody find them. Nothing, absolutely nothing suitable for a walk around a Peak District village and then lunch at a country pub with a handsome fella. A first date in the countryside, where she currently lives, is new territory. She hasn't planned and shopped for this moment.

Sebastian is gorgeous in a quiet, unassuming way. His freckles are cute, yet incredibly sexy at the same time. Surely, only more will appear as the summer continues and his face becomes more sun-kissed? Claire pulls out black jeans and a white fitted T-shirt. It's sunny and warm outside, so this should be fine. It's simple and chic and you can't really go wrong with simple and chic.

Claire spends a whole hour on her makeup, which is double the usual amount of time. She's trying to achieve a natural look, which is totally unnatural, but looks natural, which is actually a lot of work. Her long, brown curls are behaving today and are flowing down her back, in a *Disney* princess kind of way.

She's ready. Now what does she do with herself? He'll be here soon. She needs the toilet. Damn that nervous energy. After a while, in the loo, she douses herself in perfume and brushes her teeth again.

There's a knock at the door. He's a few minutes early. Why is she nervous? Has it really been that long since she's hung out with an attractive male? Yes, it really has been months and months. She's not even sure she can do polite chit-chat anymore.

Claire opens the door. 'Hello,' she says with a big smile, which she quickly turns into a small smile while smoothing down her T-shirt.

'Hi, are you ready for your grand tour? Baliston awaits!' Sebastian booms.

Claire giggles, warming to his silliness. 'I've been here a little while now. I'm pretty sure I've seen everything,' she says as she steps out of the front door.

He's wearing a similar outfit. Blue jeans and a plain white top. They could be in a *Gap* advert together. She would be leaning against him while draping her arm over him. She quickly scours his arms. They're stretching the sleeves of his T-shirt, just ever so slightly. His biceps are trying to escape and show off, and Claire has to admit that's a show she would like to see.

'Well, let's make sure you've seen all the sights.'

'So, we're going to Main Street then?'

'How did you know?' Sebastian pretends to be shocked and surprised at Claire's inside knowledge of his grand tour, of a village that she's lived in for a few weeks, where just about everything is on one singular street; the main road.

They walk side by side towards the centre of Baliston, the sun beating on their backs. It's quiet, apart from the birds tweeting, they could be the only two people in the world. She keeps getting wafts of Sebastian and he smells delicious. Soap and fancy aftershave hang in the air. Sebastian sneezes four times.

'Bless you.'

'This bastard hay fever is driving me mad!' Sebastian swears quietly and through clenched teeth, but the sentence crescendos with frustration.

'How can a farmer have hay fever?'

'My thoughts exactly.'

Claire studies his face, she's not sure what he means, but

Sebastian isn't meeting her eye.

They arrive at Main Street. She takes in the familiar homes and shop, she's pretty sure there aren't any hidden gems that she hasn't already found.

'As you can see, we have the post office SLASH shop to your right.' On the word "slash" Sebastian dramatically holds his right arm up before karate chopping it across his body.

He's different today. Much chattier and more relaxed than other times she's seen him. She's enjoying his playfulness, just being in the moment.

Sebastian continues, 'Further down we have the chippy and then even further down the road is the primary school and the pub, The White Swan, which I believe you might be familiar with?'

'Yes, I have frequented this establishment,' Claire says in her best posh voice and does a little bow.

'Well, if you'd like to follow me, we can take a closer look at the education establishment.' Sebastian is in full tour guide mode.

Outside the small school, they can hear children's voices seeping out of the open windows. Claire can't make out the words, it's a mash up of excitable chatter.

The constant hum takes her back to being in school. She would always write her name with a love heart over the "i" instead of a dot. Writing was her passion, and she would always try to write her neatest using a fountain pen, meaning her hands were often covered in ink. She would go to after-school club most days because her dad was working. He'd usually be the last parent to pick up, sprinting into the playground, still in his work clothes and smelling of bread. He'd give her a cuddle and she would bury her head in his work shirt, breathing in the fresh wheat. Dad had been there though, and supported her every step of the way. He couldn't believe it when she got accepted into uni. The first in the family to go. When he dropped her off, after fussing around her room, making her bed, setting up her TV, and even producing an extension cable from his back pocket, so she could plug in her CD player, he said, "My daughter, at university". He shook his head, pushed her hair back, then cupped her face before pulling her in for a tight hug. This raw emotion – unusual for Dad – caught Claire off guard and she started welling up. It was a monumental moment in her life and Dad was there for it, but there wouldn't be any more.

'This is where I went to school. I don't think anything has changed. You see on that wall there.' Sebastian points to the playground wall on the far side. 'Yep, you might be able to make out the word, Seb, that's me.'

'Wow, you're part of history,' Claire says in a bright voice. She focuses on Seb's name, trying to drag her mind into the present and what's happening now. A date, with a rather hunky man.

'Well, yes, I guess I am, even if I had to scratch it into the wall myself.'

'What was it like growing up here?'

'You're like an interviewer with all your questions.'

Claire thinks this is supposed to be a bit of a dig, but she very much takes it as a compliment. 'I think I've only asked the one.'

'Today,' Sebastian says, 'when I first met you, you asked about what being a farmer is like. Always with the straight to the point questions.'

'I suppose,' she says quietly.

'To answer your question. It was boring growing up here. It's so quiet. Nothing ever happens. It's a serene childhood. Lots of open space and it's safe, but not exactly exciting.' He starts to saunter towards the pub. 'Where did you grow up?'

'Enfield in London. I was in Acton before I came here.'

'Why would you come here, in your twenties, on your own?'

'Well, you're doing the same aren't you?'

'I suppose.' Sebastian stares at the floor, and they meander in silence to the pub.

'Is the tour over?' Claire finally asks. 'It wasn't very long.'

'Mmm, yeah it was pretty short. The rest is houses and farms really and of course the woods,' Sebastian says, his eyes are twinkling, he's trying not to laugh, but he's not trying that hard.

'Yes, that would be a more useful way to spend our time, you can show me how to navigate the woods. Although, I do think I've figured that out now.'

'Good, I didn't think it would take you long to find your way. It is a small wooded area.'

It's quite condescending, but Claire can take some good-hearted ribbing. It's thrilling being teased by Sebastian. It's as if the tiny platelets in her blood are dancing through her veins. Jigging about every time he smiles at her, warming her body.

In the pub they both order the steak. He gets a pint of lager and she has her usual large white wine. The place is pretty empty, but then it is lunchtime on a Wednesday.

'Don't you need to be at the farm?' Claire asks, trying to get the conversation moving.

'That's where I am most days. The farm manager is there, he'll have things under control. Today is my day off.'

'Thank you for spending it with me.'

'What's your job?'

'At the moment I've just started doing odd jobs for Hazel in the village. I think I'll go back to London at some point, I don't really know, I'm figuring it out.'

'I know Hazel. She's a nice lady,' Sebastian says.

He doesn't ask any more about why Claire is in Baliston and why she hasn't got a real full-time job. It's like he can sense she doesn't want to talk about it, or because he's reluctant about speaking about himself, he's not going to push her because then she would push him. Claire's not sure why he's in Baliston either. It sounds like he's on the farm just temporarily helping his dad for some reason.

'So, you're just helping your dad for a bit?'

'Yeah, I live in London. This is the longest I've been in Baliston for years.' Sebastian scratches his head and messes with his hair.

'I work in finance in the city, I'll get back to it, eventually.'

A fellow Londoner. Interesting. Why didn't he mention that before? Claire senses the need to move on. 'I'd love a tour of the farm one day, to see how it all works.'

'I'm sure I can show you around.' Sebastian smiles at Claire. It's that same one he gave her in the woods. A great smile, but it doesn't reach his eyes, a sadness lingers.

Their food arrives. They take their elbows off the small circular table and dig into their meals. Sebastian cuts his steak carefully. After slicing through, he inspects the middle to check for pinkness inside. Once he's satisfied it's been cooked correctly, he dips the steak in peppercorn sauce, swishing it around to completely coat the meat, and then chews methodically. Wow, he takes his steak seriously. It's like watching a Beef Sommelier at work.

I wonder where he goes out in London?

Claire allows herself fleeting glances at him in between eating her food. She notices, as predicted, the number of freckles on his face has increased since she last saw him. They're all over his nose and down his cheeks. *I bet they're all over his back as well.* She bites her bottom lip and forces her mind not to go down that path. He doesn't need her salivating over him over dinner. Her attraction to his freckles is surprising and new, but on him the tiny dots make beautiful, intriguing patterns. She wants to inspect where they go, to study his whole body, to devour every part of him. The strength of this feeling makes Claire feel quite shaky, so she closes her eyes for a couple of seconds, banishing the thought and concentrates on her steak.

'You're quiet,' Sebastian says.

'I suppose I am.' She doesn't know what else to say.

'That's what people usually say to me. But there's nothing wrong with being silent in someone else's company. There doesn't have to be non-stop chatter.'

Claire kind of agrees, usually she likes a good chat, but there's something about Sebastian which makes her nervous and her mind wander, which results in her being quiet. It's not really her usual style. She decides to show her real self instead of this quiet, meek, apparently sexually charged self. 'You're a farmer who has hay fever, how does that work?'

'Well, it doesn't, really.' Sebastian shuffles in his seat. Claire nods but doesn't say anything, willing him to continue and offer more. Eventually, softly, he says, 'I'm just here to look after my dad and the farm short-term. I'm hoping I'll be back in London soon.'

'What's wrong with your dad, if you don't mind me asking? 'Cancer.'

How awful. Sebastian must be under a lot of pressure and worry. It's becoming clear from his stunted, monosyllabic words that he doesn't want to go deep and really talk. Claire knows that feeling all too well. When there's so much pain it almost solidifies within, becoming too bulky to vocalise. 'Oh gosh, I'm sorry to hear that.' Claire pauses, studying Sebastian, who is pale and dejected. It's obvious he doesn't want to go into details about his dad's illness. 'What's your normal job then? Finance, did you say?'

'Yeah, I love numbers. I'm missing being in an office and how fast-paced it is. I've taken unpaid leave to help my dad,' he says while scratching the side of his face. 'Being back at the farm is intense in a different way. It's like being a kid again, just me and dad. We've got a farm manager and workers, but I'm overseeing everything and trying to be a nurse.'

Claire watches him as he gulps the last of his pint and taps a beer mat on the table. He's consumed by fear and tiredness. He's feeling lost like her. Life on hold while they figure things out. She can tell he isn't enjoying sharing, again like her. The silliness of earlier is gone. Claire could drink that side of him up. This side of Sebastian is different, he's sombre and withdrawn. She identifies with him, it's how she's feeling. 'What you're doing is amazing. Looking after your dad, the farm, putting your life on hold…' *If only I'd been less selfish.*

Sebastian rests his chin on his fist, closes his eyes briefly, and gives Claire a tiny nod. 'So, you were living in Acton?' he asks.

'Yeah.' The change of subject is abrupt, but it doesn't startle her.

'And you chose to move here?' His face is incredulous.

He thinks I'm completely nutty. 'My dad died, I needed… some time… out.' It's honest and not one of her fake answers she's given to various people in the village.

'I'm sorry.'

'I'm sorry your dad is poorly as well.'

The conversation stops as they retreat into themselves. Both not wanting to talk about the difficult circumstances they find themselves in, but bonding over the tiny bit they've shared with each other. They eat the rest of their meals in a comfortable silence. It's not awkward, both are lost with their own thoughts while finishing their food.

The pub is peaceful. One man is sitting at the bar with his pint, chatting to the landlord. Old black and white photos of years gone by in Baliston hang from the walls. A bus trundles by the big bay window.

Once they finish their steak, chips, and salad they move onto lighter topics and the silly Sebastian, which Claire glimpsed earlier, is back. He tells her about a sneezing fit he had the other day while he was driving the tractor. He tried to continue working on the field and put the tractor into reverse by mistake, so he was sneezing away and going in the wrong direction. He says his dad keeps rolling his eyes at him because he doesn't know how to do a lot of things, despite growing up on the farm. He never showed an interest, now he's wishing he'd paid more attention.

He hated school, people picked on him for his ginger hair and freckles. Claire stops herself from saying his hair and skin are beautiful. Her eyes betray her, though.

She tells Sebastian about her shitty admin job which she was happy to finally quit, and how the plan has always been to be a journalist, but she's not got around to that plan yet. She tells him about Saskia and their partying ways. How life had just been too much fun to get around to the serious stuff, but in reality, it had been getting less and less fun and actually boring, even before her life fell apart.

Outside the pub, he stands in front of her and looks down; he cups her chin with his index finger and gently lifts her face up, coaxing her brown eyes to meet his blue. The bags under his and the redness in hers speak volumes. Both are carrying so much.

'You're beautiful,' he murmurs.

'So are you,' she whispers back. She tries to telepathically tell him to kiss her.

He seems to understand and leans down, at the same time she pushes up onto her tiptoes. They headbutt each other. Clasping their foreheads in their hands they both grimace and laugh.

'Come here.' Sebastian guffaws.

He wraps his arms around her waist. She puts her arms on his chest, her fingertips almost reaching his shoulders. He kisses her. A series of small light kisses. No snog. No tongues. Just heartfelt, long, closed mouthed kisses. It's strangely erotic in its PG nature, and it leaves Claire wanting more. As they finally separate, his lips leaving hers, she resists the urge to draw him in again.

Sebastian is beaming. 'I'll walk you home.' He takes her hand; it feels rough and twice the size of hers. As they walk hand in hand back to Claire's house, he asks, 'What about your mum, what does she think of you moving here?'

Claire sighs. 'I wouldn't know. I've not seen her since I was little.'

'Shit, I'm sorry.'

'Yeah, she walked out. Met someone else and started a new life.'

'Have you ever tried to look her up?'

'No, she made her choice.' Claire shrinks away from him. She drops his hand and crosses her arms. *I've been down this path, imagining possibly meeting her, about tracking her down, but then*

Dad died. I'll never get to speak to him about it.

'Does she know about your dad?'

'No idea.' Claire inspects the ground. He's suddenly very nosy. Claire didn't push him on details about his dad or family, why is he pushing her about her mum now?

'Why don't you try and find her? Maybe this is the time to try to connect with her.' His eyes are earnest.

'Because I don't want to. If anyone should be looking for anyone, she should be looking for me.' Claire feels sick, she hasn't got the energy to think about her mum. She doesn't want her anyway, she wants her dad.

'Mums are important, don't give up on her.'

'Well, I wouldn't know, would I?' Claire shouts at the top of her voice.

Sebastian stops walking and stares at her, open-mouthed.

'Just stop, alright?' Claire screams and she starts sprinting home, before she turns the corner she glances back and sees Sebastian still standing there, scratching his head.

Claire runs upstairs and climbs straight into bed, under the covers. She's shaking. She's not sure what happened. Why did he keep prodding her about her mum? Why's he bothered? He's got too much going on, anyway. So has she. She's just sexually attracted to him, that's it. It probably would have been just a one-night stand, anyway. Not even that, now. She would still like to trace his body map of freckles with her lips, but that's probably to do with the fact she hasn't been close to someone, romantically, for ages.

She doesn't need him. She's not in Baliston to date. She's here for time out, to heal, and decide what's next.

She should have stayed with her first impression of him.

First impressions count for a lot.

Chapter Ten

Claire doesn't know what to feel, she's not sure how they went from kissing to having an argument on a first date.

Did she overreact? Possibly.

Did he poke his nose in where it wasn't wanted? He certainly did.

She can't figure him out, sometimes he's a jokey lad full of life and humour but that person seems to fade and a quiet, grumpy old man appears.

The day after their disagreement, in the afternoon, she goes for a walk in the woods behind the cottage. Again, she ends up next to Sebastian's farm, this time, glaring into the courtyard.

When his dad shuffles out of the house, she dips down behind a bush, her heart thudding. He's an older replica of Sebastian, although he resembles a lamp post, tall and thin. Sebastian's dad walks slowly and carefully with a blanket around his shoulders. He stands in the middle of the courtyard, takes several deep breaths, and watches a flock of birds fly over head. Then with his chin still pointing upwards, he closes his eyes and remains still. It's as if he's soaking in the outside and breathing in his farm, taking in the smells of his life before he became old and ill. Raindrops start to fall and he begins plodding inside. By the time he reaches the door it's chucking it down.

Still in the bush, squatting in mud and becoming wetter by the second, Claire sobs. She'd shouted at a man who's caring for his sick dad, on his own. She'd shouted at a man running a farm, which he's allergic to, who's just trying to find his way, trying to keep everything together.

Claire knows what it's like to appear to hold it together. To play a part, to float outside of your body, despite drowning inside. It's how she got through her dad's inquest, when she met the witnesses. They told their version of events, how they called for an ambulance, how they performed CPR. Each time a witness spoke, the coroner would then ask Claire if she had anything she wanted to say to the wannabe heroes. She had plenty. But she said "no" each time. Silence was her friend; it was the only way to keep it all in. Thank you was on the tip of her tongue, but the words wouldn't come. The man responsible said his piece. While staring at the bags under his watery eyes, Claire tried to focus on his words. He said he was doing the speed limit. He thought black ice made him skid. The smartly dressed man avoided her glare. Outwardly she was calm, inside, she was screaming, grabbing at his collar, and shouting her pain in his face.

Her trainers are soaked through. In her hiding place, she shivers. Claire should run home and get dry, but she's paralysed, unable to take the next step.

Outside the court, the crash scene helpers enveloped her, crying, wanting to offer their condolences. It was almost too much to bear. Some words came out. She nodded her head; she wanted to wail and weep, but she held back. She did what she had to do.

Now Sebastian is doing what he needs to do, to help his dad and keep the family farm going. He must be struggling.

The bush's thorny branches scratch Claire's arms, as she finally finds the energy to stand up. She feels light-headed but manages to speed walk back to Bramble Cottage.

This window into Sebastian's life is cracked and dirty. Claire puts herself in his shoes, rather than only seeing his actions from her point of view.

She doesn't get out of bed for two days.

#

A week later, it's now Friday and Claire's due to get a train to London tomorrow. The small overnight suitcase on wheels is open on the bed.

Saskia called a few days ago to announce the date of the year – 10th June – was fast approaching and preparations had begun. She paused for dramatic effect, and it took Claire longer than it should have to grasp the significance of the date. Saskia's birthday.

It simply wasn't on Claire's radar, celebrations seem unimportant. Her own birthday in April came and went with no acknowledgment, she did nothing to mark reaching her mid-twenties.

Saskia managed to persuade her to travel down Saturday morning so they can go shopping together, get ready to go out, and have a big night out, then on Sunday, on Saskia's actual birthday, go out for brunch. Claire will travel home on the train Sunday afternoon, meaning she'll spend the rest of the day travelling. *The things I do.*

Claire reluctantly puts dress options into her suitcase. For a split second she wonders whether she'll be able to see her dad while she's back, or will he be working this weekend?

Then it hits her.

When will these sudden realisations stop? When will the reflex of him, stop? Or will she get this punch in the stomach for the rest of her life?

Her phone rings. It's Saskia. Claire flips it open. 'Hello?'

'You're coming, aren't you? It'll do you good to see your friends, and its only for one night and then you can get back to boring Baliston,' Saskia blurts out.

'Yes, I'm packing now, I'll get the train in the morning. Will you meet me at St Pancras? I get in at 11.38am.'

'Bit early, but okay.'

'I'll text you when I get there.'

'Eeeeekkkk. I'm so excited. I bet you won't want to leave once I remind you of… everything.'

'I don't know about that, but yeah, it'll be good to see you and everyone else.'

'Ciao.'

And she's gone. Claire throws down a silver sequinned, short, short dress on the bed. She'll finish packing later.

Claire finds herself back in Hazel's green, velvety chair.

'Hope you don't mind me popping in. It was either watch more *Diagnosis Murder* or pack, so—'

'Not at all.' Hazel smiles.

'What jobs do you need doing next week?

'We can get to that. Have you heard from him yet?' Hazel says, wincing.

'No, think that might be it, it's probably not brilliant to argue on your first date,' Claire says, but what springs to mind isn't the argument but the kisses.

It must have been five pecks on the lips, slow, lingering, lips touching, breathing each other in, before coming up for air, and diving back in. His lips were soft, his upper arms hard. Her hands wandered up and down his arms until finally they rested on his chest. He then wrapped his arms around her waist, holding her close. Both contorting their bodies to reach each other. Him bending down; her cranking her neck up. Pulling and bending to achieve closeness. As they repeatedly kissed, she felt his hands move up her torso, close to her breasts, but stopping short, just hinting at what he really wanted to do. It's the most restrained first kiss she's ever had, and the most intoxicating. It felt like they were moments from ripping each other's clothes off, when in reality they were standing outside a pub, having had several little kisses. She can't imagine what would happen if they actually did have a full-on snog. Sex would surely have to follow. Claire feels drawn to him, but also irritated by him. She was ready to sleep with him that night. After those kisses, she wanted him, she needed him. But even just a one-night stand is now off the agenda, never mind dating.

'No, but you also kissed.'

Is Hazel some sort of mind reader? 'Yeah, I suppose,' Claire says, pushing the words out as she exhales before sipping her tea. The date had been going so well, up until that last moment.

'Maybe you could call him or send him a text?'

'No way. No way am I texting him first. He contacts me or we never speak again.'

'How very traditional of you. I'm sure he'll be in touch. He's got a lot on, you know.' Hazel peers over her cup of tea at Claire.

'I know,' Claire says in a small voice. 'I'm off to London this weekend. I'll be back Sunday though, so can come to you first thing on Monday as usual.'

'Great, I'll have a think about what I need you to do. How do you feel about going back home?'

'Well, I won't be going back to Enfield, just to Saskia's in Chelsea. Should be fun,' Claire says, convincing no one.

'Andrew's coming to see me this weekend.'

'Oh, I'm sorry I won't get to see him again,' Claire says politely while thinking the opposite.

'He's insisting on coming, he wants to do jobs for me.' Hazel sighs. 'I do want those shelves putting up in the spare bedroom and the shed is full of rubbish.' She frowns and instinctively scans the photo of her son on the mantelpiece. It's from years ago, he's in his school uniform, with dried on milk around his mouth, and terrible bed head.

'I could have helped you with the shed.'

'But not the shelves, right?' Hazel has a twinkle in her eye.

'Well, yeah, I've never put a shelf up in my life.'

'I think he's just making a point, showing that he is able to help. He's still not happy about me hiring you. It'll be nice to see him though.'

Claire nods, not sure what to say; besides, Hazel seems to be deep in thought. From the warmth of inside, they watch the rain fall, in a most unsummery fashion. It's violent, coming down hard, smacking into the pavement. It's unwelcome and surprising.

#

Claire shivers on the platform of Edale railway station. Why, no matter what time of year it is, are train platforms always freezing?

It's still raining and apparently more is forecast. According to the news on the radio in the taxi, there are concerns about possible flooding. The driver had turned it up and shook his head. Claire's sheltered from the rain on the platform, but the wind howls through the encasing grey concrete.

Much to her disappointment, her train arrives exactly on time. She wheels her case on, sits by the window, and keeps her bag by her side. There's no use getting settled, as she'll need to change at Sheffield. She can get more comfortable on the next train. Claire checks her phone. It's something she seems to be doing a lot lately. Sebastian hasn't messaged. Every few days she's been for a walk in the woods, always glancing at his farm, hoping to see him or his dad – something – but neither have appeared.

She sighs and puts her mobile away in her handbag. A leather-bound photo album pokes out. She had put it in, in case she felt like staring at the contents during the journey. Now, the urge to see Dad is strong. Claire opens it up.

The first photo is of him holding newborn Claire. He's sat on a brown sofa, his feet on an orange and brown flowery carpet. The lounge is familiar but unrecognisable at the same time. It's their family home, where she grew up, but she doesn't remember it looking like this. The house didn't take long to sell. It's probably been decorated again by now. Dad's got a massive smile on his face. She's asleep, tiny and screwed up, not yet unfolded into the world. He's got huge bags under his eyes, but he couldn't look happier. It's one of the few photos of her dad. Usually the man behind the camera, always taking solo shots of her. Did her mum take this? It must have been her. Claire stares at the image, willing it to flip so she can see her mother on the other side.

The next few photos are of Claire as a baby, gradually getting older. Lying on the floor, sitting up playing with toys, crawling, and eating in a high chair. Then there's a picture just of Dad. He's mowing the lawn, wearing stone washed denim shorts and no top. His hair is bushy and his moustache a thick slug on his upper lip. The epitome of every 1980s dad. Claire's not sure if she can remember him like this, or if her memories are actually from photos. This version is different to the round, bald man that he came to be. Claire shuts the book.

Sheffield is the next stop. Just a few hours away from entering the world she ran away from only a month ago.

Claire strokes her hair flat and bites her lip as she steps off the train onto the platform at St Pancras. The greyness strikes her, the sea of people swirling around her. To her surprise, it's comforting to be surrounded by so many people who have absolutely no interest in her. It's closeness without any conversation. She had thought a little cottage in the middle of nowhere surrounded by trees would be perfect isolation territory, but she's been having more interaction there, which wasn't the plan.

Claire frowns, her eyes scanning the faces of everyone swarming around her. Saskia is nowhere to be seen. Claire slumps over to a nearby café and gets a coffee. She texts her location and sips and waits.

Half an hour later Saskia saunters into the café, orders herself a coffee, and plonks down at Claire's table.

'Are you not getting anything?' Saskia looks down at the table.

'No.' Claire glares at her empty coffee cup.

'Well, hi. I'm so glad you're here to celebrate me.' Saskia leans over the table to embrace Claire.

Claire pats her on the back twice while her face is buried in Saskia's hair. It smells fruity. Saskia's wearing a long, flowery, white and yellow maxi dress. She's absolutely stunning. Claire feels frumpy in comparison in her jeans and T-shirt. Maybe she should have thought through her clothes more for this visit.

'It's my birthday, so we're heading to Sloane Street. I've not been for a while.'

'It's your birthday? You should have said.'

'Are you looking for anything in particular?' Saskia asks.

'No, I'll just help you find what you need. After all, you are the birthday girl. Happy Birthday by the way!' Claire gives Saskia a proper smile. She can feel her grumpiness dissipating.

'Correct answer,' Saskia shouts and laughs, putting her arms in the air.

A couple of nearby people glance over. A man with thick, black-rimmed glasses who's sipping a cup of tea, raises his eyebrows. A woman who's sitting alone, reading, takes her eyes away from her book and drags them up and down Saskia. Then, just as quickly, they go back to what they were doing.

Chapter Eleven

Claire surveys Saskia's messy lounge. Luxury paper shopping bags, tissue paper, hangers, and plastic bags are strewn across the floor and scattered over the sofa, next to where she's sitting. She pushes the mound of junk to give herself more space. The aftermath of a surprisingly enjoyable afternoon. She hadn't been looking forward to it, but they'd actually had fun. Back to Saskia's stomping ground, to their usual pastime, before everything changed.

Claire absentmindedly pops some bubble wrap, while she waits for Saskia to finish getting ready. She tries to sit up straight, so as not to crumple her outfit. It's a classic. Jeans, a nice top, and heels. There were even glimpses of her former self today; floaty and free. They spent hours going in and out of the boutiques, with Saskia settling on a little blue dress. Each burst of the see-through plastic is satisfying. Each bubble is perfect and round, but with one sharp press, is then released and flat.

'What do you think?' Saskia struts, catwalk style, through the lounge, balancing on her bare tiptoes.

'Your legs are so long.'

Saskia grins, satisfied with Claire's response. 'Remember when we went out every night?' she asks while putting on her high heels.

'In the first year? We went months and months, going out every week night.'

'But not at weekends,' they both shout at the same time.

Weekends were when the locals went out. Claire and Saskia abided by an unwritten student rule, to only go out in the week. It would be lectures, watch *Doctors*, have a nap, and then spend ages choosing an outfit and getting ready. They would amble into each other's rooms and borrow each other's clothes. Getting ready was often the best part of the evening; tunes up, dancing, and singing.

'A pound a pint was wicked,' Saskia says. 'Although I don't think I could drink a pint of beer now, I think I would be sick. Too many drank as a student.'

Claire laughs and shudders at the idea. 'I miss our "one-night-stand-debriefs". That was more of a third-year thing though.'

'Our what?'

'That's what I would call our chats in the morning, after one or both of us had brought someone home the night before. Our dissection of everything the next day.'

'Oh, the how many times, what positions… convo?'

'Yes.'

'You never told me you called it the "one-night-stand-debrief". You're such a geek.' Saskia chuckles.

'Thank you, I aim to please,' Claire says before throwing a smelly sock at Saskia.

'Yuck, Claire. Really?' Saskia throws it back.

It's a shortish walk to their favourite bar, where the birthday girl's friends and colleagues are meeting them. They walk side by side, their heels clicking on the pavement. The rain is gone, the flood warnings, forgotten. The evening is dry and hot, and there's a real summer holiday vibe. The bars are busy. Excitable chatter flows through the air. Why did she leave this life? It feels so young and fresh. Claire knows why, but she wants to forget.

Inside, it's all bright lights, yet moody. Lots of nodding heads, shouting into ears, and lust hanging in the air. Saskia's posse of beautiful people are assembled and waiting. When they see her the squealing and air-kissing begins.

'Oh hi,' Saskia's uni friend says to Claire. She hangs on the word "hi", making the short greeting lengthier. 'How are you doing?' Her head tips to one side, her mouth in a straight line.

'Fine, thanks.' Claire gives her a huge teeth-baring show of fine-ness, then points to the bar. As she pushes through the bodies to get to her destination, her chest feels tight and pure panic rises, she swallows it back down. She orders herself a large Pinot Grigio and fights her way back to the assembled birthday group. There are about fifteen of Saskia's closest friends gathered. People from uni, fellow artists that she's met along the way, and modelling mates as well. Claire's probably met them all over the years, but only on nights out when everyone's drunk, shouting over music, and dancing. Claire stands in the crowd sipping her drink, watching Saskia. It's been so long since she's done this, but it feels unsettlingly familiar. She makes small talk about painting and photographers while Saskia is in her element, lapping up all the attention. Claire hasn't spoken to her since they arrived in the bar. *Yeah, shopping was fun, but is there any real need for me to be here, now?* She's here to form a crowd around Saskia, boost the numbers, and contribute to her apparent popularity. Claire necks her wine in one gulp and heads towards the toilets.

'Claire? Hi, long time no see,' a man's voice says, as she's about to push the door into the loos.

He sounds familiar – it can't be – she removes her hand from the door and spins round. Her stomach flips. 'Chris. Hi.' Claire's instantly transported to that night, to the last time she spoke to him. When he refused to meet her at the hospital. She takes a deep breath and looks him straight in the eye. Chris is a couple of inches taller than her, his dark hair is shaved short, it used to be longer, but this simple style suits him. His dark brown eyes are clear and focused, he's not drunk. 'How are you?' She raises her eyebrows, each word full of contempt. *Yes, Chris, how are you? Let's make sure you're okay and check in on you.*

'I'm good. I haven't seen you for ages. What have you been up to?' His face drops once he realises the stupidity of his question.

Claire stays stony-faced.

'I heard about your dad. I'm so sorry I didn't come with you to the hospital. I didn't think it was that serious, and we'd split up and I was already out. I can't really remember the whole conversation. I was pretty pissed.' He reaches out to touch her arm, but Claire steps back and dodges him. Chris puts his hands into the pockets of his blue jeans and studies his shoes.

'So, you knew, but still, you didn't call?' *I don't need this. Why is he here?*

Chris lifts his head. 'Well, yeah, eventually I heard. I wouldn't know what to say. I'm sure you didn't want to speak to me,' Chris shouts as the music gets louder. 'You look great. I'm sorry for your loss.' He frowns and leans in to hear her answer.

His aftershave is the same. That sweet citrus with a hint of vanilla jolts Claire back to nights out, to going bowling, to sunbathing in Newquay. They dated for four months, before she found out he was also seeing someone else. But she needed him that night in December. She needed him to hold her, to guide her through, and keep her company.

'Like you care.' Her bottom lip trembles.

Chris's face crumbles. He reaches for her again.

'I'm fine. I'm fine.' She raises her hands up in surrender, to partition herself away from him and turns to leave the conversation. A conversation she doesn't want and didn't expect to have.

'You know I didn't want us to end. You dumped me and then expected me to come running as soon as you called?' The softness has disappeared, his face now contorted.

His aftershave is making her feel sick. It's sticking in her throat. 'You cheated on me, of course I dumped you. I didn't want to finish things, but you gave me no choice. That night I was worried out of my mind. I was seeking comfort… I was seeking reassurance… I just wanted you to be there with me. I needed you, and you said no.' Claire feels light-headed.

Chris's face smoothes out. 'I know. I am sorry about that night. I should have supported you.'

'Okay, we don't need to keep going over it again and again.'

'Technically, I didn't cheat on you. We never had the boyfriend/girlfriend chat. Things were casual.' Chris smiles. He thinks he's being charming or cheeky.

I don't want to be here anymore. Claire pulls the neck of her top away from her skin and rubs and flaps the rims of her short sleeves, trying to let air in. 'You keep telling yourself that. We were seeing each other for four months, we went on holiday together, we were not casual. So you would have been happy if I was seeing someone else at the same time as you?'

His mouth opens, and his eyes widen. 'You didn't, did you?'

'Exactly.' Claire smirks, point made. 'Anyway, I was going to the toilet—'

'Wait.' Chris stands in front of the door. 'Let's catch up. Have a drink with me?'

'No, I'm not feeling great.' That night, when her whole life was turned upside down, when she rang him for help, he said, "I'm not your boyfriend anymore". Chris refused to be by her side for one evening and callously brushed her off. He had been her boyfriend. They were at the start of becoming serious before he ruined it. He can't rewrite history. If that was possible, she knows what she would do. 'Bye. Move out of the way.'

Chris steps to the side, and she runs to the nearest cubicle.

Claire sits, stroking her hands through her sweaty hair. Her heart beating out of her chest. The women talking about hairbrushes on the other side of the cubicle ringing in her ears.

Images flick up in quick succession.

The taxi drive which took forever, the confusing hospital layout, that little, hot room they insisted she wait in.

Claire pushes her palms into her forehead, willing the flashing memories to stop, but they don't. Again, she repeatedly rakes her damp hair.

The woman on a drip, standing in the entrance smoking, the doctors and nurses with their serious faces, that organ man and his stupid clipboard. She can picture him, pushing his glasses up his nose. Even though they were in the right place, he kept pushing and pushing. Any further, and they would have gone through his skull. After she had said goodbye and before Dad's life support machines were switched off, he explained about organ donation. In a roundabout way he talked through how he wanted Alex's organs.

The spectacled man pressed her for an answer. Dad could save lives. *What about his life?*

No more time together. No more restaurant meet ups, no more chances to even cancel, no more walks, no more chats. No more them.

She should have gone to the Italian with Dad, then he would never have got a lift with Larry. He would have ordered the lasagne, and she would have played it safe and got the spaghetti bolognese. He would moan about her going out too much, and she would moan about work. Dad would ask after Saskia and Claire would try to get out of him whether he was dating or not. Would she have told him about her plans to find Mum? What would he have said? Would he have encouraged her and helped her search? Or would he have tried to persuade her not to do it, and say Mum – Laura – made her choice? *I have no idea. He was enough, I shouldn't have wanted more.*

Claire stares at the advert on the back of the door. There's a picture of a woman with her head in her hands, some statistics about domestic violence, and a helpline. The numbers and words, sway and dance. Reds and oranges, swirl and jump off the page.

He was the 2p machine expert. She would ask Dad how he always managed to win and he would just say, "A wasted youth". They would build sandcastles on the beach and then the hours would fall away among the bright lights, erratic beeps, and the jingle-jangle of money. Clutching their full cups of coppers while watching those hypnotic shelves move backwards and forwards. Backwards and forwards. Timing was everything.

His half-open/half-closed eyes, the cuts on his face, his

mango shampoo. That last conversation. "Stay safe. Bye, Daughter. See you soon".

She said she wouldn't do this anymore, that she would no longer be the girl downing wine at parties. Claire wipes and pulls up her knickers and jeans, before leaning on the side of the cubicle for a few seconds. At the sink, she splashes water onto her face. It smudges her makeup. Heading back out into the dark and loud, she catches vacuous voices while swimming through. She observes Saskia's crowd – laughing, shouting, and dancing. She doesn't need to be here. Claire speed walks outside. She leans against the glass and takes several deep breaths. Out in London and talking to Chris. The last time she was in a bar like this, having a night like this, was when it happened. When she should have been elsewhere, but she chose to do this.

'What's going on? Are you okay? Where have you been?' Saskia stumbles out of the bar, her high heels scraping with each staccato step, as she fires her questions.

Claire's heart is loud, she tries to slow her breathing. 'Just… it's like that night… being out… when Dad… I've just seen Chris.' She sounds like a child who's been crying for ages, as she struggles to breathe and talk, gasping, hiccuping the air in.

'Your ex? That knob, ignore him. Good riddance. Come back inside, get another drink before we move on. Shit, are you okay? You're sweating.' Saskia puts an arm around Claire.

'I'm going to go. It's too much being back here.' Claire slides out of Saskia's grasp. Her breathing is calming a little, but every muscle in her body is tense, working overdrive, on high alert.

'But, it's my birthday. You said you'd be here.' Saskia wobbles, her feet unsteady. She straightens herself and squints as she tries to focus on Claire. 'Just talk to me,' she says softly.

'I need to go,' Claire shouts the last word out and starts running.

When Claire reaches Saskia's flat her hands are shaky and she's panting and sweating. Her phone is vibrating in her handbag, she doesn't need to look at it to know that it's Saskia ringing, to find out where she is. Claire uses her key to get in. She got a copy a few years ago, after being abandoned by Saskia one too many times on nights out. A hot man or woman would always win, and Claire would need to leave, alone. Saskia always insisted on Claire staying with her because she's near the best nightlife, but she would rarely actually stop at her own home. There was always some new shiny thing, and Saskia the magpie, had to pick them up and follow.

Claire feels stuck. It's probably too late to get a train back to Sheffield then Edale and onto Baliston. She decides to get changed, pack up her things, and head to St Pancras anyway, there must be some sort of combination of trains to get home. Leaving London is the priority. Saskia continues to ring, so Claire answers.

'What?' Claire shouts as she opens up her phone.

'Where are you?' Saskia bellows back.

'At the flat. I'm going home.'

'Now? What? It's my fucking birthday.'

'I know, I just can't be here right now… it's too… it's too hard.'

Saskia sighs down the phone. 'Fine, fuck right off back to the middle of nowhere. Call me when you're ready to enter the real world again,' Saskia slurs.

Claire hangs up and slams the door on her way out. At St Pancras she manages to find a convoluted way home, it will take hours, but at least at the end of it she will be back in Baliston, back in the countryside, surrounded by trees, away from everything that reminds her of Friday 15th December 2006.

Chapter Twelve

Back in Baliston, Claire is once again finding it hard to get out of bed. Any progress she's made in the Derbyshire countryside seems to have been washed away by one night out in London. She looks at her phone, there are no more calls from Saskia. She feels lousy for walking out, but she'd hoped her best friend would understand. It's now clear she shouldn't have gone back; it was too soon. In trying to not let Saskia down, in trying to celebrate, and attempting to be "normal", she still managed to let her down. What an idiotic mess. Claire starts typing a text message…

CLAIRE: Sorry.
Then deletes it.

CLAIRE: It was all too much.
Then deletes it.

CLAIRE: I hope you managed to have a great birthday.
Then deletes it.

She throws her phone to the opposite side of the bed.

Claire falls asleep and when she wakes up, she has a voicemail. Her heart flutters as she hears the answer machine woman say she has one new message. But it's not Saskia.

"Hello, Claire. It's Hazel. Where are you? I was expecting you this morning. Please ring me back".

'Shit,' Claire shouts. She was supposed to be working at

Hazel's house today. It had completely slipped her mind. Now, she wants to hide even more. How has she managed to piss off everyone in her life? Just when she thinks she can't feel more alone, she becomes more isolated.

Claire's phone begins to ring, the sound makes her jump, she actually physically shifts her weight away from the mobile, worried it will be another person telling her how shit she is. She doesn't recognise the number.

While holding the phone slightly away from her ear, she gingerly answers, 'Hello?'

'Hi, is that Claire?'

'Yes, who is this?'

'It's Sebastian. I'm ringing from my landline.'

'Oh, hi.' It's the last person she expected to hear from.

'I've been thinking. I overstepped. I'm sorry. My dad had a word with me.' He chuckles, awkwardly.

He's been speaking about her to his dad? Claire smiles at this nugget of information. *He knows he shouldn't have pushed me about Mum.* 'It's okay, I overreacted. I'm sorry too.'

Sebastian lets out a long exhale down the phone. 'Do you fancy coming to the farm? I could show you around… you seemed interested…'

'Yeah, that would be nice.'

'We could have a picnic, if you like?'

Sebastian seems unsure of himself, it makes Claire want to reach down the phone and cuddle him. 'I'd like that. I could do with getting out after the weekend I've had,' Claire says.

'Why? What've you been doing?'

'Oh, nothing,' Claire says, collecting herself. 'Just girl stuff,' she cringes as soon as she says it, realising it sounds like she's started an apocalyptic period or something.

'Right,' he says quickly. 'Are you free tomorrow, at about 4pm?'

'Yes, I'll walk round.'

'I'll see you then.' He hangs up.

It's just what she needs. A welcome distraction from Dad, London, Saskia, and Hazel. She really thought she wouldn't hear from Sebastian again.

'Shit, Hazel,' Claire whispers to herself. She can't face her. She sends her a text message instead of ringing her back.

CLAIRE: Sorry. I had a difficult weekend. Forgot about today. I'll come round Wednesday morning. I hope that's ok. See you then.

Claire winces as she hits send. She's got some grovelling to do. But first, Sebastian. Claire gets out her *Sugababes* album and puts it on. *Too Lost In You* blasts out. She falls back onto the pillows and closes her eyes, humming along to the harmonies and singing the lyrics she knows. She pictures his floppy hair falling into his blue eyes. She imagines grabbing his arms as she pulls him on top of her. His muscles are hard, but his skin is soft and covered in freckles. She fantasises about him kissing her, just like he did outside of the pub. Starting with light pecks, but building to a passionate snog. His tongue in her mouth, exploring, climbing into her. Her hands wander down his chest, through a smattering of hair between his nipples, down over the ripples of his abs, and further down into coarser hair. He's just as excited as her. He groans as her hand descends, brushes, and grasps. Claire opens her eyes. The daydream feels real. Her nipples are erect, and she's wet. Her hand starts to explore. She's never been so turned on just at the thought of a man. She's now so wound up. Playing with herself is the only answer. One hand on her clitoris and one wandering around her breasts, she leisurely rubs her sweet spot, then her fingers go deeper. Caressing up and down. She conjures him back up. Enjoying the spectacle in her mind. Sebastian arrives home, at the farm, in a black Mercedes. She can't see him; the windows are blacked out. As he steps out of the car, he rips off a white doctor's coat. Underneath, he's only wearing blue jeans. It's a boiling hot day, the sun is sweltering. He starts digging. His sweaty hair is slicked back, he's mucky and too hot, but he's a hard worker and keeps going at the job in hand. Claire watches him plunge the spade into the ground and lift the soil out. His six-pack glistens, as beads of sweat drip off each angle of his body. When he notices her, he throws the tool down and walks towards her. Striding with purpose. He lifts her up in an embrace, and she wraps her legs around his waist. Claire masturbates for all of five minutes before she orgasms. Twitching as the waves pulsate through each muscle in her body while she visualises him on top of her, peering down at her, while he's inside her. She goes for a shower to cool off. Another *Sugababes* song thunders out of the CD player.

There's a text from Hazel waiting for Claire when she gets out of the shower.

HAZEL: Not to worry. Hope you're ok. Andrew came round. We can talk on Wednesday.

That doesn't sound ideal. Claire sits on the bed in her towel and straightens the twisted towel on her head. She studies her toes and rubs them against each other. So, she's pissed off Saskia and Hazel, hopefully they'll come round like Sebastian. She can't shake the sinking feeling deep within though. Claire weighs up going round to see Hazel now to apologise, it's the right thing to do, but she doesn't feel brave enough.

Once she explains, Hazel will understand.

Maybe.

Chapter Thirteen

As Claire saunters through the woods towards the farm, she feels good. Of course, everything is still a mess. London was a complete disaster, but strangely she's starting to feel lighter. She hasn't heard from Saskia, and she's dreading going to see Hazel tomorrow. Today though, she feels like a normal twenty-five-year-old about to meet a hot man, not the young woman she's become, with a crushing and suffocating weight pushing her down. She feels pretty hot herself, in her tight-fitting, powder blue, showing-plenty-of-leg summer dress. Her long, curly, brown hair is extra springy and shiny. Claire can feel it bouncing as she walks between the trees. The breeze keeps blowing strands into her lip gloss, and she has to pull them free, but even this doesn't annoy her. Her makeup gives off natural and effortless, but is anything but. Hopefully Sebastian likes what he sees.

Today, they need to not get into an argument. Surely, if that happens again, that will be it. People bang on about how there's a fine line between love and hate, but you really are supposed to have fun on dates, especially first dates. There's loads of advice and famous quotes around about finding love. They don't include, "spend your first few dates arguing and eternal happiness will be yours".

The red-tiled roof is in the distance. She's nearly at the farm. She knows exactly where she's going. A lot can change in a short time. Claire strolls across the courtyard, then realises she's actually heading for the back door, and stops in the middle of the expanse of space. Wouldn't it be rude for her to knock on the back door? She should head to the front door, wherever that is. Claire's only seen this side of the farm, and this isn't even the main bit. Out of the courtyard and around the Derbyshire stone farmhouse, she walks, while running her fingers over the bricks, feeling the roughness and different shapes. The front of the home takes her breath away. It's wonderful, if a little rough around the edges. It's everything she'd imagine a farmhouse to be. The stone, the symmetry of the windows, the olde-worlde feel. It feels like a family lives here. Many families over many years, making a living from the land.

Claire knocks on the large wooden front door. It's brown, but faded and flaking, painted years ago. Mud is caked to the bottom from boots scraped on the lip. As she waits and moves back from the dirt, she notices a cluster of gnomes next to her, to the left of the door. One is fishing, one has a watering can, one is standing while smiling insanely, and another is knitting?! *Who is the gnome collector?* She wants to take a closer look, but also doesn't want Sebastian to catch her near a gnome again. She obviously can't be trusted.

Sebastian answers the door. Claire pretends to be staring at some poppies rather than the gnomes, before noticing him. She can tell he's just got out of the shower; his hair is still wet. One half is slicked back, combed in place, the other is falling into his eyes. They're even bluer than usual, if that's even possible. He must have been out in the sun because his freckles have multiplied. He looks like a model who's turned up for a countryside shoot for a glossy magazine. She swallows the urge to ask him if he's ever modelled before. *Play it cool.* In his stone-washed jeans and plain black T-shirt, it's a glimpse of the London Sebastian rather than the Baliston Sebastian. Claire's sure of it. The whole ensemble, his presence, everything, makes her feel wobbly. She's not sure what she was expecting, but this works, this definitely works.

'Hi.' He smiles.

'Afternoon,' Claire says brightly to match his greeting. She reaches out to lean on the door frame, then changes her mind, deciding to rest her hand on her hip, but that doesn't feel right either so she folds her arms.

They both stand, smiling at each other. Claire on the doorstep, and Sebastian on the threshold. This feels like a big moment. She knows they need to get it right this time, and she can sense he's thinking the same.

'Oh, sorry... come in.' He steps aside and motions for her to enter.

Claire hops inside, and she's immediately standing in the lounge. There's a huge open fire and mantelpiece. Seventies wallpaper is peeling and yellowing in places. There're two massive sofas and a small chair in the corner. It appears they used to be a pinkish salmon colour, but have dulled with use and are now more beige. The overall effect is a well-used, welcoming home. There's a cough from the corner. Sebastian's dad is in another small chair adjacent from her, slightly around the corner. She hadn't noticed him. The chair is swallowing his tiny frame. He's wearing a jumper and has a blanket over his legs, even though it's a lovely hot, sunny day.

Sebastian's dad smiles when he sees Claire. 'Hello me duck, have a seat.' He slowly points at the large sofa in front of the fire.

'Would you like a drink?' Sebastian asks.

'Just water, please,' she says quietly.

Sebastian leaves the room.

'So, you're Claire then?'

Claire nods.

'I'm Robert, Sebby's dad.' He straightens his blanket and tries to sit tall. 'Sorry, I didn't get up when you came in, today isn't the best day.'

'How are you? Sebastian told me about...' Claire doesn't want to say the word cancer.

'The chemo was an absolute bugger, but the doctors seem

happier since…' His eyes well up then dart around the room, as he tries to stop the building tears from falling. 'Enough about me, what do you do?'

'Not much at the moment, I'm doing some work for Hazel Wilson.'

'Lovely woman. And you've recently moved to Bally?'

Claire smirks. She's never heard anyone refer to Baliston as Bally, and Sebastian has turned into Sebby. 'Yeah, I've been here a month or so.'

'But you're from London, Sebby tells me? He's obsessed with the place, can't wait to go back. Don't know what I would have done without him though.' Robert nods at Sebastian as he walks in with three waters.

Sebastian has a quizzical expression on his face. 'I hope you're not grilling her, Father!'

'Of course not. Nice to meet you, Claire. Sebastian, I need to rest.'

Sebastian puts down the waters on the coffee table in the centre of the room and then helps up his dad. Robert starts to walk but Sebastian is basically carrying him, taking most of his weight.

As they get to the door on the opposite side of the room, which leads to the stairs, Sebastian says over his shoulder, 'I'll be back in five.'

Claire can hear the stairs creak as they gradually make their way upstairs. She lets out a long sigh, that was intense. She's never seen someone so ill. Up close, it's shocking. Sebastian seems attentive and full of love and care for his dad. It's admirable and adorable. Not many people would do what he's doing. Just for a second, her doctor's coat ripping reverie springs to mind. Photos on the mantelpiece catch her attention, and she wanders over to the fireplace. There's Sebastian at his graduation, throwing his mortar board into the air. There's a picture of Sebastian with his dad and what must be his mum, they're sitting at an outside table, surrounded by food, and they're all laughing. Claire gazes out of the window at the rolling fields, the crops seem to go on forever. How does Sebastian's dad usually manage this place? How is Sebastian managing now? She knows there are workers and a farm manager, but still, it's a massive responsibility. The idea intimidates her, she can't imagine being in charge of something so vast.

The stairs start creaking again, so Claire quickly checks her reflection, smoothes her lip gloss, and studies her teeth, then turns around. Sebastian is standing at the bottom of the stairs, rolling his shoulders, he clicks his head backwards, and holds it back, studying the ceiling for a few seconds.

'Hello again. Is he alright?'

'Yeah, he's fine, he just gets tired very quickly. He'll be asleep for a couple of hours now.'

'He said the doctors are happy following his chemo?'

'Yeah, things are actually starting to look more positive.' Sebastian rubs his eyes. 'And so, for my next tour… the Jones Family Farm!' He opens up his arms and spins around. 'There isn't much to see really, once you've seen a field you've seen them all.'

'It's interesting, I've never had a nosy around a farm before.' Claire sips her water and follows Sebastian out of the front door.

He turns to lock the door, and while Claire waits for him, she notices the gnomes again.

'Sebby?' Claire singsongs.

'Why are you calling me that?' He pretends to be angry, but his dimples reveal a hint of a smile.

'Your dad let me in on that one.' Claire pokes her tongue into her cheek, while trying to suppress the urge to laugh.

'Well no one calls me that, just a few family members, that's it.'

'Okay, okay. Anyway, Sebastian… what's with the gnomes? I didn't realise you were such a fan.'

'You can stay away from them.' His face is full of fun and then it changes. 'They were my mum's. She thought they were funny or ironic, or something.'

Claire doesn't know what to say next. She's been wondering why it's just him and his dad, but she's not wanted to pry. She'd thought maybe Sebastian's parents were divorced. The possibility of his mum being dead had entered her mind, but she had shoved it away, hoping it wouldn't be true. She chooses to stay quiet and waits for him to continue.

'She died when I was ten.'

'I'm sorry. So, you get it.'

'Yes, I do. I know it's hard. It does get better with time though, but of course you're never the same. I'll always miss her. Grief is different for everyone.'

The urge to climb onto her tiptoes and throw her arms around him, is strong. They lock eyes and offer each other a little reassurance. She's never felt so seen. Claire can feel herself falling for him, which she knows is ridiculous, but nonetheless it's how she feels. Sebastian's the opposite of Chris, he's nothing like him, this can work. *I need to block Chris out of my mind. I'm just scared of falling for someone again.* Bumping into him in London has really rattled her. Just because that relationship didn't work out doesn't mean this one won't either. Claire swallows down her second-guessing doubts.

'So.' Sebastian walks down the garden path towards the large field at the front of the house. 'We're an arable farm, which means my life has been muck spreading and spraying recently. I'm gagging less and less. I'm taking that as a win.'

Claire looks at him blankly.

'You don't actually want to know about the farming side, do you? You just want to nosy around the buildings and look at the view, right?'

'Right.' She giggles.

They walk around the other side of the farmhouse to some outbuildings near the courtyard.

'This is where we keep the tractors. You see this one? It was my grandad's. She's a beaut.' Sebastian beams at the old-fashioned, red tractor. It's small and has a flat tyre.

'Are you getting into the farming then?'

'No, not really. Parts of it were fun when I was little, but it's not for me.'

'Will you be going back to London soon?'

'Yeah, soon as I can. Dad is improving, but I can't go yet.' Sebastian marches off in front, Claire quickens her step to keep up. He hops over a stile, and she follows, frowning.

'Ta daaaa!' Sebastian is very pleased with himself.

Laid out is a red and white checkered picnic blanket with a wicker basket set on top, next to it are two champagne flutes and a bottle of champagne. It's like something out of a film.

'Shall we?' Sebastian holds out his hand for Claire, she runs over to him and puts her hand in his, she grips on tightly as he guides her over bumpy ground.

#

Claire sits with her legs folded to one side, and sips champagne while taking in the view as the bubbly stuff tickles her throat. It's a beautiful, sunny day, the hotness beating down. Surrounded by green, she watches a rabbit hop across the field in front of her, it then launches itself into a bush and is gone.

'I didn't know what sandwiches you like, so I made a few different kinds,' Sebastian says as he takes out food from the wicker basket. 'So, we've got cheese salad, smoked salmon and cream cheese, and plain old ham.' He looks at her to gauge her reaction.

Sweet, he's nervous. 'They all sound lovely. Can I have a salmon one, please? You made all these?'

'Uh-huh.' Sebastian is distracted, trying to find the right sandwich for Claire.

'Excellent. Get you, I'm impressed.'

Sebastian puffs out his chest and puts his hands on his hips in a *Superman* pose. Claire giggles, while self-consciously pushing her hair out of her eyes, she then wipes a finger under each eye, to make sure her eyeliner hasn't smudged.

'There you go, smoked salmon.' Sebastian hands Claire her sandwich.

They sit for a few minutes, munching on their sandwiches and sipping from their champagne flutes.

'So, you said your dad is improving?' she eventually says quietly, while opening her eyes wide, willing Sebastian to open up.

'Yes, he's responded better than they thought to the chemo. It wasn't looking good, but now the conversations are different, they're much more positive.' Sebastian fiddles with the corner of the picnic basket as he talks. 'It's such a relief.'

'I bet. That's brilliant.'

'Anyway, what have you been up to in nothing-ever-happens Baliston? Getting to know the locals?'

'I am going to speak to Simon about the gnome.'

'I know, that's not what I meant.'

'Oh. Well, Hazel's lovely, but I've been keeping to myself, really. Here is where I'm meant to be. It's doing me good, I think. I needed a break from London.'

'Let me get this right, before everything went downhill after the pub...' Sebastian pulls a pained face. 'You told me you worked in administration but what you really want to do is journalism?'

I'm impressed. He was listening. 'Yeah, that's the dream. I think I'm finally ready to really give it a go.'

'Good for you. Yeah, go for it.' Sebastian grins. 'I can see that for you actually, you do like to ask a lot of questions.'

'That, I do. Is finance your dream job?'

'I wouldn't go that far, but I do like it. Hopefully, my job is still waiting for me. They've been very understanding, but I think they're losing patience.' Sebastian returns to fiddling, this time with the cling film which had been around his sandwich.

Silence hangs in the air. *Shit, what do I say now? I can't tell him he won't lose his job.* 'Right,' Claire says loudly, 'let's do a getting to know each other quiz, job talk is boring.' She claps her hands and stands up.

Sebastian laughs and puts his head in his hands. 'What? Do we have to stand up?' he says while lifting his head.

'Sure, yeah, why not?'

Sebastian gets up. 'Ask away, I suppose.'

Gosh, he's tall, and those shoulders and arms… 'Have you ever been arrested?'

'No.' He purses his lips, suppressing a smile.

'What's the wildest thing you've done?'

'I did the world's highest bungee jump in New Zealand.'

'Really?'

Sebastian nods, grins, and raises his eyebrows.

'Wow.'

'What about you? What's the wildest thing you've done?' he asks.

'Hey, this is my quiz, and you're doing the answering.' She puts her hands on her hips and leans to one side, while pointing one leg forward, aware that it's a superb angle, making her legs seem longer and more shapely.

'Answer this and then I'll answer more.' He folds his arms, and somehow the upper part looks even bigger.

Claire rolls her tongue around her mouth and averts her eyes. 'Okay, the wildest thing…' she ponders, 'skinny dipping in the sea in the middle of the night.' She watches him as he takes in her answer, searching his face for signs of him thinking about her naked.

'Nice, I think that's a better answer.' He stares straight at her, and she holds his gaze.

'Right, next question. How old were you when you lost your virginity?'

'Oh, we're going there, are we? Eighteen, when I went to uni. I was a late bloomer.'

'What's your biggest secret?'

'Probably that. I've never told anyone that before.'

'Well, thank you for choosing to tell me.' She peeps up at him, craning her neck, drinking him in.

'It's the pressure of the questions. How about I ask you a few more? I've only asked you one.'

'Oh no, I couldn't possibly answer any more. I am a woman of mystery.'

'Oh, really?' Sebastian grabs Claire by the waist and pulls her towards him, wrapping his arms around her. He looks down at her, and she looks up at him. Blue meeting brown eyes, his eyelashes are impossibly long and curled, hers are never like that, even with mascara.

Claire reaches to put her arms around his neck, but he's too tall, instead she rests her hands on his shoulders, the tips of her fingers just touching the sides of his neck. She goes for it and kisses him. It's more urgent and rushed than before. There are no gentle pecks this time. Their tongues completely explore each other's mouths, their heads tipped to one side. Her breasts rub on his chest, her erect nipples, begging to be touched. She yearns and aches for him. They stop snogging and pull away from each other, their breathing heavier. She can feel he's hard against her. Claire reaches down and starts stroking and exploring him. Sebastian looks deep into her eyes as her hand brushes up and down the outside of his trousers, teasing, giving him a taste of what could be to come. While grabbing her in for another kiss, his hands begin to wander. He cups one of her breasts and tries to massage her nipple, she can only just about feel it through her padded bra, it makes her want more. He moves both his hands down, rubbing over both her breasts, before wandering down to her waist again, his big hands taking her in, before ending up on her bum. He's leaning down to reach and Claire then finally wraps her arms around the back of his neck. He lifts her up, drawing her into him. She wraps her legs around his waist, the kiss still continuing, becoming more frantic. His dick is now pressing between her legs and she can feel she's wet. She pushes down on the hardness, imagining him inside her.

He lets out a low groan. 'Fuck,' he whispers.

Sebastian slowly drops to his knees and lowers Claire down to the blanket. He moves to go on top of her, but she pushes him back. He unfolds his legs and lets himself fall backwards until he is stretched out on his back in front of her. His arousal is clear against his jeans. His T-shirt has wrinkled up, revealing his abs. Claire can see a line of hair at the bottom of his stomach. *God, he's gorgeous.* She smiles at him and while holding in her own tummy; she slides her knickers off under her dress. Carefully, she places the lacy pants on the picnic blanket, slightly under the basket, hidden from view. He watches her, taking in what is about to happen. She starts to undo his trousers, unbuttoning him and beginning to slide open his zip.

'Wait,' he says.

He pulls her in close again; he sits up and beckons her to straddle him. Sebastian puts his fingers between her legs and starts to stroke. She buries her head in his shoulder as he caresses and she rocks on his hand. Claire opens her eyes and peers across the field. She had forgotten they were outside, near Sebastian's farmhouse, surrounded by trees, crops, and bushes. Only nature is witnessing their passion, *thank god*. She again closes her eyes and plants tiny kisses on the side of his neck. She breathes deeply into his ear when he finds the right spot, encouraging him to continue.

'Come on,' she says, she's had enough, she needs him, now. She grabs the top of his already undone trousers and drags them down to his ankles. 'Have you got protection?' she whispers.

He silently reaches into his pocket and retrieves a condom. Claire lies down on her front next to him and glances away while he sorts himself. She can feel her dress is bunched up around the top of her thighs, the lower part of her bum peeking out. Claire thinks about touching herself, the aching deep down becoming more intense, the anticipation driving her crazy. Instead she traces the checks on the blanket with her pointing finger.

'All set,' Sebastian says in a gruff, deep, yet quiet voice. He pulls her in again. 'You're beautiful,' he says.

It's so genuine and so heartfelt, his eyes intense, it catches Claire off guard. 'So are you,' she gazes back at him, just as intently. It's like their first kiss, the same words spoken, but it means more now.

She climbs on and gently slides him inside her. He groans, and she gasps. As she rocks back and forth, he reaches for her breasts, but they are still hidden and wrapped up in her dress. Sebastian tugs her dress and bra down, and caresses, for the first time skin on skin. She leans over him, and he puts a nipple in his mouth. Sucking and nibbling. The combination is almost too much for Claire. She's almost there, she can feel it building, almost, almost. Then he comes. She was very close but hadn't quite got there. *Damn it. I'll let him off.* Next time. Claire dismounts, smooths her dress over her legs, and puts her boobs back in her bra and dress. She lies down next to him and puts her head on his shoulder. He whips off the condom and pulls up his trousers before snuggling up to her.

'Well, that was unexpected,' he says.

'Mmm,' she says. *Says the man who organised the most romantic picnic ever and had a condom in his pocket.* Not that she's complaining.

'You're amazing.'

Claire opens her eyes and smiles at Sebastian. She could just fall asleep in the sunshine and spend the rest of the day lying on this picnic blanket, breathing him in. It's the most relaxed she's been for a long time.

'How are you really doing?' Sebastian asks, concern written all over his face.

'Good, I was close, but... it was amazing.'

'What?' Sebastian sits up and Claire does the same. 'I meant how are you really coping with everything, since your dad?' He tucks a stray hair behind her right ear and then another strand behind her left ear before cupping her chin in his hands.

'Jesus, really... now?' She can't believe he wants to talk about this now. 'Not exactly pillow talk.'

'Well, we haven't got any pillows.' He chuckles, then all humour drains from his face. 'It's just... I know what it's like to lose a parent. You can talk to me.'

'Sorry, yes, thank you,' Claire says. The birds are tweeting, and she suddenly feels uncomfortable, the ground is bumpy and full of stones. The image of Dad in that hospital bed flashes into her mind, she closes her eyes for a couple of seconds to banish the thought, but it's like it's burned into the inside of her eyelids, because there he remains. Dad. There but not, him but not, seemingly alive but not.

'I don't know if I deserve your sympathy. It's all my fault.' *There I said it.* Claire feels physically sick after finally confessing to someone. But why is she telling him and why now, after they've just had sex? Fucking hell, one fuck and she turns herself inside out, offering her complete self over to him.

'What is?'

'My dad,' Claire can't quite believe she's saying it, finally, what's been going round and round in her head, she's telling Sebastian and saying it out loud. 'I was supposed to meet him, the night he died. We had dinner plans, but I cancelled. He didn't drive to work that day because he was expecting to meet me in the evening. We would have had wine and got a taxi at the end of the night. Instead, he got a lift with Larry from work... and... they... crashed,' she says, her eyes fixed on her shaking hands. She's not sure why she's saying it now. Sebastian had asked about how she really is. This is how she really is. Dealing with the absolute loneliness of missing Dad while also beating herself up for basically killing him.

'Claire, it's not your fault. There was nothing you could have done. It was an accident.' Sebastian stares at her, he won't take his eyes off her.

'Yeah,' is all she says. She pulls up her knees and buries her head in her arms, her body tightly balled up. Claire knows deep down there's nothing she could have done, she couldn't have stopped what happened, she didn't know, but she can't help thinking, what if? What if she hadn't cancelled? Would he still be alive now? Or would he have died suddenly in a different crash or in a different way? Was it his time? Would she have had longer with him if she'd gone for dinner? Would she have died too? She knows she didn't make the crash happen, but that doesn't stop her from feeling guilty. If she wasn't so selfish, would he be alive today? 'I was so wrapped up in going out with my mates and possibly starting to search for my mum.' She jerks her head to gauge Sebastian's reaction, but his expression stays the same. He's listening. 'I was going to tell Dad that night and get his take on it. I should have treasured that man.'

'I'm so sorry this happened, Claire, but there's nothing you could have done.'

It's all she needs to hear. They hug, and they stay cuddling for a long time, absorbing each other's grief and struggles. In each other's arms they talk and take in the bright blue sky, every now and then pointing out birds as they fly over, Sebastian telling Claire the names and marvelling at her lack of ornithological knowledge. The whole time it's just them and the sound of the leaves gently rustling in the breeze.

After a while she climbs back on top of him, and this time she gets there, with bells on.

Chapter Fourteen

Claire is still glowing from the picnic date as she makes her way to Hazel's house.

It really was the most amazing date ever.

Sebastian's nervousness over the sandwiches, opening up to each other, and him listening and comforting her. It was pretty special. Sebastian talking about his mum's death and then encouraging Claire to talk about her dad. He really cares and believes the crash wasn't her fault. They connected on a raw and deeply personal level. After unburdening herself to Sebastian she feels less heavy, less isolated. No longer drowning but treading water instead. She slept amazingly last night. The sex, their chat, seeing where he lives, and meeting his dad have had a loosening and easing on Claire.

Although today, her muscles are tenser and tighter, and her stomach is churning. Hazel is waiting for her. Claire feels awful that she let her down and pissed her off. Hazel is the last person she wants to upset and leave hanging. As she waits at her elderly friend's front door, she does her usual inspection of the garden, ready to marvel at its neatness, but it's different. It's still by anyone's standards very together and well-kept, but the grass doesn't look like it's been carefully curated. It's tidy, but is a little overgrown compared to its usual uniform appearance.

Claire is frowning at the front garden when Hazel answers the door. 'Hi,' Claire says.

'Come in,' Hazel replies in clipped tones.

The welcome is frosty at best. Claire sits on her favourite

velvety, green chair. 'I'm sorry I didn't come on Monday. I really am.' She launches straight into her apology, sensing no small talk is needed or indeed wanted.

Hazel sits on the sofa. She perches on the edge and doesn't sit back, as though she's ready to leave at any second. 'What happened?' Hazel pinches invisible bits of dust or fluff – well, god knows what, there's nothing there – from her black skirt. Her hand repeatedly forming into a pincer grip as if she's holding a pen and then flicking into a spider shape as she gets rid of the imaginary dirt. It's done with such vigour and violence that Claire can hear Hazel's nails and fingers rub together as she flicks. It's almost as if she's clicking her fingers and summoning an explanation from Claire. Impatience rolls off every movement. It's really a rather excellent impression of a completely hacked off headmistress.

Claire gulps, hard. Her mouth is dry, and she gets the urge to laugh, so she presses her lips together. Nervous energy does the most ridiculous things. The last thing she needs to do now is laugh. She glances at the sword on the opposite wall and at the surrounding photos. Lots of toothy grins. Hazel's support system waiting for her explanation. Hazel is fast becoming her support system. *Have I really messed this up? I need Hazel in my life.* 'I went for a night out in London, and I got really upset. It just all reminded me of the night my dad died, I couldn't cope.' It's the truth and, it's straight to the point. Claire strokes the velvety arms of the chair, seeking the comfort she usually finds. Today, it feels rougher and not as accommodating. The brown material, peeking through from underneath the velvet, where many arms have rested, is uncomfortable and inhospitable. Claire stops fiddling.

'I'm sorry to hear that, but I need someone reliable. I think we are going to have to part ways.' Hazel's bottom lip trembles, she lifts up her chin and swallows, waiting for a response from Claire.

Claire opens her mouth and leaves it open for a while before snapping it shut. *She doesn't want me anymore?* The rejection is like a swift punch. Claire feels physically winded, a pain shoots through her stomach and breathing is a struggle. Her body is responding in the same way it did to the night out in London. She slowly breathes in through her nose and exhales a gush of air out of her mouth, focusing on the simple act of taking in oxygen and releasing carbon dioxide, to fight off the impending panic attack. She's come to rely on Hazel, she feels safe talking to her about anything and she's fun, Claire feels like a better person around her.

'Andrew is still keen to help, so I'm going to let him.' Hazel nods her head in one brisk action, her mouth is clamped shut. She smooths her skirt with both hands and again starts brushing away imaginary crumbs or dust or fluff.

'Really, that's it?' *Just like that she's getting rid of me? This is why I never fully trust anyone.* After finally opening up Claire can't believe Hazel is now casting her aside at the first problem, at the first sign of trouble. She's spent months in her own head, speaking to no one about how she truly feels, not knowing how to deal with the mounting guilt and grief. But she'd seen something in Hazel – a kindness, a wiseness, which disarmed her. Hazel is these things, isn't she? It doesn't feel like it in this moment. Claire can feel rage and upset stirring within her. She feels sick and shaky.

'For the job, yes,' Hazel says. 'I would like us to remain friends.' Hazel stares at a photo of Jack. It's clear she really wants her husband right now.

Claire wells up. The building emotions crash and wash over her. 'Thank god, so I can still come round for a cup of tea and a chat?' Her armpits and hands are sweaty. She tries to rub the sweat from her palms.

'Of course. I'll be fucking mad if you don't,' Hazel shouts in pretend fury. She waggles her finger at Claire, visibly relieved for a bit of humour and to still have a friend.

'I am sorry, Hazel.' *She's still my friend, she's not casting me aside, not really. Who cares about the stupid job. I just want my seventy-*

nine-year-old friend, who really is becoming my best friend, well, alongside Saskia… hopefully. 'I haven't imagined it, have I? We are friends? We have a laugh, and we talk, like, really talk.'

'Yes, of course we're friends, and you not working for me doesn't change that.' Hazel smiles. 'Besides, you make me young again. It's magic.' Hazel waves her arms around and tickles the air with her fingers, as if she's sprinkling fairy dust.

'You're magic to me. You make me feel like I can actually get through this. You're keeping me sane at the minute.' Claire chuckles but she's serious. She's come to rely on Hazel. When something happens, she needs and wants Hazel's take on it. This must be what it's like to have a mum. If that's the case, she was right to never search for her actual mum, as she's found Hazel, instead. *Hazel is sacking me, but she's not giving up on me.*

'A magical duo.' Hazel sighs. 'I know you're sorry. I appreciate you apologising. Why was London so bad?' She sits back in the sofa and makes herself comfortable, her posture and demeanour totally changing. The headmistress has gone, hopefully never to be seen again.

'I don't know, it just reminded me of when I got the call from the hospital about Dad. In a bar, surrounded by people.'

'What happened?' Hazel says softly.

Oh yes, I haven't told her. 'Car crash.'

'I see. Thanks for sharing.' She reaches for Claire's hand.

Claire is again messing with the pile of the velvet, pushing it this way and that, watching as the nap creates different patterns and catches the light in different ways. She stops, takes Hazel's hand, and rubs her friend's wrinkles and bumpy veins. 'I seem to be doing a lot of that at the moment.'

Hazel raises her eyebrows.

'Me and Sebastian had a chat as well. He gets it.' Claire fights a grin which is threatening to spread across her whole face. She also tries to empty her brain, otherwise she'll be thinking about the picnic and she won't be remembering and focusing on the sandwiches. Other things certainly spring to mind when she thinks about yesterday. She's sure she'll never look at a picnic blanket in the same way ever again.

'Oh, so it's back on then?'

'Yeah, I guess it is.' Claire knows there's a glint in her eye.

'Cuppa?'

'Yes please. I'll make it.'

Chapter Fifteen

Claire and Sebastian have been texting non-stop. It's been over a week since the picnic sex, and they haven't seen each other. He's been too busy on the farm and with his dad. She likes the idea of him rumbling along in his tractor, on his own in the middle of nowhere, typing away to her. Yesterday, in their last few messages they stumbled upon their next activity.

SEBASTIAN: Tell me. What's your favourite film?

CLAIRE: It was Dirty Dancing, me and Saskia have watched it thousands of times. But since seeing The Notebook a few years ago, I think that might be my favourite now. What's yours?

SEBASTIAN: The Notebook? Never heard of it. Never seen it. Mine's a classic. LETHAL WEAPON.

CLAIRE: Not sure you can call Lethal Weapon a classic, but then I haven't seen it.

SEBASTIAN: It's a date then.

CLAIRE: Eh?

SEBASTIAN: A movie date. U and me tomorrow. We watch both films at yours. I'll bring popcorn. AND we decide which is best.

CLAIRE: Deal. You're on.

Sebastian is taking the afternoon off; his Auntie Cath will make sure his dad is okay and the farm staff will be busy on the farming side of things. Claire's been allowing herself to daydream about him, replaying their date, the picnic, the chatting, and the wild outdoor sex. She's never done anything like that before, she's always got down to things in bed.

Past boyfriends have asked her to try different places, but she's never really been up for it. The ex, Chris had wanted to do it in a nightclub toilet once, and Claire had been tempted and had almost gone along with it. For a moment the idea seemed adventurous and raunchy, but when they walked in, it was dirty and seedy. Claire marched Chris straight back out. It's infuriating that Chris keeps swimming around her head. *I wish I hadn't bumped into him. Just because he cheated on me doesn't mean Sebastian will. This is different.* With Sebastian, the adventurous sex happened organically. Well, she's sure he'd been hoping it would happen, and as soon as she saw the picnic set up, her mind had gone there, if only for a second. They just had to have each other, it had been building up, all the arguments and the little kisses on their first date.

Claire's back to not doing very much since Hazel sacked her. But she has been scanning the media jobs section in *The Guardian*, to see what's out there. There's nothing suitable at the moment, plus she's not ready yet, but she's heartened by the act of looking. It's the first time she's searched for journalist jobs since she left uni. Maybe it's time to start putting herself out there?

Sebastian will pick her up soon. They're going to drive to *Blockbuster* and rent both films. Claire hasn't got a copy of *The Notebook*, she went to see it at the cinema three times and has been meaning to buy it on DVD. Sebastian's copy of *Lethal Weapon* is at his flat in London. She might have seen a bit of it one Christmas, but that could have been *Die Hard*. Those type of films merge into one.

But before Sebastian comes to get her she has just about enough time to go see Simon about his smashed-up gnome. She's been putting it off for weeks now, but she can't leave it much longer. It's drizzling as she makes her way down the main road, the perfect weather for a movie day.

Claire arrives outside Simon's bungalow. There's a new gnome in the old gnome's place. This one is holding a green watering can, but basically looks like the red spade one's brother. He's still got the long white beard and pointy red hat. Claire is thankful she has no urge to kick it, she's now in a very different place to when she did obliterate a gnome. The pain and Dad are still ever present, but it's not all-consuming.

Sebastian is now dominating her thoughts, maybe that's not a good thing? She makes a mental note to play it cool and not get too carried away with her new romance.

Surely, you can't swap grief for passion, and everything's better?

Hopping from one obsession to another, jumping from a pit of despair to kissing and giggling at a boy's texts. In fact, what is she doing? Is she even ready for any of this? But it is fun and distracting, which feels better than the alternative.

Claire knocks on the front door. Simon answers almost instantly. He's younger than she'd imagined. Probably in his fifties. He has brown hair with speckles of white and grey at the sides. He's short, slim, and well presented; wearing a shirt, tie, and green jumper. It matches the gnome's watering can.

'Hi, I'm Claire. I live at Bramble Cottage.'

'Hello. Simon.' He rests his hand on his heart. 'What can I do you for?'

'Well, um... I'm a friend of Sebastian's, you know him, don't you?'

'Er, yeah, Robert's lad.'

'He suggested coming to speak to you.' Claire takes a breath, *how is she going to word this?* 'Your gnome—'

'Oh, you heard about that,' Simon interrupts, 'terrible business, mindless vandalism.' He shakes his head.

'Yes, I wanted to speak to you about that. It was me. I was having an awful day and was very upset, and I'm afraid I kicked and smashed the gnome,' Claire speed talks, before she changes her mind.

'You did it?' Simon's eyes widen.

'Yes.' Claire inspects her sandals.

'Okay, and you're telling me this now, why?' Simon stands up tall and pushes back his shoulders.

'I wanted to say I'm sorry. I really am. I should have come to see you earlier; I've been plucking up the courage. I never should have done what I did. Sebastian has been saying I should come down and speak to you and explain. He said you'd understand.'

'I appreciate the apology. You know I'll have to explain to the Parish Council, they were looking into organising some patrols around the village.'

'Yes, that's fine.' How embarrassing. Everyone is going to know. What will they think of her? Well, they're just going to have to move on and find something else to gossip about. She won't be here forever, anyway. 'Of course, I will pay for your replacement. I see you already have one. How much did it cost?' Claire asks in a business-like manner, any humbleness dissipating. She shifts back into self-preservation mode.

'It was forty-five pounds, I only buy the best.'

Claire's mouth drops open, before she gathers herself and starts rummaging around in her handbag for her purse. She finds two twenties and a ten-pound note and offers them to Simon.

He hesitates, before taking the notes out of her hand. 'Thank you, I appreciate your honesty. It's the correct and honourable thing to do, to take responsibility for your actions.'

'Yeah.' Claire fiddles with the zip on her purse. 'Sorry, again. It won't happen again.'

'Good. Say hi to Sebastian. Don't go corrupting him. He's a good lad.' Simon nods and smiles and with that, he's gone.

Cheeky bastard. But she knows it's what she deserves. As she walks back to her cottage to wait for Sebastian, the drizzle stops, and an earthiness fills the air. Claire breathes in that after-the-rain smell.

#

'You're quiet,' Sebastian says when they've been in the car for ten minutes without any chit-chat.

'Mmm, I guess I am,' Claire says. She's been concentrating on trying to get out of her funk while watching the cows and sheep through the passenger window. In the field they've just passed half the cows were lying down and half were standing up. What's that saying? If they're lying down it means it's going to rain? Or is it the other way round?

'Well? What's up?' Sebastian glances at her, and then back at the road.

'I went to see Simon.'

'YES!' Sebastian shouts. A huge smile on his face. 'Well done, you.'

'He was nice, but obviously a bit pissed off and confused.'

'He's hardly going to pat you on the back, is he? I bet he accepted your apology though?'

'He did, but he also said he's got to tell the Parish Council, as they're planning some patrols.'

'Really? Has it gone that far? Was he pulling your leg?'

Claire frowns. 'No idea, I thought he was serious.'

'He's a nice man, he won't want to make an example of you or anything.'

'Mmm,' she says.

Claire goes back to her window gazing. She feels like an idiot. She tries to tell herself it's no big deal. Sebastian saw her do it and look at them now, he's still given her a chance and they're more than good. She studies his face. He's focusing on driving.

His eyes and eyebrows in concentration mode. The clouds have now disappeared making the sky an all-encompassing clear blue, to match Sebastian's eyes. They're quite unbelievable. Claire's eyes dart back and forth, at him and then past him and out of his window, then again at him and then past him, out through the glass. Amazing, actual sky-blue eyes. Next, she explores his freckles, hunting for patterns, like she's eagerly following a treasure map. His hair is flopping down into his eyes again, and he keeps flipping it back with a little twitch of his head, it's the most adorable yet sexy thing ever. Claire has to stop herself from reaching out and brushing his hair back for him. She imagines doing just that, he then pulls her towards him, she straddles him, and they start to kiss.

Ridiculous.

It's like she's got the mind of a horny teenager at the moment.

She can't distract him, he's driving. What a stupid thought. If she climbed on top of him they would certainly crash. Crash. Again, she sees her dad in the hospital bed. Lying there. The most important person in her life transformed into a recognisable stranger. She's haunted by that room and the machines, feeling like it's from another life, instead of months ago. This image though, of her dad, motionless in white sheets, is imprinted into her brain. Claire doesn't need to remember that version of her dad. If only there was a way of pressing a button and deleting this particular memory. Its existence is complete torture. She tries to conjure up her dad in happier times, but once the hospital bed image pops up, she has a battle on her hands to banish it.

Claire realises Sebastian is witnessing the horror in her mind, he's staring, with a questioning expression. They're at a set of traffic lights, he's been watching her, seeing her relive her life fall apart.

'So,' she says brightly, 'are we nearly there?'

'Yeah, just round this corner. I forgot the popcorn, but

they should have some there.' He goes along with the jovial conversation.

'Of course, what would *Blockbuster* be without popcorn?!'

'Are you ready for the best film of all time?' Sebastian asks. 'Are you?'

#

Claire closes the curtains and plunges the lounge into darkness. Sebastian walks in from the kitchen with a bowl in each hand, carrying the must-have essentials of popcorn and wine gums.

'I can't see a thing in here,' he says.

'It's to get the cinema experience,' she says to the outline of Sebastian. Claire's eyes haven't adjusted yet either.

They both make their way to the sofa from opposite ends of the room and sit down with the bowls between them and start shovelling popcorn into their mouths.

'What are we going to watch first?' Sebastian asks. He pushes the popcorn into his cheeks to enable him to talk, his face is hamster-esque and his speech is still muffled.

'I think you just asked me, what are we going to watch first?' Claire frowns. How can he still look gorgeous while being a greedy pig? In fact, it makes him more adorable. *Shit, I've got it bad.*

Sebastian nods. 'Mmm-hmm.'

Claire laughs. 'Anyone would think you've not eaten for days. Let's watch *The Notebook* first. Let's start with brilliance and then we'll be able to cope with your rubbish.' She wrinkles her nose and grins at him, waiting for his reaction.

'I don't need any order tricks; my film speaks for itself.' He nods, pleased with his response.

Claire puts in the DVD and the movie begins, a sunset over water appears and slow classical music accompanies the scene. She folds her legs up onto the sofa and gets comfy. Sebastian is close but they're not touching, the bowls of treats are in the way.

During the opening credits, she sneaks a glance at him. He's focusing on the screen. She loves that he's giving her film a go and is willing to do something that really isn't his cup of tea, but he'll do it for her, to make her happy.

He realises he's being watched and turns to Claire and smiles. 'Watch the film!' he raises his voice in mock annoyance. 'Or are you bored by your own film already?' He widens his eyes, acting shocked and dismayed.

'Of course not, you're just a little distracting.' She flicks her hair.

They settle into silence as the film properly gets underway. In the movie, when Noah climbs onto a Ferris wheel to get Allie's attention, to ask her out, Sebastian says, 'That's like when I asked you out in the pub.'

'I don't remember you climbing anything.' Claire says between laughs.

'Well, no, but they had a little bit of a rocky start, like us. She wasn't showing any interest, so he had to go big. It took guts for me to come up to you in the pub. You were unsure about even getting in my car after you fell off your bike… and yet… I carried on and made a big gesture—'

'By walking across the pub to talk to me?'

'Exactly. That's a big move around these parts.'

'Watch the film.' She playfully slaps his arm.

Claire notices Sebastian's smile when Noah and Allie dance in the street to no music. It's a romantic moment and she can see, much to her delight, it's captured Sebastian. Later in the film, Allie and Noah go on a beach date and she starts cawing and flapping like a bird.

'What is this?' Sebastian puts his hands over his face and continues watching through his fingers.

'Shhh!' Claire throws a cushion at him.

And after a montage of Noah and Allie arguing lots, but also being crazy about each other, Sebastian whispers, 'You and me.' He points his finger at Claire and then at his chest.

Sebastian moves the bowls off the sofa onto the floor and beckons Claire. He puts his arm around her, and she leans her head on his shoulder. She breathes in his oaky, musky, manly aroma.

He traces circles on her arm during the sex scene.

Sebastian pulls Claire closer and gives her a squeeze when Allie almost crashes her car into another car. In return, she rubs his arm and snuggles into him.

When Allie and Noah are older, the movie reaches its gut-wrenching, weep-inducing climax. Claire wipes away her tears and self-consciously lifts her head off Sebastian's shoulder to glance at him and he's crying too. He roughly scrapes his hand across his eyes and giggles to himself when he realises Claire has clocked his emotional reaction to the story.

'Well?' she says as the closing credits roll across the screen.

He slowly nods. 'Surprisingly good. Not just a chick flick. An actual enjoyable watch. Now though, it's time for something that's not as sentimental, but probably twice as fun.' Sebastian rubs his hands together.

'Straight away?' Claire exhales dramatically. 'Okay, let's do this.'

'We don't have to watch it, really.' Sebastian chortles.

'No, a deal is a deal.'

'Very honourable.' He ruffles her hair like he's petting a dog.

'Hey,' she shout-laughs.

'I've been thinking. Do you want to drive out to Dovedale Stepping Stones? Maybe in a few days?'

'Don't you need to be at the farm?'

'I can be out for a few hours. In fact, I think Dad would prefer that I did. He says I'm suffocating him and that he needs to have some space. I suppose that must mean he's feeling better than he was.' Sebastian shrugs.

'Dovedale Stepping Stones? Should I know what that is?'

'Yes! They're iconic and a fun way to get across a river.'

'You want to take me to a bunch of rocks?' Claire tries to suppress her teasing smirk.

'I know how to show a girl a good time.' Sebastian pushes his hair out of his eyes. 'It's really pretty and a nice walk. Not the most exciting thing in the world, but it's something different. And romantic…' He embraces her, which leads to a long and sensual kiss.

Claire comes up for air. 'Sounds great,' she says. It really does. They kiss again, and *Lethal Weapon* is soon forgotten.

Chapter Sixteen

After rumbling over several cattle grids, Claire and Sebastian arrive at the large car park for Dovedale Stepping Stones, which is full of cars.

'It looks busy, especially for a random week day,' Claire says as she takes off her seatbelt. There are couples and young families milling around, keen to explore.

'Well, it's a popular tourist attraction,' Sebastian says while scanning the area. 'I'm saying that like I know what I'm talking about.' He laughs. 'I haven't been here since I was a child, but I remember there being lots of people then, as well.'

Claire can feel a warmth in her chest. He first experienced this as a child, and now he's brought her here. There's a short walk to the stepping stones. They amble along the beige path; the loud and fast-flowing River Dove is to their right, and the hills crowd around them at every angle. Bumpy blankets of green and grey. It's like they're walking through a valley, heading towards the centre, which is just out of view. The grassy and rocky hills are breathtaking, and despite the chitter-chatter of other tourists, the drama of the landscape still has a peacefulness about it.

The Dovedale Stepping Stones are a set of slabs, positioned closely together, to allow people to cross the water. The crossing is made up of about fifteen stones, some are bigger with enough room to fit a few people on, but one in particular is about half the size of the other stones and looks precarious for even one person to stand on. The rocks are natural and irregular and have been shaped by many feet brushing by over many years. She can feel the history as they queue for their turn to cross. The river, an opening between meeting mounds, a collision of nature.

'Nearly our turn,' she says to Sebastian, as the queue moves forward and more visitors have a go at stepping across. Returning her gaze to the river, the stone crossing is smaller and shorter than she thought, the clear water is quite narrow and shallow. Some people are steady and cautious, taking careful, slow strides, while others leap and jump. Claire glances at Sebastian again, he's frowning. 'What's up?' she asks.

'It's just… it looks different.' Sebastian crosses his arms and then a grin slowly spreads across his face. 'I remember it being bigger. Maybe everything looks bigger when you're a kid.' He shrugs.

'I can see how this would have been a challenge for a child and a real adventure. Think it might be a challenge for me too,' Claire offers with a chuckle as they step forward again, getting closer to the water.

The image of her jumping onto what she thought was a large shiny stone, when she was young and out in the countryside with her dad, pops into Claire's head. The utter horror of discovering it was a cow pat. The muddy dirt smell and the mess are so fresh in her memory it could have been yesterday, the event seared into her brain. She thinks about telling Sebastian about it, but then decides to keep it for herself. Hopefully these actual stones go a little better.

Claire hops along the uneven rocks, treading carefully as she goes before stopping in the middle to take in the River Dove in all its glory. Green yet rocky hills are in every direction. It's like she's walking on water, she's close to the shimmering liquid, yet hovering above on the weathered and worn boulders. The water is rushing by. A nearby mallard tries and fails to swim against the flow. Sebastian is ahead of her, showing her how it's done. Claire peeks back to where she's just left behind and realises she needs to keep moving as the queue continues behind her. Sebastian is a few stones in front when he sees she's stopped. He backtracks.

'You're going to cause a traffic jam,' he says while gently taking her hand.

'Thanks for the help, but I need to balance.' Claire lets go of his hand, preferring to have both her arms free to hold out like a scarecrow in order to negotiate the sometimes slippy stepping stones. *I've got this.* 'You're being a true gent,' she adds, not wanting to offend him.

Sebastian smiles. 'I try my best. Come on.' He steps across the ancient blocks once again.

He's quicker than her, so she tries to move along at a higher speed, but she worries about falling – even though the water is shallow – and slows down. She's happy to see his tall frame moving with ease, his broad shoulders and muscly bum in perfect view. She's revelling in the attention from Sebastian. It's lovely to have someone else take the lead, organise the day and plan everything, she just has to follow.

'Not bad, right?' Sebastian says once they've successfully crossed the river.

'Yeah, fun,' Claire says and puts her hands on her hips, while taking a few deep breaths.

'I'll make you an outdoorsy person.' He laughs.

'I am an outdoorsy person?!'

'You're definitely town mouse trying to be country mouse and only kind of enjoying it.'

He's perceptive. 'Yeah, I like it round here for a change, but you're right, London is home. What about you?'

'What do you mean?'

'Where's home for you now?'

'Well, Baliston is proper home, but my life is in London.' Sebastian squints. 'Shall we carry on walking for a bit?' He nods his head towards the seemingly never-ending beige path, which disappears into the distance. A green sign points in the direction Sebastian is facing. It says the meandering track goes to Milldale, which is two and a half miles away. That sounds like a bit of a hike. Claire bites her bottom lip.

Sebastian follows her gaze. 'Don't worry, we won't go that far. There're some steps I want to show you. It's so cool at the top, you can see for miles. It's not far. The steps were built by Italian prisoners of war.' He raises his eyebrows at Claire and then starts striding down the path.

Has he been researching this place? He really is taking this whole tour guide thing seriously. The thought of him planning their day out and investigating the history of Dovedale Stepping Stones and the surrounding area simply melts Claire. Okay, if he's going to be so sweet, she can put in the effort and climb a load of steps for some unknown reason.

Claire quick steps to catch up with Sebastian. 'Okay, I'm in, show me the sights.'

He grins at her, and they march on.

'How is your dad doing?' she asks.

'He's doing much better. Oh, I've been meaning to ask you. Bit short notice now. Can you hang out with him for a few hours tomorrow morning? I've got loads of stuff to get done on the farm and I don't like to leave him for too long, plus Auntie Cath has been helping out a lot lately…' He opens his gorgeous blue eyes wide.

Claire is taken aback. It's a big ask after, what, four dates? He must see them going somewhere if he's asking her to care for his dad. He knows she's not really doing anything at the moment, not since Hazel gave her the heave-ho, but still.

This is a big deal. It makes her glow from within.

'Yeah, I can do that, he seems nice.' It means she gets to see Sebastian again tomorrow.

'Thank you, I owe you one,' Sebastian says. He then becomes distracted when he notices a couple of splashes of water on the face of his silver watch. Using his thumb to wipe the drops away and the bottom of his top to polish up the glass, he checks the watch is still working. He's transported elsewhere, completely focused, and the rather intense conversation they were having is forgotten.

Claire tries to pull him back to her. 'Nice watch. Is it damaged?'

Sebastian stops frowning and re-focuses on Claire. 'No, I thought it was for a second, but it's fine. It was a present from my mum. The last thing she gave me.' His Blackberry begins to ring. 'Just one sec.' He holds up his pointing finger briefly and wanders off the footpath onto a patch of grass near to the water.

Claire welcomes the break and wanders a bit further up the track to sit on a rock. The last thing his mum gave him, no wonder he's protective over his watch. She's pleased he told her, a very private nugget of information, shared.

What's it like to have an active mum? One that gives you presents? A mum that you knew and miss?

Claire takes in the scenery while also watching him. He walks up and down and in circles, kicking his legs up into the air, chatting away while studying the grass. He's talking business. She hears "spreadsheets" and "Giles has the numbers". Sebastian ends the call and walks to where Claire is waiting for him.

'Everything okay?'

'Sure, brilliant actually. It was my boss, checking in. He's keen to get me back, which is a relief. They haven't replaced me.' Sebastian runs a hand through his hair. 'It feels like I've been gone a long time.'

'That's great.' Claire feels a pang of something. Is this going somewhere, or is he going somewhere? Too early to ask, she remembers her promise to herself about playing it cool. 'It's great that you've got such a great career. I've started thinking I should get one of those!' Claire laughs, she really must stop saying "great", she sounds like an overexcited Labrador, well if it could talk.

'Yeah, it's great.' He teasingly jabs her in the ribs with his elbow. 'If you want to be a career woman, you should go out and do it. Do whatever you want.'

'I suppose, it's just with everything that happened before Christmas—'

'Yeah, but you graduated four years ago, right?'

'Yes,' Claire hangs on each letter, elongating the word.

'So, get on with it.' He gives her another playful jab.

He's not wrong. She does need to take control of her life. Even before everything happened, the same was true then, she's been coasting for years. There's always an excuse to not put herself out there and play it safe.

'Any thoughts on tracking down your mum?' Sebastian says, his face is serious.

Claire can't believe it, she braces herself to have a go at him, to tell him where to go, again. How dare he bring this up again? Wasn't she clear about how she felt about this? Then she realises his lips are tightly folded, restraining a smirk. Cheeky sod. This time she tries to jab him in the ribs, but he's quick, he grabs her elbow and pulls her towards him. He leans down and kisses her. She goes to wrap her arms around his shoulders but remembers she can't reach and rests her arms on his chest. Their bodies press together, the kissing becoming more urgent. Her hands wander to his bulging arms, caressing his muscles. His hands wander to her bottom, he cups each cheek. Claire then remembers where they are, in a very public place, she shrinks away, feeling very self-conscious about a very showy snogging session. She rubs her mouth with the back of her hand, her lips feel sore. Sebastian hasn't shaved and is all stubbly.

'Prude.'

'Whatever,' Claire says, but she's smiling.

'Right, let's go for this walk,' he says.

'To the walk,' she shouts and points to the path stretching out in front of them. Being silly with someone really is the best medicine, of course it helps if the person you're being silly with is bloody beautiful.

While gulping for air, Claire takes in her surroundings after climbing what must have been hundreds, if not thousands of steps. They really are high up; they could be at the top of a mountain.

They're even standing next to a stony and craggy peak which is smooth in places from hands and feet climbing to the top. They're on their own now, the crowds left behind.

'Let's stand up there.' Sebastian points to the rocky crest. 'You can't really tell how high we are near the steps.'

Claire's pretty sure she can, but she nods and follows him. At the top of the summit, near to the steps, she clings onto Sebastian. It's steep. They're above the neighbouring grassy hill, which is dotted with trees.

'Wow,' she manages to say through gritted teeth.

'You wanna stand back near the steps?'

'Oh, yeah.'

At the steps, he says, 'Sorry, if that was too scary.'

'No need to apologise, I'm glad we did it, I just didn't want to hang around there for long.' She titters. Her legs feel wobbly.

'This area is called "Lover's Leap". The legend is a young woman heard her lover had passed away in the war. Desperate with grief, she jumped... but her life was saved when her skirts got caught in the undergrowth.'

'How sad,' she says while surveying the distant trees on the hill next to them.

'She lived though, she was saved, something caught her and saved her life.' He pulls her towards him. They gaze into each other's eyes, Sebastian craning his neck down, and Claire craning her neck up.

They both lean in at the same time.

The kiss is tender and Claire's convinced, full of love. There's a lump in her throat and for once she feels like crying happy tears.

Chapter Seventeen

Making her way through the woods, Claire strolls to Sebastian's farm, so much more relaxed than the first time she encountered these trees. That day feels unreal now, like a bad dream. At least she met Sebastian that day. She feels calm and happy in his company, the madness of this year becoming more distant. He's thoughtful and kind. Caring for his dad and planning their dates. A gentle soul who treasures a watch his mum gave him years ago.

Dad is still occupying her mind a lot of the time, but she's managing, she's getting out, and living her life. So many things make her think of Dad, including being amongst trees. On walks, when she was little he would ask her if she knew the name of each different tree they came across. He'd get her to inspect the leaves and then present her guess. He'd do this for a few minutes before stopping, walking in silence, and suddenly, without warning start quizzing her again, trying to catch her off guard. She can't even remember the names now, she knows Oak, but that's about it. Oak trees have the best leaves, those bumpy edges bring her joy and another memory of her dad.

She's starting to realise that night probably wasn't her fault. Yes, she shouldn't have cancelled on him, but even if they had met up and gone for a lovely dinner, maybe he would have still died. Maybe it was his time? Claire's not sure if she believes in people having a "time" to die, but she really is trying to let go of the guilt. She had, after all, cancelled on him many times before. He knew she loved him. If she had gone to the dinner, she would have had that time with him, and maybe he would have lived for a few more months, years? Or maybe he was destined to be involved in a crash in some way that night, no matter what. Claire could drive herself crazy thinking about the "what ifs". She's trying to think about it differently, what happened has happened, it's tragic and awful, but there's nothing she could have done about it. This is what she's beginning to consider, there's an acorn starting to grow and form, which holds her not blaming herself. She's still not quite convinced. Grief is a wretched beast. All she really knows is that she misses him.

Her mind unexpectedly flicks to her mum. She can understand why Sebastian would think she should try to find her. By the sounds of things, he had a great mum who was taken too soon. He would have looked for her if she had walked out. But Claire's mum isn't her, she left years ago, and there's been nothing since. She half expected to hear from her when Dad's obituary was put in the paper, but still the silence continues. That's a stone best left unturned, Claire knows she doesn't need that kind of person in her life, especially now that she hasn't got the support of her dad.

Claire finds herself at Sebastian's front door, she's been so lost in her own thoughts, she's not sure how she got here. She glances at the gnomes and gives them a little nod then knocks on the door.

'Good morning,' Sebastian whispers. 'Dad is asleep at the moment, come in.'

Claire steps inside. Is he going to give her a hello kiss? He doesn't. 'What's your plan for today?' She stands in the middle of the lounge and twiddles a loose thread on her top.

'I've got so much to do in the barn and the fields. Thanks so much for doing this. If you're here and I know Dad is fine, it means I can get on with things. I don't have to keep coming in to check on him.'

He seems harassed and not focused on her at all. Claire's fine with that, this isn't a date. She's just helping him out, this is a huge honour, he's trusting her with his dad. 'Right, what do I need to do?'

'Leave him sleeping, he'll probably shout when he wakes up. Go get him up and bring him down to his chair. He needs to take two of these tablets at 1 o'clock.' Sebastian waves an orange, see-through tablet pot at her and places it on the coffee table. 'Don't touch the tablets with your hands, they're actually kinda radioactive, use plastic gloves, they're in the kitchen under the sink.'

'Okay,' Claire says. This is more serious than she'd anticipated, she really is going to be Sebastian's dad's nurse for the day, she's in way over her head.

'You'll be fine, it's nothing complicated, and he's not as bad as he was.' Sebastian closes the gap between them and rubs the outside of both of her arms.

She glances up at him. 'Right. Good.' Claire repeatedly rubs down the cuticles on her thumbs with her fingers, before clasping her hands together. He kisses her on the forehead and then quickly withdraws and starts lacing up his boots.

Okay, that was a bit like an uncle kissing his niece on the head, passionless, but he's distracted.

It's fine.

'Make him some lunch too. There's some leftover chicken in the fridge, to make a salad with. He'll moan, but he needs to be eating healthily. I'll be back before tea, so I can sort that.'

'Okay, I can do this.' Claire nods her head, her focus on the red carpet.

'Of course you can, your main job is to keep him company really, and you're fantastic company.'

He finishes putting on his boots and again comes to find her, to be close to her. 'Come here, sexy nurse.' He looks deep into her soul, puts his arms around her, and pulls her to him by clasping her arse. They kiss. This is no uncle kiss, this is nothing but passion. His hands move from her bottom, up to her face, caressing her body as they go, brushing past her breasts. His fingers are in her hair, his palms on her cheekbones, her curls are dangling in his grasp as he gently massages her scalp. She can feel his attraction. She wants him now. Her breathing is heavy and laboured. He pulls away, his eyes penetrating her. She can see his mind is racing. He shakes his head and adjusts himself in his trousers. 'Fuck, you drive me crazy. Sorry, I've got to go. Let's continue this later.'

Claire just nods, and he leaves. She feels turned on and abandoned at the same time. What a welcome. What a start to the day. She walks to the bottom of the stairs and can hear Robert snoring upstairs. Okay, he's still asleep. No witness to their lust and no need for her to be a nurse yet. It's odd being in Sebastian's childhood home, basically alone. They've only really just started dating. This feels like a huge leap forward. Circumstance has made this happen, but he asked her. He didn't have to ask her. This has to be a step forward in their relationship, whatever it ends up to be, but it's such an untrodden, unusual path, Claire isn't sure how to feel.

What Claire does know is that this is an excellent chance to have a snoop, her curious, wannabe journalist senses are tingling. As if she's going to hang about on her own in his house without having a ferret around, she simply has to. She makes her way around the lounge. Claire can tell she would have liked Sebastian's mum, there's a warmth about her in the photos scattered around the room, she reminds her of Hazel. There seems to be the same caring yet carefree spirit about her. Claire stops and wonders how could she possibly know that from photos, just one captured moment which in itself is fake and posed. She concludes it's her eyes, you can tell a lot from someone's eyes and hers are kind. She's seen the lounge before so she wanders into the kitchen, her first time in this room.

It's fantastic, there's no other word for it. The dream country kitchen. A rustic hanging pot rack takes centre stage, dangling from the ceiling. Below, in the centre, is a huge island. There're two farmhouse sinks, and beautiful wooden cupboards surround the room. On the far side is a huge open fire with Welsh dressers either side, displaying posh plates and rows of glasses. There's a wooden table, with six chairs around it, but it seems like nobody's eaten at it for a while. It's covered in papers and open files. It's as though someone's taken some very organised folders and chucked them at the table. Claire has a cursory glance. It's financial stuff relating to the farm. Bills, Government forms, bank statements, and invoices for supplies. Claire drags her eyes away. She wants to snoop to a degree, but this is private and isn't Sebastian's stuff, it's his dad's. Is Sebastian struggling to keep things afloat? Or is this his dad's rather messy filing system?

It must have been lovely growing up here, with two parents, when Sebastian was little and devastating when his mum died. A real family home, the type you see in films. Claire opens a few draws and finds cutlery, a junk draw full of wires and batteries, and a larger pan draw full of, well, pans. Just the usual. The table is a mess, but the rest of the kitchen is spotless. It's extremely clean, there are no dishes on the side, the sinks are gleaming, and you glide along the floor tiles. Has he done this for her, or is he always this domesticated?

The next room is the utility, and it stinks. It's full of farming clothes and mud. Claire quickly closes the door on that one. Nothing to see there. There's a study and a swish laptop. Surely, that's Sebastian's? Is he still doing some work for his job as well? When will he go back to London, and when will she go back? For her, most likely when her six-month rental contract is up, she can't see herself staying for longer.

'SEBASTIAN!' Sebastian's dad yells from upstairs. Shit, does he even know she's here?

Claire runs upstairs and tries to guess where Robert is. She opens one door – the bathroom. She opens another – a bedroom, the bed is empty, and it smells of Sebastian. She scans the room, trying to take it in.

No, no, no. This isn't the time to be nosy now.

She opens another door, and finally she's in the right one. Tiny Robert is lying in the middle of a huge double bed. 'Um, hi Mr Jones, it's Claire,' she says through the crack of the door.

'What? Where's Sebastian?'

'He's working on the farm and asked me to hang out with you for a bit and make you lunch.' Claire wants to shrink away, have the carpet rip open, and swallow her. Anything not to be here in this moment.

'Oh yes, he did tell me.'

Thank fuck for that. 'Anything I can help you with?'

'Yes, can you help me sit up? I'm a bit stiff.'

'Of course.' Claire hurries over, props up his pillows, and helps him into a sitting position. It's an easy manoeuvre, he's so thin, there's no weight to move.

'Thank you, and call me Robert.' He smiles, there's some colour in his cheeks. He appears better than the first time she met him. 'Well, this is awkward, isn't it?'

Claire laughs. 'Unusual, yes, but I'm happy to help.'

'Take a seat for a second.' Robert pats the bed.

Claire perches on the edge and sits up straight.

'So, you're dating Sebastian?'

'Yes.'

'He's a good lad, not much of a farmer, but a good lad.'

'Do you miss being out on the farm?'

His face crumbles. 'Oh yes, I can't wait to get back to it. It's all I know. I'll be there in a couple of weeks. I have to be.' He tries to flatten his hair which is sticking up at the back, he pats his head a few times and then gives up.

Claire smiles, a couple of weeks seems ambitious, but she nods agreeably. 'Shall we go downstairs? Sebastian said you like to be in your chair in the lounge, and I've got to give you your tablets soon.' Claire looks at her watch.

'Okay, I'm fine to walk downstairs, but can you just walk beside me, just in case I need a little help.' Robert's face twitches into a cringe. Claire can see he's struggling with needing to ask for help, just like Hazel, just like herself.

'Yeah, that's fine.' Claire stands up and observes as Robert gets out of bed. He's more nimble than she was expecting. It's as if he was more poorly when he was half asleep, but now he's fully awake, he's improving before her eyes. He steps down the stairs carefully and slowly, not needing Claire to help him. She puts a blanket over his knees once he's in place in his chair. He's done well, but there's a tiredness in his eyes once he's sitting. Getting downstairs was a huge effort for him, which he managed to successfully hide, until now.

'Sebby tells me he took you to Dovedale Stepping Stones?'

'Yes, proper tourist stuff, and your son is an excellent guide.'

'Good, I'm glad you're enjoying yourself.' Robert fidgets with the blanket on his legs and takes a deep breath, his exhale is loud and dragon-like. 'I'm sorry about your dad.'

The sentence takes Claire's breath away, she hadn't been expecting the conversation to go in that direction. The mere mention of her dad has a draining effect on her body.

'Sorry, love. Sebastian told me.' Robert's face is full of concern.

Claire can hardly bring herself to look at him, she still can't stand the overly empathetic expression that people insist on giving her. It's too much. It's too real. 'Thank you.' She flicks her eyes up at him.

'Are you managing okay, here on your own?'

'Yeah, I needed some time out, away from… everything.'

'Well, you picked the right place to get lost in. I've lived here all my life, why would you leave?' Robert gazes out of the window, admiring his fields and the forest in the distance.

'Sebastian did,' Claire says, she's not sure why she sounds so confrontational.

'Yeah, he's never been that interested in farming. If his mother… if she'd still been here… I think he might have stayed.'

'I'm sorry. You must miss her.'

'I do, I always will. It gets easier to deal with though, with time.'

She can feel Robert's eyes boring into her scalp. Claire stops studying the carpet and raises her head. There's understanding in his teary eyes. He knows what it's like to lose the main person in your life. Of course, she'd heard this before, "time is a great healer" and all that. She can see that it's true, even in the short time since it happened, months on she isn't how she was days on, but time takes time. She doesn't want to feel like this anymore, but concurrently she feels as if she's honouring her dad by wallowing and grieving. It's exhausting, and Sebastian really is a welcome distraction. His dad, not so much.

'Thank you, Robert,' is all Claire can muster. 'It's almost 1 o'clock, I'll get your lunch and tablets ready.' She heads towards the kitchen, thankful to leave the room.

'What's for lunch?'

'Chicken salad. Sebastian's orders,' Claire calls back from the kitchen.

'Blasted salad, I'm not a guinea pig,' Robert mumbles in the lounge.

Claire giggles and instantly the image of her and Dad eating pie and chips at the football enters her head. She does like Robert, he comes across as the firm but fair type, the type of man she respects and can get on with and his son, well… she shouldn't be having those thoughts while making lunch for his dad.

#

Claire and Robert are watching TV in the lounge when Sebastian finally returns from the fields. They've both been completely involved in *Hollyoaks* for the last twenty minutes, but Robert quickly turns it off when footsteps can be heard approaching the front door. Claire starts to protest as Robert reaches for the remote and the off button but stops when she realises the reason behind the abrupt finish. She doesn't want to get caught watching her guilty pleasure programme either. Who'd have thought they would have the same taste in telly? Claire was quite shocked when Robert stopped flicking the channels and settled on the soap about twenty-somethings. Maybe he just likes watching all the attractive people go about their dramatic lives, who knows?

Sebastian arrives and kicks off his muddy boots onto the mud-caked doormat. He frowns at the quiet room.

Claire and Robert both meet his eye.

Robert slowly removes his hand from the remote control.

Claire stifles a giggle.

Sebastian appears suspicious, and for a moment she thinks he's going to feel the TV, to see if it's hot, but he doesn't. That may have been her paranoia getting carried away.

'Hi.' Claire gets up and then sits back down again. He isn't the bloody queen.

Sebastian takes a deep breath and removes layers of clothing. 'Hello,' he monotone mumbles. 'How you feeling, Dad?'

'Fine, more than fine, actually. Claire is excellent company.' He nods and grins.

'Good,' is all Sebastian says. He finishes removing his jacket and jumper and then cracks his knuckles while leaning on the wall next to the front door.

'My god lad, I've told you to stop doing that,' Robert growls and glares. 'You'll end up with arthritis if you don't pack it in.'

Sebastian jumps then stops abruptly and puts his hands by his sides. The spitting image of a small boy playing soldiers who's been told to stand to attention. 'I see you're feeling better,' Sebastian starts off saying loudly but by the word "better" he's muttering.

'Yes, well, actually I am feeling a little tired now, can you help me upstairs?'

As Robert shuffles through the lounge, Sebastian follows him with his hands slightly raised, ready to catch his dad if he falls. If Robert turns around he drops his arms, but then as soon as his dad faces forward again, his catching hands are once again ready.

'I'll just be a minute,' Sebastian says to Claire.

Robert stops abruptly. 'Thank you for today, Claire,' Robert says while blinking in slow motion. He's exhausted.

'You're welcome, Robert.'

He nods and continues his journey to the stairs.

Claire waits in the lounge, listening to the creaking floorboards and Sebastian and Robert's grumbles to each other. She's standing by the window, looking out at the fields, when Sebastian comes back down.

'Thank you for today, I got loads done.'

'No problem, I like your dad. He says it as it is.'

'He sure does.' Sebastian collapses into the sofa.

Claire sits next to him, perching on the end, her back as straight as a ballerina's. Poised and waiting.

'I'm done in, I'm going to have a bath and call it a night, I think.'

The image of him in the bath is distracting until she understands he wants her to leave. It's been a positive day, but now her insides are sinking, making her feel empty. She'd hoped they might spend the evening together, maybe have some food and see where things go... apparently that isn't going to happen.

'Don't look like that,' Sebastian says. 'I'm just tired.'

'Okay.' Claire puts on her shoes.

'Auntie Cath is coming round on Saturday, which means I'm free. Would you like to go horse riding? There's a stables a couple of miles outside of the village.'

'Yeah, that sounds like fun. I've only ridden a few times though.'

'That's fine. We'll go on a short hack... walking... maybe some trotting. I'll text you. Thanks again.' Sebastian puts his hands on her hips and draws her close before kissing her forehead. Great, another kiss-your-elderly-relative-kiss, but he lingers, making it closer to an I-fancy-you-kiss.

Once he pulls away she tips up her chin and reaches up, on her tiptoes, to kiss him on the mouth. She's ready for a snog, but she gets a peck. Her arousal from their passion earlier in the day is still lingering. She's ready to pick up where they left off this morning, she's been on edge all day. He's definitely not there though.

'Really give the door a tug on your way out and then slam it to make sure the latch is on.' Sebastian is already trudging away.

Claire watches him disappear upstairs. She stands by the front door, still in his lounge, in disbelief. Pretty abrupt, he's treating her like a member of staff, a nurse who's looked after his dad all day and who he obviously isn't going to spend any time with. She's literally letting herself out. He's just tired, he's had a long day, he's just worried about his dad. Claire can come up with a list of excuses, but all she knows for sure is that right now, she doesn't like how she feels in this moment. She slams the door as hard as she can and breaks a nail in the process. The loud crash-thud is satisfying, but how she feels is far from it.

Chapter Eighteen

By Saturday, Claire has convinced herself that everything is fine, and she was overreacting when Sebastian basically asked her to leave.

Was he rude? Yes.

Was he dismissive? Yes.

Could he have been more thankful and attentive? Yes.

She's willing to forgive though. Sebastian's got a lot on his plate and he'd had an exhausting day and she hasn't exactly been at her best all of the time in front of him. In fact, most of the time she definitely hasn't been her best self. That stupid, smiley gnome enters her head and them shouting "fuck you" at each other. She knows better than anybody that people make mistakes, especially when outside forces hurt you, upset you, and put you in a bad mood. He has text her about today, like he said he would. At least she's now spent some time with his dad and got to know him a bit. That's connection, that's forming a bond. Getting to know someone's family is a big deal and something she can't offer him.

Saturday afternoons were for Dad. Every home game down at Enfield. Away games at home with the radio on, still eating pie and chips, not from the stadium, but made by Dad. It was tradition; it was theirs. Claire could take or leave the football, but watching Dad watch the game was her favourite thing to do. It was very entertaining! Her quiet, softly spoken dad morphed into an animated, shouting one-man show. Screaming at every decision, chanting the fruity chants, singing, and clapping. He absolutely loved it and lived for his team winning. It was the one father-daughter activity that remained from childhood to adulthood. She hasn't been back since. There's no point without him. In fact, in the seven months since everything changed, Claire hasn't done much on Saturday afternoons, usually choosing the sofa, her duvet, and chocolate. A couple of times she's tried turning on the radio at match time, but the commentator's voice strikes like a knife, instantly recognisable, the pain jolting through her whole body. Why would she listen on her own? Dad was devoted to Enfield. She only ever took part to spend time with her dad. It was the one constant in their lives. Sometimes it would be the only time they'd see each other for months, never making any other plans, busy with their individual lives.

Wait, it's the end of June, the season will be over. She would usually have known that. A rock forms in her throat, making it hard to swallow.

In the summer she would go round to Dad's for lunch and instead of watching or listening to twenty-two men kick around a piece of leather for ninety minutes, they would chat, watch a film or *Star Trek* or play cards. It was carved out time, each week, to be together. Now, Claire is going to go horse riding with Sebastian, an activity with someone else on a Saturday afternoon. A big deal, not that he knows it.

The outfit for the ride? Jeans and a T-shirt. Classic. A simple and plain outfit, but she takes extra care over her hair and makeup. Concealer, foundation, powder, and blusher with some eyeliner and mascara, all to create an illusion of making no effort. She thinks about tying her hair up, but then remembers she'll be wearing a helmet, so lets her curls flow. Sebastian is at the forefront the entire time she's getting ready. Even him shouting at her about the gnome, she now remembers fondly. He's truthful and was trying to get her to own up and correct her mistake. At first, she welcomed the constant obsessing, to think about something and someone else was refreshing, a distraction from her inner torment and grief. Now the obsessing alarms her. She's falling for Sebastian, but she has no idea how he feels. She plans to broach the subject today, in the most casual, indirect way possible. There's no way she's going to ask him to be her boyfriend. She has to play it better than that. Asking him outright isn't an option. She can't appear to be as keen as she actually is. She doesn't want to scare him away.

There's a knock at the door. Claire checks herself in the mirror one last time then runs down the stairs, before remembering her aloofness plan and sauntering down the remainder of the stairs. On opening the door, he's standing there with a huge smile on his face, clutching some poppies. She suspects they've been picked from his garden, but he's arranged them nicely and swaddled them in flowery wrapping paper.

'For you,' Sebastian says and holds out the red flowers.

'Thank you, they're lovely. I'll put them in some water. Come in.'

Sebastian steps inside and blasts out three sneezes.

'Hay fever still bothering you then?' Claire shouts from the kitchen above the rushing tap.

'Mmm.'

'Are you ready for horse riding?' she says, re-entering the lounge after putting the poppies in the one vase she owns.

'Sorry about the other day. Farming doesn't put me in the best mood. Dad had a word again.'

'Very wise, your dad.'

Sebastian smiles a broad, genuine smile. 'You're not wrong.'

He strides over to her, and she's reminded again of his tallness and the sheer size of his chest. She becomes suddenly very aware of her own body, how her hair is falling and where her hands are. Claire feels fidgety while basking in his attention. She grasps his hands and pulls him towards her, their bodies now touching, she reaches up to kiss him. Every time their lips meet, it's so much more than just their mouths pressing together. Claire's never experienced kisses like it. The closeness of Sebastian, the outdoorsy, oaky smell of him, the urgency as they explore each other, makes her want to drag him into bed. It's pure lust. She's never fancied anyone else this intensely. Their connection is strong and deepening. She's pretty sure he feels the same. She can feel it every time they embrace. They're growing a love for each other.

He pulls away.

Claire can hear her own breathing; his breathing has quickened as well. She's mentally undressing him, and she can see from the look on Sebastian's face that he's doing the same. Although there's a puzzlement in his eyes, the beginning of a frown, fine lines starting to crease between his brows.

Do they have time? Claire peeks at the clock above the fireplace.

Sebastian follows her gaze. 'We're booked in for the trek,' he says quietly.

'Okay, let's do the planned day,' Claire tries to sound enthusiastic. 'We could come back here after?' She runs her hands down his chest and briefly brushes the top of his trousers.

Sebastian takes a deep breath and mumbles something that Claire can't hear. 'Yeah, we could,' is all he audibly says. Sebastian coughs and rubs his face. He's stressed. Claire dismisses it as sexual frustration.

They're both quiet on the drive to the stables, both turned on, but not satisfied. Claire shuffles in her seat. Sure, waiting is frustrating, but it's also kind of thrilling. She remains in a mildly turned-on state, all her senses working in overdrive.

As they rumble over the gravel car park, Claire takes in the stables. You would never know it was here. There's a small sign on the road just before you come in, but she's not sure she would have spotted it on her own. There are two rows of brown stables. Most of the stable doors are half open at the top, with horses peering out. The animals seem eager to say hello and get going. A few other cars are parked up, and there are people hanging around and chatting. They must also be going on the hour-long trek through the farmland and trees. A woman, with very mucky jodhpurs on, tells everyone to head to the tack room. She says it's a small room, past the horses and is where everyone should try on riding hats. Sebastian takes Claire's hand as they meander between the horses, it takes Claire by surprise, and she hopes her hand isn't too clammy. He's holding her hand. He wants to walk around holding her hand! His large palm and slender fingers around hers feels protective and loving, she could get used to this.

Claire stops to stroke the nose of a brown horse with a white stripe down the centre of its head. 'Who's a good boy?' she says in baby talk.

'You talking to me?'

Claire jumps back, dropping Sebastian's hand. She looks back into the stable, past the horse and there's a man inside, mucking out the side of the stable the animal isn't standing in.

'I didn't see you there, I thought there was just a horse inside.' Claire laughs.

'Sorry, I didn't mean to scare you. I'm Terry.' He tramps over and offers to shake Claire's hand. He's small and slim, about the same size as her. She suspects he's older than he appears, his brown eyes don't belong in his boyish body.

'Ginge!' Terry says.

Claire frowns at him. What? Terry is talking to Sebastian. Sebastian is glaring at Terry. Claire can't read Sebastian's face. Is it an in-joke? Is he angry? He's trying to put on a poker face, while there are a million emotions going on inside of him, but it's not clear what he's feeling.

Sebastian's eyes seem to darken, no longer crystal blue, but grey. 'Hello,' he says.

'How have you pulled her?' Terry points at Claire. 'You like carrot tops then?' he asks her.

Claire has no idea what to say. Have they been transported back in time to the school playground? What adult greets another adult with "ginge" and "carrot top"? It's so ridiculous she doesn't know whether to laugh or shout, and to make matters worse, Sebastian seems to have frozen as well. They're both standing motionless, silent, and bewildered, while this tiny man insults Sebastian.

'We should go, we're booked in for a horse-riding trek,' Sebastian says to Terry. He sounds formal, business-like, and cold.

'Alright ginger pubes, you lucky bastard.'

Claire and Sebastian march towards the tack room. Claire peers over her shoulder and scowls at Terry's screwed-up face. He winks at her and then goes back to shovelling shit. She glances up at Sebastian. His shoulders are pushed back, and he's standing tall. He seems to have become even bigger. He's ruffled his hair, making it impossible for her to see his eyes. They're hiding behind a curtain of strawberry blonde.

'That was weird,' she finally says.

'Yes.'

'So, you know him?'

'Yeah, just some knob from school.'

Sebastian's chest is going up and down. He's taking very slow, very deep breaths through his nose, similar to a cartoon bull. His hands are clenched, making fists and his knuckles are white. He's trembling, he's clasping his fingers together so tightly, they've become shaky. He doesn't say any more. That's all Claire's going to get out of him, it's as if dark grey clouds now hang over him. She's surprised that he didn't say an insult back. Not really his style though. Sebastian had mentioned something about not liking school when he'd given her a tour of Baliston, but now she's just witnessed, despite years passing, the full picture as to why. He did say that his hair had been a problem. But was he really, actually, badly bullied? How awful was it? She wants to ask, but she daren't. Since the conversation with Terry, Sebastian has made himself physically larger and shrunk into himself at the same time.

The trek is brilliant and is perfect for a beginner like Claire. Plodding along, she takes in the trees, fields, and views while spotting birds of prey (she's not sure if they're birds of prey, but they're big and kinda dinosaur-like), squirrels, and rabbits. She's thankful there's nature and general gorgeousness to see because she basically does the ride alone. Sebastian is there, but he isn't. Others on the ride are talking amongst themselves, there's a lot of chatter. Kids pointing out rabbits to their parents, a couple talking about the new kitchen they're having fitted, and one man repeatedly telling his wife what the optimum position on a horse's back is, constantly telling her to sit forward more or sit back more. Sebastian is quiet for the whole hour. Claire attempts to involve him in light chit-chat about what they're doing, but he barely grunts back. Claire wishes she could time travel back a few hours to them kissing in her lounge. They would decide to bin off horse riding, and she would lead him upstairs to her bedroom.

Chapter Nineteen

Sebastian is in a mega grump, and it's riling Claire; after all, he's only just apologised for his last bad mood. Remember, tolerance. Deep breath. She was a complete mess when she met him, and he's been patient and forgiving.

He switches off the engine outside her house and his car rumbles and groans into nothingness. They haven't spoken for the entire journey back. The day started in such a promising way as well. After her failed attempts to get him to converse on the horse ride, Claire eventually stopped trying, and stubbornness by both parties prevailed on the drive home. She rocks her feet back and forth, toes to heels, wriggling her toes inside her trainers. The mud and grit beneath crumbles and scratches as her soles obliterate the muck. Sebastian looks in her direction, a questioning and annoyed expression on his face.

'Thank you for taking me horse riding. Shame you weren't there,' Claire spits out. She glares at the strawberry air freshener dangling from the rear-view mirror. It's still swaying slightly, momentum from the motion of the car still powering it. The sickly stink tickles her nose. Bramble Cottage catches her eye, and she stares at the house instead of the stupid strawberry. Turning from him, rejecting his gaze.

'Sorry I was quiet, it was a shock to see Terry,' Sebastian says.

An apology, this I can work with. Claire softens. 'Are you going to come in?' She feels for him. Being bullied is a terrible thing. Witnessing the scared and ashamed boy inside him was completely unexpected and shocking. He must have been bullied around the time his mum died. How did he cope? She puts her hand on his thigh and strokes up to the crease. Despite basically going horse riding on her own, her lust from earlier hasn't faded.

Sebastian shuffles in his seat. 'I don't think that's a good idea.' He shifts his body towards the door, away from her, and refuses to look her in the eye.

Did he just recoil from me? Claire snatches her hand away and picks at dry skin on one of her fingers.

'My dad is on the mend, he's doing really well, getting better each day, and my Aunt Cath says she can help more when he needs her, as she's retiring soon, not that he'll need much help going forward,' he says in a fast, rambly fashion.

'That's great news.' Claire frowns, *why does it feel like this isn't good news?*

'So, I'm going to go back to London in a week or two.'

'I'm happy for you,' she says while trying to ignore the sinking feeling in her stomach. He's leaving? Already?

'I'm going back to my life. I've never been so eager to get on a tube and get back into the office.' It's Sebastian's turn to study his hands.

He's going back to the life he had before he came back to Baliston, before he met her. *I need to know how I fit in.* 'You'll still be visiting your dad, though, won't you? And I can come to London, I'll be back there, eventually.' He hasn't mentioned yet how they'll move forward, so she takes the initiative and points the options out. The sinking feeling seems to be now rising to her throat. No need to ask him about being boyfriend and girlfriend, this is the perfect way to find out about the future; figuring out the logistics of him being in London and her being in Baliston for the next few months.

'It's been fun, it really has…'

Claire's eyes widen. *He's not, is he?* Surely not, she literally cared for his dad days ago, they were close to sex hours ago.

'…A holiday romance that I'll always remember, but now I'm going back to the real world. I won't have time for… dating.'

Fuck. Fuck. Fuck.

He's dumping her? She did not see this coming. They were finally on the right path, weren't they? Has she imagined their deep connection? "A holiday romance". Shit. After she opened up about her dad, he knows what she's been through, what she's still going through. They connected over their pain. Didn't they? They've both lost a parent. Both had to cope with unimaginable grief at a young age. They've had the best time getting to know each other. He's sexy and quiet, but funny and hardworking. He's dumping her. But these last few weeks have felt meant to be.

'Is this about that twat at the riding place?' Claire's voice is getting louder. She can't figure this out, where is this coming from? Is his pride really so hurt by an old school bully that he needs to get rid of her, the witness to his hopelessness? Surely, that's not it.

Has he been killing time until he can go back to his real life? Something to keep him busy while he's bored in the countryside, looking after his dad. Oh, that new girl, she seems lonely, she'll do, she'll entertain me for a bit.

'Of course, it's not about fucking Terry.' Sebastian runs a hand through his hair, his nails noisily dragging against his scalp. 'I've been thinking this for a while—'

'Before or after Dovedale? Before or after you asked me to care for your dad?' Claire searches his face for answers.

'I know, I know. We've been having fun. I shouldn't have asked you to look after my dad, that was too much, too soon. I just don't think I'm a relationship sort of person.'

Claire had an inkling things shifted that day, when he came home after working on the farm and she was sat watching telly with his dad. That freaked him out. Sebastian had invited her in, but then when he actually witnessed her being in his family home and being comfortable there, he rejected her. 'But I thought… this was something… the kisses are just so…' she trails off, humiliated. He's not a relationship person? It would have been helpful for him to have mentioned this.

I've been questioning the timing and whether I was ready or in the right place and just as I decide to get out of my head, he retreats into his. He probably noticed a shift in her behaviour and his commitment-phobic alarm started blaring. She doesn't get it, his dad is fine, he's going to have more time now, London isn't far, and she'll be moving back there at some point.

'You're a lovely girl, you really are.' Sebastian wipes dust off the dashboard.

Really? REALLY? 'Well, thank you so much.' Claire screws up her face into a smile dripping with sarcasm. 'This is coming out of nowhere,' she whispers, more to herself than him.

'Like I say, you're a lovely girl. I've never met anyone like you.' He finally meets her gaze. 'I just can't have a girlfriend right now. Looking after my dad has been draining. I need to think about… me… about getting my life back.'

'Right,' Claire says.

'Better to end things now before we get too deep.' Sebastian nods, confirming his decision.

Too late. She can't believe she was going to broach a conversation about where they were going. She thought they were heading for a relationship. How can she have got it so wrong? The thing is, she doesn't think she has. He is just as into her, isn't he? He's just spooked, isn't he? 'Have a nice life,' Claire says in an eerily calm and sweet way.

She slams the car door so hard she hurts her hand. The deep pounding of metal-on-metal echoes around the street. She can sense Gareth twitching at his curtains. Sebastian speeds off. Not even a second glance.

Claire goes back to the familiar. Back to bed to cry. As she collapses into the pillows her first reflex is to ring Saskia, but they're still not speaking. Not since she fled London.

No potential boyfriend.

No best friend.

No Dad.

Alone in Baliston, just as she planned, and it feels more awful than ever.

Chapter Twenty

The next day, Claire is reeling, questioning every moment with Sebastian. She's mentally gone through every interaction, every conversation, every touch. HE'S the one that kept trying with HER. Her walls were up. She didn't want to connect with anyone; she wanted to be alone. That was the whole point of moving to Baliston. But he had fought for her, ignored the arguing, the shouting, the grief, and kept on trying to get to know her. This had meant a lot. She thought it meant something. They shared their pain, shared their pasts, shared about losing a parent, and most of all, they've had a bloody blast! She's laughed and laughed and laughed. It was special.

Surely, she hasn't made that up?

It was special.

His behaviour now can't change that. Surely, he doesn't ask any old fling to help look after his dad? Yeah, go to a club, get pissed, pull a fitty, have a one-night stand then get them to care for your dad the next day. A solid plan and totally normal. Claire chuckles despite herself.

She feels completely confused and let down, but nothing is as bad as what she's faced, so she knows, deep down, she will be okay. Her time in Baliston is making her stronger, she's sure of it. She'll have a bath, go for a walk, and then visit Hazel. Claire needs to talk to her friend. A friend she's not seen for weeks because of being wrapped up in Sebastian.

Hazel answers her door with a frown. 'Oh hi, I wasn't expecting you, was I?!'

'Just thought I would pop round and say hi,' Claire says as she steps into the hall.

'You've been crying,' Hazel says to Claire's back as they make their way into the lounge.

'Nothing gets past you.' Claire manages a little laugh.

'Trouble in paradise?'

'You could say that.' Claire heads into the kitchen and gets herself a glass of water, takes a small sip, and then chucks the rest down the sink.

'So, now you've got time for good old Hazel.'

'It's not like that,' Claire says loudly as she turns away from the sink to face Hazel who is slowly storming into the kitchen.

Hazel gives her a curt smile. 'I know. Don't forget I was young once.' Hazel raises her eyebrows and then points at the back door. 'I've just managed to do half an hour of gardening. Heaven.' She closes her eyes on the word "heaven". 'It's lovely out there. Do you fancy sitting in the garden?'

'Yeah, that would be nice.' Claire reaches for her sunglasses, which are balancing on the top of her head, and puts them back on, retreating back into a darker world, away from the bright cheeriness of the beautiful summer's day. The blistering sunshine stubbornly continuing. She may as well go outside and bake her flesh, maybe the sun can burn away his touch, his soft kisses, and help her forget.

'I made some lemonade yesterday, I'll bring it out.'

'I can get it for you.'

'No, it's fine, go outside and relax. I'll be there in a minute.'

Hazel will never change, she's still fighting for every bit of independence she can. Claire admires her strength, if she can learn to be half as strong as Hazel, she knows she'll do just fine. Maybe some will rub off on her, she bloody well needs it right now.

Hazel brings out a huge jug of lemonade and two glasses on a small round tray, carefully placing them on the wooden table before going back inside to retrieve something else. It's glorious, like being abroad. Claire crosses her arms, slumps in the uncomfortable wooden garden chair, and pushes her sunglasses closer to her eyes. The garden is as pristine as the front, with large bushes, pansies, and trinkets dotted about, but thankfully no gnomes. Hazel returns with an array of different biscuits on a plate. Bourbons, custard creams, chocolate digestives, rich teas, and pink wafers. She plonks them down, and a couple fall off onto the table. Ignoring the mess, she sits down and crosses her legs in a slow and deliberate fashion. She surveys Claire, again like she's a naughty pupil in her office.

'I've messaged you a few times. I've had nothing back,' Hazel says, as she scratches the corner of her eye.

'Sorry, I got caught up in it all, in Sebastian,' Claire mumbles, feeling like a stroppy teenager.

'That's fine, of course. I was just starting to get a little worried plus I thought you might be mad about me sacking you.'

'No, not at all. Sorry for making you think that. I wasn't thinking. I was just thinking about Sebastian.' Claire sits up straight and puts her glasses back on the top of her head.

'I get it. I know what it's like to be young and in love.' Hazel gives Claire a genuine smile full of kindness.

'How have you been, Hazel? How are things working out with Andrew?'

'Great, he's doing everything I ask. I thought he would be forgetful and disorganised, but he really is proving me wrong.' Hazel beams.

'I'm glad, maybe it's good that I let you down,' Claire offers.

'Mmm,' is all Hazel will say on the topic. 'Stop changing the subject. Why have you been crying?'

'Sebastian is going back to London.'

'Okay…'

'So, he's ended things. Ended us.'

'Really? I am surprised.'

'He said he's going back to his life and now the "holiday

romance" is over. That's what he said we are or rather were, a "holiday romance". But don't worry, I'm "a lovely girl…", not so lovely for him to continue seeing me, mind,' Claire rants, her upset turning to pure anger.

'Odd, I thought he was really into you.'

This makes Claire feel better. Hazel thinks the same as her, she isn't going mad. A blossoming relationship had happened, it was happening, Sebastian had just put a stop to it, abruptly.

'You've had fun though?' Hazel asks.

'Yes,' is all Claire can muster. She starts crying again which is really very annoying, she rather prefers rage, it hurts less.

Hazel gets up, lugs her chair next to Claire's, and puts her arm around her. 'You don't need a stupid man right now, anyway. It's your time. Focus on you. You needed this break here, but that's not going to last forever. You need to think about what you're going to do next. What you want. You can achieve just about anything, if you put your mind to it.'

Claire nuzzles into Hazel's shoulder and lets the tears flow. Hazel holds her. To have someone comfort her while she cries is a foreign experience, she can't remember the last time she cried with someone. Ever since her dad's accident, she's cried alone. She moved away from London, to cry alone. However, Claire is discovering things don't seem so wretched and dark when she shares. To let someone else catch her sobs is freeing.

A butterfly lands on the table next to Claire and flaps its orange wings, the intricate patterns loop and form to give the impression the creature has two large pairs of eyes on its delicate wings. Claire focuses on the lower set, at the bottom, pretend blue eyes flutter back at her. The insect then takes off, darting around the garden, hovering in the sunshine's gaze. On its own adventure.

'I never put myself first and I regret it,' Hazel says.

'How do you mean?' Claire asks while blowing her nose and dabbing her eyes.

'I wanted to be a fucking jeweller, didn't I? I love my jewellery.'

'Why didn't you do it?'

'Life got in the way. We married young, and I was very busy with four children. I don't know why I didn't do it as the children got older. It just felt too late by then.'

'You could still do it.'

'No, my hands are old, they don't work as well as they used to.' Hazel studies her hands, running a finger over her bulging veins and liver spots. 'Anyway, that's not my point. You want to be a writer or journalist, don't you? Go for it.'

'Yeah, I have always wanted to be a journalist. And about the writer thing… I'm not writing a novel.' Claire grimaces.

'I know, love.' Hazel winks.

Claire opens her mouth in shock and coughs after taking in too much air too quickly. 'I suppose it's time I followed my dream. I've only been putting it off for years.'

'Yes, girl. Get yourself fucking out there.'

#

Claire walks the long way home, to enjoy the brilliant weather, instead of cursing it. Meandering through the village is calming, sitting at home surrounded by four walls sometimes really isn't. Instead of walking down the main road she goes the back way, across some fields, following the narrow muddy path, listening to grasshoppers in the long grass. Even seeing the public footpath sign makes her think of Sebastian.

Ridiculous.

She knows she'll have to move on. You can't make someone care, you can't make someone want to be with you, no matter how much you want it.

Hazel's right, she should focus on herself, they had fun but now it's over and she needs to work out what she wants and map out a future for herself. She'd hate to have regrets one day and think she hadn't reached her full potential. Fuck Sebastian and his stupid "holiday romance". She hears kids laughing and realises this route passes the small children's park. There're only two swings, a slide, and a climbing frame. Claire's walked this way a few times before, and there's usually some teenagers sat on the swings looking moody and chatting, but today two young girls are running around, giggling, and being boisterous together. A man, presumably their dad, shouts that it's time to go home and they skip off. Claire can no longer see them by the time she reaches the park. One of the swings is still rocking back and forth. Claire wants to have a go. She looks around. There's no one. She sits down on the black rubber seat and grabs the chains either side. Everything feels smaller. She remembers what Dad taught her. Legs straight and forward, then tucked underneath and backwards. She gradually picks up speed and soon enough Claire is swinging through the air. She thinks back to when everything seemed bigger. The wind in her hair, going higher and higher, wondering if she went much higher would she eventually go over the bar and completely up and over? The swing creaks and squeaks and the sun pummels down on her head and shoulders. Claire tries her best to empty her mind, to be completely in the moment, like a child. To not think about Sebastian or about Hazel or Saskia or even her dad. Just to be here, in a field in Derbyshire, on a hot day on a swing. The tears dripping into her smile.

After a while, a sweaty Claire stomps home, having found solace in the park, but now needing the cool and quiet of her cottage. As she gets near to her street, she reaches into her handbag for her key and is almost at the front door when she sees a man sitting on her doorstep. She reacts to the unexpected visitor, sitting in the shadow from the house, by flinching and stepping back. 'Hello?' she says, while squinting into the sunlight. It can't be who she thinks it is.

'You're home. Hi,' Sebastian says. 'I've been waiting for you.'

'Why?'

'I feel bad about how things went down yesterday, and I want to say bye properly.'

'Goodbye, Sebastian. Let's not drag this out. Things don't end nicely. It's fine, you've made your feelings clear.' Well, they're not actually clear, they're confusing as hell, but Claire's got the message. He doesn't want to be with her anymore.

'At least, this way, we end on a high.'

'But why would you stop on a high, wouldn't you just enjoy the high?' she realises as soon as she says it, that it sounds like she's begging him to stay with her, but she would never do that. Claire simply doesn't understand. She pushed him away at first but as soon as she's allowed him to pull her in, he pushes her away. 'You're a head fuck.' She laughs then the snivelling starts, which is absolutely mortifying. She doesn't want to cry in front of him. Claire wipes her face and lifts her chin.

He just stands there, a statue of a man. Sebastian has shut down, just like her dad used to, when things got too deep or too difficult.

Dad always struggled to help her with her homework, but it became more and more obvious as she got older. When Claire was revising for her GCSEs she tried to broach the subject, first talking about how he often brought paperwork home from the bread factory as he couldn't get it finished during his shift. It was the first time she dared to mention the word, "dyslexia". He went bright red and left the room.

'Thanks for calling round, Sebastian. I need to go in now. Excuse me.'

Sebastian steps to one side to give Claire access to her front door. 'Bye, Claire. I'll remember this summer forever,' he whispers into her ear.

Startled by the closeness, she darts her head to look into his eyes.

He's on the verge of tears himself. 'Hay fever,' he says and wipes his face with the back of his arm.

'Bye, Sebastian.'

Chapter Twenty-One

Three Months Later...

Friday 12th October 2007

Claire gets out another dress from her wardrobe and holds it against her body in front of the full-length mirror. Up and down, she studies her reflection and concludes it's too summery and puts back the flowery little number and selects a short red dress. Perfect. It'll be great with black tights and boots and her bright red lipstick. Hopefully she won't be over or under dressed.

What exactly do you wear to an eightieth birthday party? She's never been to one before, but surely the usual party rules apply?

Claire looks in the mirror again, and does a double take, as she's pleasantly surprised by her own reflection. Her eyes are bright and clear, her cheeks rosy, and her skin glowing from her outdoorsy lifestyle. She presses her nose against the mirror; the point touching the cold surface, the deep sadness she's seen for months and months, is no longer glaring back at her. The thought makes her well up, and she chuckles at the irony.

Over the last few months, Claire has been taking Hazel's advice and focusing on herself. Applying for loads of journalism jobs and for weeks hearing nothing back. But, as she's honed her CV and application style, she's started to get replies. In fact, she has two interviews for trainee positions in London next week. It's unbelievably exciting. In between scouring the job market, Claire has been enjoying exploring Derbyshire, going for long walks and pub lunches, mostly on her own, but sometimes with Hazel. Getting out and about seems to be helping Hazel's mobility. A short walk eases the stiffness in her joints. They usually put the world to rights while taking in the outdoors. They've also been on an afternoon tea tour, finding new spots to go to all the time, plotting the bus route together before gorging on tiny sandwiches and beautiful cakes.

Claire has been so busy, she's almost forgotten about Sebastian, almost.

Well, that's what she's telling herself, anyway.

He has been on her mind more lately though, especially with a trip to London on the horizon. Her mind wanders to the last time they saw each other. Those words… "holiday romance" are such an inadequate description of what they had. That isn't what he really thinks, she knows it isn't. After breaking down her walls, she became available and then he ran away. Maybe one day they can come back together? Maybe once she's back in London, she could try to get in touch with him? But of course, she's getting ahead of herself, she needs to land herself a job before she goes back, that's the most important thing right now. She can't help reminiscing about the stepping stones and how he kept checking if she was okay, about how he rang her and apologised after they argued on their first date, when she was so rude to him. He understood and forgave. Such a kind heart. Such soft lips. She remembers being wrapped in his arms, her face against his chest.

Today is about Hazel though, and her eightieth birthday party. Her family have organised a celebration at the village pub's hall, which apparently is behind the main building, Claire didn't even know it was there. It promises to be a big shindig with half of Baliston going and all Hazel's children and grandchildren attending as well.

The orange, brown, and red leaves dance and sway in the wind outside, the rustling sound startles Claire at first, but once she realises, she smiles. She shivers and closes the window, shutting out the cold as well as the noise. While at the glass, she takes a moment to absorb the trees and fields stretching for miles into the distance, taking comfort from the warmth of the cottage, while admiring the wildness outside.

Her stomach continues to churn. She'll see Hazel's son, Andrew, again tonight, but that's not the root of this feeling. Dad's birthday is also coming up, two days after Hazel's. Hazel will be surrounded by her family, while he's not here. She couldn't believe it when Hazel told her, her birthday is on 11th October, she had to get her to repeat the date. What would he have done for his birthday? He would have been fifty-three this year, while Hazel is eighty. How is that fair? How does it all work?

Claire tries to imagine what she'd be doing now if her dad was still alive, if that night in December had never happened. She would still be living in London, in Acton, in the same admin job. He'd be working at the bread factory in the day, but he would want to celebrate in the evening. He'd go for a few pints with his mates one evening and he'd want to see Claire on another. She can see it now, he'd invite her for dinner at his and she would say he can't cook on his own birthday and she'd suggest going out, nowhere fancy, but a treat just the same. Just the two of them, so many years, just the two of them. At times a lonely existence, but they had each other, they hadn't ever really needed anyone else. A quiet life in their bubble.

'Today is about Hazel,' Claire chastises herself, trying to move her mind on from the men no longer in her life. She wants to celebrate the woman she was hired to help, who ended up being the one to help her.

#

Claire hates arriving somewhere on her own, she should be used to it by now, but she never knows what to do with her hands or how or where to stand. Should she walk up to the first person she sees and say hello or stand in a darkened corner, waiting to see someone she recognises? As she enters the hall, Andrew is the first person she sees. Great.

'Welcome, Claire,' Andrew says, his arms outstretched. He gives her a bear hug.

'Hello, Andrew. How are you?'

'Brilliant, ready to party.' Andrew puts an arm in the air and does something resembling a jig.

'Where should I put this?' Claire holds up a small box, wrapped in red paper.

'Over there.' He points to a table in the corner. 'We're asking everyone to put the presents on there.'

Claire nods and walks over to place her present down. She puts it at the front, in the hope it doesn't get lost among the huge boxes.

They'd been out shopping in Ashbourne when Hazel had spotted it in a shop window. A silver necklace with an emerald pendant, she'd been struck by its beauty and simplicity but had balked at the price. Claire's inheritance has dwindled since being in Baliston, being spent on simply living, on the rent, food, and bills, but as soon as she saw Hazel's face transform at the sight of the green stone, she was itching to get her purse out. So, the next week she went back to Ashbourne and bought the necklace. Claire can't wait to see it hanging from Hazel's neck, she just knows she's going to love it. Dad would want her to have something special, after all, Hazel has really been there for Claire and continues to be such a wonderful friend and almost like a mum.

Claire steps back over to Andrew. 'When is Hazel getting here?'

'She's due to arrive in about fifteen minutes.'

'Did you manage to keep it a secret? I don't think she had any idea the last time I saw her.'

'I don't think she knows, or she's trying to be nice and pretend she doesn't know. You can never tell with her. She thinks Sarah and Heather are taking her out for a meal.' Andrew steps from one foot to another, like he's desperate for the toilet.

'I'll get a drink before the big surprise.'

Andrew nods as Claire makes her way to the bar.

'A Pinot Grigio please, large.' Claire pulls out a ten-pound note from her teeny tiny handbag.

'Hello, Claire. You look lovely.'

She spins around to confirm the familiar voice. 'Robert! Gosh, you look great.' His cheeks are chubbier, there's more colour to his face, and he seems at least two inches taller. It's lovely to see Sebastian's dad looking well, but she's not seen him for ages, not since, well, since she was dating Sebastian.

'Oh, thank you.' He strokes a hand through his thinning hair. 'I feel great, well, better than I have done in a while.'

'Are you back working?'

'Yes.' His whole face lights up.

'I am glad.' She reaches out for the bar, to steady herself.

'I was sorry to hear about you and Sebastian. I had high hopes for the two of you.'

'Yes… well…' Claire's not sure what to say. She wants to be polite, but she also doesn't want to dissect what went on.

'He mentioned you the other day actually,' Robert says quietly, moving closer to Claire.

'Really?' Despite herself she wants to know what Sebastian has been saying about her.

'EVERYONE IN POSITIONS PLEASE!' Andrew's voice echoes around the hall. 'Back of the hall and quiet. Get ready to shout surprise, she's going to be here in a few minutes.' Andrew claps his hands, rounding everyone up, herding the guests like sheep.

That's the conversation over then, the moment gone. Claire smiles at Robert, and he continues to try to get the bartender's attention before moving. Claire makes her way across the hall. Saved by the Andrew shouting. What was she supposed to say to Sebastian's dad? It's brilliant to see him healthy and enjoying life, but she really doesn't want to discuss what went down.

But what was he going to say?

Does this mean Sebastian still thinks about her?

Is he regretting his decision? *I mustn't get carried away, forget it.*

Everyone huddles together and are mainly quiet apart from a few whispers and giggles. You can feel the anticipation in the air, it's all tingly.

'SURPRISE!' everyone yells in unison as Hazel treads through the door with her two daughters. She's startled then immediately emotional as she sees all the familiar faces waiting just for her. Hazel peers up at the "Happy 80th Birthday" sign and gives it the finger. Good old Hazel. She's absolutely gorgeous in a long, grey ball gown. It's fluffy, there's netting and sparkles and apart from the colour it could be a wedding dress. The complete ensemble suits her perfectly, not many people could pull it off, but Hazel does with grace and elegance. Claire's feeling a little teary herself. Her chest could burst with the admiration and love she has for this lady, who came into her life just when she needed her.

'Alright, treacle?' Claire says into Hazel's ear in an East End laddish voice. 'Not too shabby, right?'

Hazel hugs Claire, then surveys the room and says, 'Not too shabby at all.'

'You knew though, didn't you?'

'Course I did.' Hazel winks and is then beckoned to the other side of the room, she's in demand tonight, which makes sense at her surprise eightieth birthday party.

Claire takes a seat at an empty table on the edge of the dance floor and watches several small children dance and slide on their knees. Occasionally, she'll check for Hazel in the room, she's always in a different part, speaking to a different person. Buzzing around, thriving and vital to the party atmosphere. Hazel is having the time of her life. People light up when she approaches, entranced by her many and varied stories. The eighty-year-old is glowing, it makes Claire simultaneously smile and wipe under her eyes, unsure whether she's going to laugh or happy-cry. Instead, she chooses to take a deep breath, while nodding and tapping her foot in time to the music. She might have to get her dance moves out later.

'Hi, are you Claire?' a woman who must be in her fifties says, she looks familiar. 'I'm Elizabeth.'

Ah that's why, she's Hazel's other daughter. Claire is used to seeing the twelve-year-old version of Elizabeth which hangs in Hazel's lounge. 'Yes, that's me. You really look like your mum.'

'Thank you. I've heard lots about you.'

'Really?'

'Yeah, you've really helped Mum, in a really difficult time in her life.'

'I can say the same about her.'

They chat for a bit about Hazel, Baliston, and Elizabeth's children before Elizabeth carries on working the room, saying hello to the many guests.

Claire is content with sipping her wine and watching the evening. A room full of people all for one amazing person. One day, she hopes to have a room like this.

Chapter Twenty-Two

At home, after the party, Claire sits on the edge of her bed, kicks off her high-heeled boots, and calls Saskia. It's been months. It's gone midnight, but she'll be up.

Saskia answers but says nothing.

'It's Claire. Hello?' She bites her bottom lip.

'I know,' Saskia replies in a flat tone.

'I miss you. We never don't speak for this long.'

'I know. I'm sorry.'

'What?' Claire twitches, then freezes. *Did I hear that right?*

'I know you've had it rough. I shouldn't have gone off on you like that.'

Claire tries to digest the words, in the whole time she's known Saskia, she's never apologised. Her involuntary response is to feel sick. 'Thanks. Sorry I left your birthday night out.'

'I'm over it.'

Claire frowns. She's not sure if that's quite true, but at least it sounds like Saskia wants to move on. 'Good. Guess where I'm going to be next week?'

'Here?' Saskia's voice distorts with loudness.

'Yup, I've got a couple of interviews for journalist jobs.'

'Wow! Yes! Finally. You go, girl,' Saskia high-pitched squeals.

And just like that, Claire has her best friend back.

#

Claire breathes in the car fumes and peers up at the massive office buildings while listening to two teenagers next to her swear it out. *I've missed this.* Being amongst the throng felt claustrophobic when she left, but now simply feels like home. She's missed everything being on her doorstep, being able to buy gorgeously over-priced coffee, and the hustle and bustle. The feeling of being in the thick of it, like if anything is going to happen in England, it's going to be here, in London.

Of course, all these positive vibes are being helped by two interviews going swimmingly. Her first interviews in years, her first interviews for journalist positions, and she was on it, putting on a great, confident act and showcasing all her swotting. It's all she's been doing for weeks... reading about the history of the newspapers, the editors, past articles, looking at the circulation figures, who they target... everything. She's been studying all day every day and then going round to Hazel's to be tested, and she's a hard task master! Hazel decided to go for a Jeremy Paxman-type approach for her interviewing style, and boy is Claire thankful for it now. Hazel's grillings were far worse than what she'd actually ended up facing. The interviews were a nice chat compared to Hazel's interviewing technique. Hopefully, just hopefully, Claire has got at least one of them in the bag and she'll be able to start on her trainee journalist journey. The pay is shit and less than what she used to be on, but hopefully it's just the beginning. It feels like she's at the start of something, of doing what she's always wanted to do, but never really felt quite ready.

Claire rounds the next corner, and their coffee shop is in front of her. It's closer to the corner than she remembers. She spots Saskia immediately. She's sitting in the large floor to ceiling window, perched on a high stool. A heady mix of Tyra Banks and Vivienne Westwood. Gorgeous and fashion forward in a zebra print short dress, with a leopard print fluffy jacket. The outfit shouldn't work. Claire is sure it would look terrible on her, but Saskia's beauty carries it off. Her long legs on display, her hair big and bouncy, and her makeup absolutely flawless and on trend. Claire pauses for a second to take in her friend. It's been too long. While she's standing on the pavement, staring, Saskia looks up, sensing someone is eyeballing her and her face breaks out into a massive smile. With big, dramatic hand waves Saskia beckons Claire in, several people frown at her, but Saskia doesn't notice, her focus is completely on Claire.

'You're back, back in the promise land! It suits you.' Saskia gives Claire an all-encompassing hug.

'Thank you, it's good to be back.'

'You look hot. Is that what you wore to the interviews?'

Claire peeks down at what she's wearing, as if to remind herself what she put on hours ago. The outfit is a grey jacket and skirt combo with a black shirt/blouse thingy. It's plain and simple, but very expensive. Claire and Hazel went shopping in Manchester to find it. It fits perfectly, accentuating her small waist. The outfit is plain, but with small details which make it spectacular. The black stitching around the sleeves, the waist and hem, add a little something and make a fashionable and young statement rather than an old and boring one. It cost Claire a small fortune, but she knows Dad would approve of her spending her inheritance on making a future for herself. She feels beautiful and powerful in the outfit, enjoying clicking in her heels around the capital, feeling every inch the journalist, she one day hopes to be.

'Thanks, yes, I got the outfit for the interviews.' Claire strokes down her skirt and takes a seat next to Saskia.

'It feels like forever,' Saskia says.

'Yes.'

There's an awkward silence. Claire's not sure whether they need to talk about what happened more or to just leave it and act normal. She doesn't know how to navigate this. They don't usually go deep, but that seems to be changing.

'I know I was a dick on my birthday. I just wanted you to

be there. But I should have been more understanding. I know I don't get it. I haven't lost a parent.' Saskia wipes her top lip, sweeping away beads of sweat.

Claire listens, taking in the words. Saskia has put it perfectly, and it's exactly what she needs to hear. She knows Saskia has been there for her in her own way, ever since Dad died, but they've never had a heart-to-heart. 'I appreciate that. I wish I'd been able to stay for the whole night.' *I can't believe I had a panic attack.* 'I think I'm getting there, though.'

'I'm glad. I just saw red when you walked off, leaving me.'

'Which is what you usually do.' Claire can't quite let it go, past resentment refusing to be forgotten. Deep down, she's still pissed off. She disappeared on a night out, once, after it triggered memories of the night her dad died. Saskia has disappeared many times on nights out because, quite simply, she wanted to get her end away.

'I don't.' Saskia pouts. It's reminiscent of a toddler sulk, but within seconds is more model at a photoshoot.

'Anyway, you were with other people and I was very upset.' *Did she mean the apology? I need to turn this around.* 'I understand you feeling angry. Remember that Halloween night at uni, when we were dressed as witches and you pulled that really tall guy? I was so fucked off with you when I saw you heading for the door with him.' Claire chuckles, feeling nostalgic for their uni days. They really had some adventures together.

'Your face actually went bright red.' Saskia tips her head back and laughs loudly. 'He was a great big hulk of a guy. I had to follow him. He was gorgeous.'

'He was, his long flowing hair as well. He looked like he had time travelled from the past,' Claire puts on a silly *Star Trek* opening monologue-type voice, 'sent back in time to seduce Saskia.' Her dad's favourite programme, something she loved to tease him about. 'Abandoning on a night out is usually your thing. That was the first time I've done it, and for very different reasons.' Claire is suddenly serious. She really is struggling to let this go. They need to talk it through.

'Slut shaming, nice, real nice.'

'I'm not slut shaming. You can fuck the world for all I care. Maybe just let me know, before you disappear, maybe ask me if I want to get a taxi with you? Maybe just check I'm okay before you wander off.' Claire can feel collective rage pumping through her, for every time Saskia has abandoned her. Each instance buried, now coming to the surface.

'You're the one that's disappeared now. You've retreated into a bloody field. How am I supposed to check on you there? Ask if you're okay, when half the time you've got no signal?!'

They both glare out of the window, refusing to look at each other. They stare at two business people, talking and gesticulating. Are they in a business meeting which is getting heated, or are they a couple who've met for lunch, who're now on the tip of an argument? Claire glances over at Saskia. She can see from her expression that she's wondering the same.

Saskia's eyes are glassy. 'I am really sorry.'

'I know, I'm sorry for leaving too.'

'When I'm on the pull, I kind of forget about everything else. The thrill of meeting someone new just kinda takes over. It's been that way since Max... until recently.'

'I know... I do know that... you know?' Claire stumbles over her words.

Claire would never dare mention his name. Max. Everything always leads back to Max. The drinking, the sleeping around. Ever since he caught Saskia kissing a woman in a nightclub, she hasn't been the same, she's just got wilder. For about a month after the break up, Claire and Saskia became like hermits in their teeny flat. They chatted and watched films. It did wonders for their degrees, as they were on top of their coursework, for once. Saskia cried a lot. Claire held her and listened. Then one day Saskia was back to her normal self. She no longer wanted to talk about it, and they left the flat again. They went out more than ever. The fact that the split was because of something that she did, because she cheated, she's not been able to forgive herself. The fault was hers. It's about time she got over her university boyfriend. It's been years, but grief is a wild beast which attacks everyone in different ways. Max is no longer in Saskia's life, and she craves him, unable to let go. Hopefully, the need is fading and she can see a future without him. Grief never fully goes, but Claire is discovering it does become less sticky. One day you're trying to walk through the mud, barely able to move your feet, the brown goo is pulling you down, and you can't see a way out, but as time keeps moving, so do you, you find a way, and you start to put one foot in front of the other.

'Shit, that's too deep.' Saskia takes a deep breath. 'How did the interviews go?'

'Really well. Hopefully, I'll be back in London soon.'

'Thank fuck for that. I was starting to worry you'd packed it all in and settled in a retirement community at twenty-five.'

There she is, Saskia back to her normal self. 'How are you, anyway?'

Saskia raises her eyebrows and touches her hair, relishing the moment to finally talk about what's going on with her. 'Good, that campaign I was on about isn't happening, but I'm still getting lots of work and there could be something else in the pipeline... plus... I'm dating someone.' Saskia lifts her shoulders up as if to brace herself.

'Really?' Claire is flabbergasted. Saskia bringing up Max is a complete first and now this? She hasn't known Saskia date anyone for years, not since uni and everything went wrong with Max. For ages, it's been one-night stands and an odd date here and there, but actual proper dating hasn't entered Saskia's life in a very long time. 'Who, how long, where, when, what?' Claire claps her hands in anticipation of mega gossip.

Saskia takes a deep breath and rolls her shoulders, revelling in the attention and pausing for dramatic effect. 'He's a model as well. I met him on a shoot a month or so ago. He's called Stuart. He's from Derbyshire way, actually. He moved to London about a year ago to try to make it as a model. He's beautiful...' Saskia says, before looking down and murmuring, 'and kind.'

'Wow, that's a lot of info at once. Where's he from originally?'

'Um, Stoke.'

Claire laughs. 'That's not Derbyshire. Stoke is in Staffordshire. Still, yeah, quite close to where I am.'

'Same difference. He cooks, he takes me out, he calls when he says he's going to call. There's no messing about and no games. It's... it's... refreshing. Oh, and his dick is massive!'

The frowny people from earlier are now at it again. A woman who is feeding a baby in a high chair tuts loudly.

'Saskia!' Claire pretends to scold her and then whispers, 'Really?'

Saskia folds her lips, closes her eyes, and nods slowly. The picture of smugness.

'But not too big?' Claire feigns concern, but she can't stop her smile spreading.

'No, not scary, just right.'

'Maybe I'll meet him soon?'

'Yeah, you can. He's picking me up from here.' Saskia glances at her watch. 'In about fifteen minutes.'

'Oh,' Claire says quietly while folding her arms.

'You'll love him. What happened with that Sebastian guy, anyway? The hunky farmer.'

'We dated for a bit. He's back living here now, actually. When he decided to move back, he dumped me.'

'Dick.'

'Uh, yeah.'

'So, he's not a farmer?'

'No, he works in finance. He was in Baliston to look after his dad. His dad is much better now.'

'Even better, I can get on board with finance, farming not so much.'

'It doesn't matter now, anyway.'

'As I said, dick,' Saskia says and rolls her eyes before giving Claire the once-over.

'What?' Claire says, brushing her jawline and stroking her hair. Saskia has a weird expression on her face. 'Is there food around my mouth? Urgh, what's in my hair?' She starts batting her hair, making it swing wildly.

'No, stop.' Saskia halts the incessant hair-rounders by pushing Claire's hands down into her lap. 'Sebastian really hurt you, didn't he? You've still got feelings for him?' She tips her head to one side, her face serious.

'And I thought I was hiding it so well.' Claire clasps her lips together, making her cheeks dimple either side. 'I was falling for him. I'm still shocked he ended it, if I'm honest.' She swallows and tries not to picture Sebastian describing what they had as a "holiday romance".

'You're gorgeous, intelligent, fun… he should be begging you to stay with him, not dumping you. It's his loss.' Saskia nods her head firmly.

Claire contemplates her friend. 'Thanks for the vote of confidence… it's… I wish—'

Just then a man walks in, and Claire immediately knows it's Stuart, and she's pretty relieved for the interruption. She wants to meet Saskia's new man and not talk about Sebastian, who doesn't want her. Stuart's tall, very tall, maybe six-foot-five, with very broad shoulders. He almost seems as wide as he is tall. He's wearing a very tight, white T-shirt, so tight that you can see he's got pecs and a six-pack underneath. He's classically tall, dark, and handsome, but the most striking thing about him is his razor-sharp cheekbones, protruding from his face. They're so high and prominent. Everything about him says model.

'Stuart,' Saskia shouts and waves him over.

'Hiya, I'm Stuart, you must be Claire. Saskia never shuts up about you,' Stuart says in a thick Stoke accent. His voice really doesn't match the exterior, but the mix is kind of endearing.

'And I've just been hearing lots about you.' Claire finds herself looking down, without realising, and sure enough, there's an impressive bulge in his jeans.

'We've got to go, but you'll be back again soon, won't you?' Saskia asks as she gets down from her stool.

'Hopefully,' Claire says.

'Are you going back to Baliston now?'

'Yeah, my train is in a couple of hours.'

'Okay, let me know what the plan is. I can't wait for you to move back,' Saskia shrieks.

'Nice to meet you, Claire. I was hoping you could tell me loads of embarrassing stories about Saskia. Maybe another time?' Stuart says. He's practically being dragged away by Saskia.

'They'll be no need for that.' Saskia darts a "keep your mouth shut" evil-eye at Claire.

As they leave hand in hand, Claire chuckles and shouts, 'Another time, Stuart. I've got plenty to tell you.'

Several people watch them go. They're a striking couple. Claire gets up to order a coffee. In the excitement of seeing Saskia, she'd forgotten to get a drink. She casually sips it while sitting in the window and watching the world go by. To think about what she said in the interviews, to think about the whirlwind meet up with Saskia, and to think about leaving Baliston. Alone, again, with her thoughts.

He would be proud of her. Dad would every now and again ask her what her degree had been in, like he'd forgotten what she studied. She would snap back at him "Journalism" and then she would realise he was doing it again, reminding her of her passion and what she wanted to do, in a silly, annoying fashion. He didn't want her to stagnate and carry on in admin, just because it was easy and paid the bills. There's a certain freedom in going to work and leaving it at the door and not giving it a second thought until you're there again the next morning. A job you don't care about means you can go out and not worry about being fresh the next day, but it's also mind-numbingly boring and soul destroying. If he could see her now, he would be so proud. *What did I study? Journalism, Dad. I'm nearly there.*

Claire's phone vibrates on the long thin table. She picks it up and flips it open.

'Hello, Claire?'

'Hi, yes, Claire speaking.'

'Hello, it's Janet from the *Ealing Star*.'

'Hello, Janet,' Claire manages to push out while simultaneously holding her breath.

'I'll get on with it. No small talk.'

That doesn't sound good. I knew I messed up that court reporting question.

'We'd like to offer you the job.'

I'm a bloody-fucking-bitching genius.

Chapter Twenty-Three

She should be packing, but she can't face it. It's been the longest and shortest six months of her life. Claire's leaving Baliston to start her new job as a trainee journalist at the *Ealing Star*. Every time she thinks about it, it's like an electrical bolt zaps through her body and a wooden spoon starts mixing her intestines. They think she can do the job, but can she? Can she remember her training from uni? Can she remember all the media law stuff? What can you report from a first magistrates' court appearance? What's a section 39 order again? Claire glares at the media law book on the shelf near her clothes rails. She resists flicking through and swotting again. She knows the answers. She just needs to relax, and maybe pack. Does she really need all this stuff? Maybe she could just leave it all here?

This is the perfect time to go and see Hazel.

Claire opens the light green door and peeks her head into Hazel's house. *She should really lock her front door.* 'HAZEL. IT'S CLAIRE.'

Hazel eventually wanders into the hall from the lounge and makes her way to the front door to greet Claire. 'Well, just let yourself in. I've been doing a crossword, don't know why I bother, it's so blimmin' hard.' Hazel throws her arms into the air, realises she's still clasping a biro, and puts the lid back on while shaking her head. 'Come in, come in.'

Claire sits down in her favourite chair, while Hazel hovers. 'Your party was brilliant,' Claire says.

'It was, wasn't it? I had a fabulous time but was a little tipsy by the end. Sorry, I didn't talk to you much. There were loads of people to natter to.'

'Oh, don't worry, I was people watching most of the time. You know some characters.'

'Well, of course.' Hazel thrusts her head back and puts her hands out as if she's about to launch into jazz hands. She then stands up straight before lowering herself onto the sofa. Claire waits, letting Hazel focus on the task in hand, noticing the wince and the pain in her eyes, letting her deal with her ageing body before continuing the conversation. Hazel settles herself before jumping up in her seat. 'Oh, thank you, by the way, I can't believe I haven't thanked you yet. Thanks so much for the necklace, obviously you know I like it,' she says while holding the emerald dangling from her neck. She yanks it out under her chin and looks down, smiling.

'You are very welcome. It looks even better on you.' Claire reaches out to inspect the emerald and then lets it drop gently onto Hazel's chest. 'I'm procrastinating by popping round. I'm supposed to be packing.'

'It's that time already, is it?'

'Yes, back to London. It feels like the right time. Baliston has done its job.' Claire glances at her elderly friend and around the room. The green velvet of the chair in her hands, the smiling faces on the walls, and the trinkets of a full life surround her. A lump forms in her throat.

'I'm pleased for you.' Hazel reaches over and squeezes Claire's leg. 'I'm so proud of you for getting out there and getting that job. I hope you love it.'

'So do I, imagine if I hate it?' Claire laughs, trying to ignore the boulder in her neck and the wetness in her eyes. *Hazel is proud of her.* She never thought she would hear those words again, words usually uttered by her dad. Words that should be uttered by a parent, but Claire has Hazel.

'You'll fly,' Hazel shouts as she walks into the kitchen to put the kettle on.

'I would still like to visit you. You've become a great friend.'

Hazel leans on the kitchen door frame as she wipes a mug with a tea towel. 'I think we came into each other's lives at the right time. But don't worry about traipsing back here to see me. You'll be too busy digging up the dirt.'

Once again, Claire can see Hazel is desperate not to be a burden, not that she ever could be to her. 'I want to. How about every other weekend? Saturday afternoons?'

'You've got yourself a deal. But don't worry if it doesn't work out how you plan.'

'It will. It's important to me.' *I won't abandon you. You don't do that when you care. I can't lose another Mum.* 'You're important to me,' Claire says more quietly.

Saturday afternoons have always been family time. With Dad, it was watching Enfield Football Club play. With Hazel, it'll be a walk in the countryside, a cup of tea, and a gossip. She never thought coming to Baliston would mean gaining a new Saturday afternoon companion.

'It would be good to go for a Saturday afternoon walk,' Hazel says, shiny eyed.

'That's exactly what I was thinking.'

'Jack liked to do that. It became something of a habit.'

'I used to watch the football with my dad on a Saturday afternoon.'

'Well, Saturday afternoons are perfect then.' Hazel shoves the tea towel into the mug, ambles over to Claire, and reaches for her hand. 'You really are getting better at talking about your feelings.'

'I know, it's surprising every time.'

'It's better though, isn't it?'

'It sure is.'

'I'm going to miss you popping in like this.' Hazel releases Claire's hand and goes back to drying the mug.

'Me too, but don't worry, I will be visiting,' Claire says before noticing a brochure on the coffee table. It's for the University of Derby. 'Are you thinking of becoming a student?' She laughs as she picks up the glossy booklet.

'I am actually,' Hazel says in a high-pitched voice. She raises her eyebrows and waits for Claire's reaction.

'Really? What are you going to do?'

'Well, I'm just looking into it at the moment. There's a part-time Silversmithing course. I thought I might give it a try, see if the hands can hold up.' Hazel puts down the tea towel and mug and glares at her hands before stretching them by making a fist, then spreading her fingers, making a fist, then spreading her fingers.

'Yes, give it a go. So, you might be able to make some jewellery?'

'Yeah, that's the idea.' Hazel's eyes are full of emotion. They're glistening with joy.

She's actually going to do it. Hazel is going to go for her dream after a lifetime of waiting. Something just for her. *Maybe I actually have helped her too. She's not only helped me.* 'I want to be you when I grow up,' Claire says. She could burst with pride. 'A student at eighty. They're going to love you.' They really will.

Chapter Twenty-Four

What do journalists even wear? Claire wants to look professional and well-dressed, but she could be squashed together with other reporters at a press call or be spending hours writing shorthand in court. Being comfortable is key. Claire is tempted to put on heels, but opts for flats. She could be on her feet a lot, literally running for a story. The story comes first, not fashion. She nods her head as she puts the ballet pumps on, happy with her decision and dedication to the cause. Claire tries to eat some toast but only manages a few bites and a swig of fresh orange juice. Her stomach is doing too much dancing and sloshing about. Her first day in a real newsroom. Shit! She did news days at uni when they pretended to be a live newsroom for the day, but she's never actually been part of a real newsroom. The prospect is exciting, yet completely terrifying.

She gets off the tube with plenty of time for the short ten-minute walk to the *Ealing Star*. She tries to stride with purpose and confidence, but she has neither.

What the fuck is she doing? How much will they expect from her? Will they throw her in at the deep end or hold her hand?

Well, she's about to find out.

Briefly, she stands in front of the rather unimpressive and unassuming building before rushing inside, eager to get this first bit of the day done. The receptionist picks up the phone and calls the big boss, Janet, and she appears five minutes later.

'Welcome, Claire,' Janet says, her arms outstretched as she booms through reception.

'Thank you, Janet, it's good to be here and finally get started,' Claire says, getting up from her seat in time for when Janet reaches her.

'Well, let's do just that and get you started.' Janet walks off and Claire follows her. 'I'll take you to the newsroom and introduce you to the News Editor, Steven. You should have met him already really, but he was on holiday when we had the interviews.' Janet tuts under her breath. 'Steve,' she shouts across the newsroom as Claire follows her, weaving in and out of desks, navigating the open plan set up. A few people lift their eyes from their screens, but when they don't see anything of interest, they go back to their computers. The walls are painted white and the scratchy, wiry carpet is grey. A line of muted TVs flash on the wall behind Steve, showing different news channels. Coffee and sweat lingers.

Most people are quietly tapping away at their keyboards, and there's also a meeting taking place in the corner. Five journalists appear to be discussing a story, and it's getting quite heated. One is passionately on the edge of shouting, telling the rest why a Council story is important, and explaining it's not an old story, but a big update on an ongoing story. Claire is so busy staring at the huddle that she almost collides with Steve's desk. She just manages to catch herself in time.

'Steve, this is the new trainee, Claire. I've got to dash,' Janet says to Steve, already backing away and heading back to her private office on the opposite side of the huge room. 'You're in safe hands, Claire.' And with that, she's gone. The one woman that Claire has met and knows in this place has scarpered.

Claire turns to the news editor. 'Hello, I'm Claire Morris.'

'Yes, Janet has been filling me in. Sorry to miss you at interview. We're just about to have our morning meeting. Come along, I'll fill you in on your training programme after.' Steve is already up, out of his seat, heading towards the gathering of arguing journalists. 'It's an ideas meeting and we discuss the top stories and who's working on what.'

'Great,' Claire squeaks the word with forced brightness and enthusiasm, when all she wants to do is run out of the nearest exit.

'Everyone, this is Claire, the new trainee. Claire, everyone.' Steve gestures at the three men and two women. 'You can introduce yourselves properly after.'

One woman smiles at her, the other is looking at Steve. The men glance at her and then continue scribbling in their notepads.

'Right, what have you got for me?' Steve grabs a black marker and stands in front of a white board with the word Monday written on it.

'I'm still working on the Council redundancy case studies,' Smiley Woman says.

'Is anyone talking?' Steve asks.

'I think I'm going to have at least two. One that has worked there for thirty years and a youngster as well.'

'Great, you need to get moving. We need to run it this week. We need the exclusive.'

Smiley Woman nods.

'I'm looking into the spate of shed fires there's been recently. I've got an interview with the station manager this morning at one of the scenes. Should make good pictures,' the other woman says.

'Good, Rebecca. Show me when you get back.'

Rebecca, right that's one name I now know.

'Jason, isn't there that sentencing today?'

'Yeah, the Hanwell murder. Just looked at listings. It's due to start soon. In fact, I need to go.' Jason grabs his coat and hot foots it out of the room.

Steve nods and adds MURDER SENTENCING to his list of stories. 'I want to do an FOI on the number of female refuse workers. I've never seen one in Ealing. I think it's all men. Might be a nice piece. If there is a binwoman, a human-interest interview… "what's it like in a man's world?" In fact, let's bang out a load of FOIs. It's time-consuming, but usually gives us some original stories. Claire, that can be one for you today.'

'Great,' Claire says, her eyes wide. She seems to be stuck on that word, but she can't think of anything else to say. She's trying to wrack her stupid brain about what a fucking FOI is. Did they do that at uni? She can't remember. She'll just pretend she knows what it means and hopefully glean the meaning as the task is described to her.

'Of course, you've got mandatory training and introductory bits to do, and then you can crack on.' Steve points the pen at her before moving on.

'I'm still trying to set up that profile piece with the Assistant Commissioner. A year in the job and all that. What are her priorities? Plans for Ealing? There's talk of this afternoon. It should come off,' the blonde man says.

Steve writes POLICE PROFILE on the board. 'Kabir, what are you working on?'

'The Fire Service sent a press release about their new fire dog. He's wearing those special little boots, which protect his feet. They've sent pictures, lots of quotes. I'm writing that up.'

'The first for breaking news!' Steve studies the ceiling in an exaggerated eye roll, then writes BOOTS.

The third man starts talking about something to do with a recent stabbing, and Claire tries her best to listen and concentrate, but she can't help fading him out as the panic begins to rise. She's completely out of her depth. This is proper. She has her story ideas – prepped for the interview – stashed in her bag, but left that on Steve's desk and can't for the life of her remember a single idea. Calm, she needs to calm down. Then maybe her brain will work and she will have an actual fucking idea if someone asks her. Surely, she should be offering suggestions, but she feels like a deer in the headlights. Overwhelmed, completely overwhelmed. But surely, they won't expect too much from her. She is only a trainee after all, but at the same time they will expect some level of competency, not a potato in smart clothes.

During Claire's quiet meltdown, the meeting appears to end, and people start getting up and going back to their desks. No one comes over to her and introduces themselves. She attempts to make eye contact, but fails. They're all far too busy and important. Oh, if she could just have an ounce of their confidence. Surely, they'll warm up, she'll make friends, they're busy, that's all. Claire swallows, straightens the collar of her blouse, and follows Steve back to his desk.

'You'll be sat next to Katie,' Steve points at Smiley Woman. *Yes!*

'Here's your log on details. It probably won't work, so call IT. The number is on a poster on the wall. Once you get into your email, I've sent you links to all the introductory training you need to do this morning. Do all that first and then get cracking on the FOIs. Do the bin one and then come up with some other ideas and get the emails sent. We have an FOI template which you'll need to use and adapt for each one. Katie can show you where on the system that is. I've got an editors meeting now, can we talk through your plan tomorrow?'

'Yeah, sure,' Claire says.

Steve already has the phone receiver to his ear.

Claire treads over to the empty desk. There's a monitor, keyboard, and phone, the whirring computer is underneath the table. Katie's desk is mayhem by comparison. Covering half, maybe more, of the faux wooden surface are Council minutes and press releases. They're piled up or spread out in fan shapes. On the clearer part, there are framed photos, pens, and a yellow banana and a brown banana nestled together.

'Hi, I'm Claire.'

'Hi, I'm Katie. I'll be with you in a sec. I'm just listening to the voicebanks.' Sure enough, a monotone voice is coming from her phone, which is on speaker. The disembodied man is talking about pumps and aerial ladder platforms.

Claire nods, voicebanks she knows. She listened to them during news days at uni. It's where the police and fire service record incident updates for the media to dial into, listen, and report on. A police officer rattles off the details of a road traffic collision. Claire coughs.

'Boring, boring, boring.' Katie hits a button on the phone and turns her attention to Claire. 'So, it's your first day. You live nearby?'

'Acton.'

'Oh, I'm there too.' Katie smiles.

'How long have you been a journalist?'

'Two - no, three - years; since I graduated, really.'

Claire nods. She should have been a journalist for a few years by now too, instead she's been procrastinating, out partying, and then hiding in Baliston. The last few years run through her mind as she stares at her desk's engineered wood grain. The lines have a hypnotic quality.

Katie lowers her head to catch Claire's eye. 'If you have any questions, if you want to pick my brain, or you just want to know where the toilets are, then ask away.'

Claire pulls herself together, takes a deep breath, and drags her hair away from her face by flicking it over her shoulders. 'Thank you. Where are the toilets, actually?'

'The Ladies is behind you, past the coffee machine, worth knowing where that is too.' Katie goes back to whatever she's working on.

Claire pushes the large grey door and chooses the cubicle furthest away. While washing her hands, she studies her reflection. Her eyes are sparkly, she's having a good hair day, each curl is doing its thing, and her skin is clear. *I'm ready. I can do this.* Dad would have given her a pep talk this morning. It would have been a thirty-second phone call, but it would have meant so much. She knows what he would say. She doesn't need to hear the words; she knows. Claire straightens her blazer and leaves the mirror behind.

Claire manages to log on without needing to phone IT, find her email, and access the online courses. They involve a lot of videos and multiple-choice quizzes, covering data protection, privacy, social media use, basic media law, and a shorthand proficiency test. It's lunchtime when she finishes, having passed them all. She noticed a sandwich shop nearby on her way in; she thinks of it as her stomach starts growling.

'When is lunch?' she asks Katie.

'Lunch? What is this thing you speak of?' Katie laughs at Claire's puzzled face. 'There isn't a set break time. We all just grab some food when we can. You are supposed to get an hour's break each day, but no one really takes their full break. I usually take half an hour and then eat at my desk.'

Claire searches Katie's face for a hint or clue that what she's saying is a joke, but she's deadly serious, and kind, sharing this in-house anti-break mentality. 'Okay, thanks for letting me know, I'll just go get a sandwich.'

'One day, we'll try to go at the same time. It's hard to do though, as Steve doesn't like everyone out at once in case we miss something.'

'I'd love that, if we can. You can tell me all the office goss.'

'That would take much longer than half an hour.' The phone rings and Katie answers it.

Claire treats herself by buying a salmon and cream cheese sandwich and a coffee before sitting at one of the few tables inside. As she munches on the much-needed food, her mind wanders onto Sebastian. She keeps finding herself thinking about him. Back in Baliston it had gradually become easier to block him out, but now she's back in London, he's her go-to person to daydream about.

They're in the same place again, in the same city.

Claire's in a better frame of mind, coping, and he's not caring for his dad anymore. Surely, this could be the time when it could actually work? *I bet he looks killer in a suit.* She imagines him in a pitch-black designer suit, tailored to fit his body perfectly, his hair slicked back, with just one stubborn strand falling into his eyes. He keeps pushing it back, sweeping his hand through his hair, but it keeps sexily falling into his eyes, like Elvis Presley in his films from the sixties. A crisp white shirt, a red tie, and a strong yet musky aftershave, the type that almost drowns you when you catch a whiff. In the office, assertive, in charge. Claire licks her lips. A flashback to him lying down on the red and white checkered blanket pops into her head, and she has to stifle a giggle. She flaps her blouse with one hand and smoothes down her hair with the other, having come over all hot and bothered.

Maybe she could give him a ring? Pretty ballsy, but she would get more of a feel for where he's at, much better than a text. Does he still think about her? It all ended so abruptly. What they had can't surely be a normal fling for him. She's had flings before and they were nothing like that. It was special, but did he ever feel that way? Does he still think about her? Claire needs to know, although she usually lets men come to her, and never texts or rings first.

She glances at her watch. It's been almost half an hour since she left the office. One more bite of her delicious sandwich and a sip of her now cold coffee and then she speed marches back to her desk.

Right, FOIs, they sound scary and like she should know what they are. 'Katie, where's the FOI template?'

'It's where we write the articles, saved in the folder KEEP.'

Claire finds the template. Of course! Freedom of Information, that's what it stands for. They did briefly cover making the requests in uni. They're used for getting more detailed information, which press offices at public bodies won't just give to you in a phone call, as it requires more digging and more work. The requests are great for getting stats, and if you think of the right question, you can get information that you would never normally find out, and an original story. However, as Steve said, it's time-consuming and often boring work. First up is contacting local Councils about the number of female refuse workers and then to think who else Claire can contact and about what, which will have interesting results and make a story.

It's 4 o'clock when Steve approaches Claire, for the first time since the morning meeting. 'How are you getting on, Morris?'

Claire looks up at him from her seat. 'I've done all the introductory courses, I've emailed all the local Councils about the refuse workers, and I'm now working on some other FOIs of my own.'

'What are you thinking?' Steve rubs his chin and leans against an empty desk.

'To ask the Police about the number of fatal stabbings over the last five years, looking at each year and the ages of the victims, the Council about the number of accidents on the borough's roads and the top five roads where there have been the most accidents, and to ask all London Borough Councils – how many lollipop men and women do they employ, and how many did they employ five years ago and then we can compare how Ealing is doing when compared to other parts of London. I've heard there are fewer about, that they're not really a priority anymore.' Claire takes a deep breath after rattling off her list and forgetting to breathe.

'Have you sent all the requests off?'

'No, nearly there,' Claire says, while studying her notepad.

'Good work, Claire. Let's see what we get.' Steve starts making his way back to his desk. Over his shoulder he says, 'Oh, we'll do your trainee plan tomorrow, okay? I want you going out with reporters and going to court, all that.'

'Great, thank you.' *Fuck I said great, again.* Claire's stomach does a little flip at the thought of going to court. She's never done it and media law is scary. Dad's inquest is the nearest she's been. But going out with reporters is a dream, a chance to learn, and an opportunity to actually talk to some members of the team. Surely, they'll speak to her if they're showing her the ropes?

Katie watches Steve saunter to his desk and sit down. As soon as he's sitting and out of view, she swivels her head round to Claire, like a meerkat in the wild. Her eyes are wide and bright, and her lips are folded as if she's bursting to say something.

'What?' Claire asks, leaning forward in her chair while resting her elbows on her desk.

'You got a "good work" out of Steve, on your first day!' Katie raises her hands to the sky, before laughing into them. Her fingers are tight around her mouth, muffling the sound of her giggles.

'That's good, right?'

'Er, yeah, it's good, it's fucking unheard of,' Katie says while shaking her head.

You were right Dad, I can do it.

Chapter Twenty-Five

'What we need is a good murder,' Jason says loudly as the morning meeting finishes and everyone makes their way to their desks.

Claire gasps, but no one else really reacts. There are just nods and smiles or nothing. She fiddles with her hair, sits down at her desk, and scans the room. They'd all been moaning that there isn't much about. They're all scratching around for stories, but Claire can't help but be shocked by Jason's comment, but she seems to be the only one.

After a week at the *Ealing Star*, it's taking a little time to adjust to the dark humour. Journalists wishing for bad things to happen, so there's a story. Well, they don't – she hopes – actually want people to get hurt; they don't really want the awful event to take place, but they all want to cover a huge breaking story. It's taking some adapting, but Claire is finding her feet. Her time in admin is serving her well, she's organised and great at spotting typos, and her fresh perspective on the world means she keeps bringing in story ideas that nobody else has thought of. Most evenings are spent trawling the internet and reading other newspapers in the hope of sparking a brilliant idea. She's not sure she can keep this up long-term. She's been working non-stop, and it's tough. It's only been one week since she started. It feels much longer. She's managed to have decent conversations with most of the newsroom, there's still one or two who are completely unapproachable and uninterested, it's like they're not going to bother with her until they know she's definitely sticking around and then they'll make the effort to speak to her.

When Claire first met Katie, she thought she seemed kind and sweet and friendly, and her first impression was spot on. She's so lovely and Claire is so pleased she's sitting next to her.

Kabir is kind of nice too, he's a laugh, but is crazy ambitious and never really has time to have a proper chat as he's always on the hunt for THE story which will change his career and mean he can go national. He's always chasing, searching, or staring at job adverts.

Rebecca is older and has been a journalist for decades. She can barely work the computer system, but she's a brilliant writer.

Jason is disorganised and forever running about, having forgotten about a press call or court appearance, but he always gets the story.

Steve is a firm but fair boss, an inspiring journalist, though he's not so good at the HR side. He still hasn't taken Claire through her training programme. He keeps putting it off; he doesn't seem to care about it, he's just completely focused on the newspaper and what stories they're covering. Claire's starting to wonder if the plan even exists, but she doesn't really care if it does or doesn't, as she's learning by just being in a newsroom and shadowing the other reporters.

Despite it being, on the whole, a positive first week, Claire is glad when the clock approaches 5 o'clock and it's acceptable for her to start packing up her stuff. She's exhausted. The amount of concentration and learning she's done has been intense.

'Well done on completing your first week, Claire,' Steve says as he passes her desk, with his coat folded over his arm.

'Thank you, I've enjoyed it. My head is full, though.'

'I'm glad to hear it.' Steve smiles and makes his way to the lift.

'Fancy a quick drink?' Katie asks her.

Claire's about to say no, but this is her first social work invite and she should make the effort. 'Yeah, just the one. I'm knackered.'

'Yeah, just the one. I'm cooking for my boyfriend tonight.'

Katie switches off her computer and throws her notebook on top of the swamp of papers on her desk.

They go to the pub nearest to the office, even though it's an old man's drinking pub. It's very traditional and not the expected destination for two twenty-something women. On the plus side, it's quiet and they get served straight away.

'Is this where you usually come?' Claire says, while taking in the grubby floor and sticky bar.

'Yeah, when we come for a drink after work. I know it's a shithole, but it's close to the office and a couple of the regulars are a laugh.' Katie leads the way to a table. 'How have you found your first week?'

'Good, my head hurts. It's a dream come true to finally be in a proper newsroom.'

'I'm so glad you started. The office is too male, far too many men, we need more women.'

Claire laughs. 'Glad to be of service.'

They chat away about their lives, where they like to go out, and where they go shopping. Claire briefly mentions living away from London for a bit in Baliston, but she doesn't go into specifics and she doesn't mention her dad. She wants to keep things light; she wants to talk about what other twenty-five-year-olds are talking about. She wants to pretend with this new person in her life that the last year didn't happen.

Katie drinks the last drop of her half of lager. 'Well, I'm going to have to love you and leave you, I'm afraid. I'm going round to John's and I've promised to make him my famous risotto, which takes ages to cook. You okay?'

'Yeah, I'll finish this and then head home.' Claire points at her wine and smiles.

'See you Monday.' Katie puts on her coat and waves.

Claire sips her wine, taking her time as she starts to relax. She could go to bed right now. She's worn out, but her mind is buzzing with all the details of her first week as a trainee journalist and she knows there's no way she'll sleep yet. She takes in the room, the red wallpaper, the black and white photos of an old London, the old men drinking pints and playing cards, and the tall man ordering a drink at the bar. The tall man ordering a drink at the bar... when did he come in? She hadn't noticed him. Her eyes fall to his broad shoulders, and she admires his muscly arms. He's wearing a suit and looks like he's come straight from the office.

Could it be him? His hair is darker, maybe because it's got wax in it. Surely, Sebastian wouldn't be in a place like this, would he? The man turns round, pints in hand, one for himself and one for his mate, waiting at a small table.

It's not him.

He's nothing like Sebastian. Probably wishful thinking. She still hasn't called him despite often daydreaming about their possible reunion. What if she rang him now? What's the worst that could happen? He tells her to go away, and that's not even that bad. At least that would be a final answer, a resolution. Claire could ring him now. The pub is quiet. She's on her own. It's outside of work hours and before anyone really heads out, he should answer. Is it sad to call on a Friday evening? Shouldn't she be busy with her own fabulous social life? There's always a reason why she shouldn't call. She always manages to talk herself out of it. Claire searches for his name in her contacts and hits the green button before she chickens out.

'Hello?' a female voice says.

Claire is dumbfounded. Has she got the wrong number? She almost hangs up immediately, but speaks eventually, 'Hello, um, not sure if I've got the right number. Can I speak to Sebastian please?'

'You've got the right number. Who is it please?' the woman's voice is clipped, breathy, and posh.

'Claire.'

'Claire who?'

'He'll know.'

'Oh, that Claire. SEBBB!' the woman shouts into the phone.

Claire winces and jerks the flip phone away from her ear. *The woman knows who I am. I'm "that Claire"?* She then presses the mobile close to her ear when she hears the woman and supposedly Sebastian having a hushed conversation. Something about "time" and "respect".

'Hello? Claire?' Sebastian says.

It's him. She's finally speaking to him. It feels so long, but like hardly any time has passed. 'Hi, Sebastian,' Claire says, lowering her voice, trying to sound sexy.

'Claire, is that you?' Sebastian sounds confused.

'Yes, it's me,' she says in her usual voice.

'This is a surprise; it's been months. How are you doing?' Sebastian says brightly.

'I'm good. I'm back in London now.'

'Oh.'

Well, he doesn't seem to be breaking out the champagne. 'How's your dad?'

'He's doing really well, thank you.'

He could be talking to his grandma. Fuck this polite chit-chat. 'I thought I had the wrong number at first,' Claire says through gritted teeth while glaring at the open front door of the pub.

'Oh yeah, sorry about the confusion. Cassandra answered the phone, as I was in the shower.'

Cassandra. Shower. 'I just thought I would say hi, seeing as I'm back in town.' Claire necks the rest of her wine.

'It's good to hear from you. A real surprise, I thought I'd never speak to you again, especially after the way I left things—'

'Not to worry,' she interrupts, eager not to re-hash the moment he dumped her.

'We should meet up. It would be so nice to see you,' Sebastian says quietly.

'I wouldn't want to eat into the time you and Cassandra have together.'

Sebastian laughs. 'You wouldn't be.'

'There's no need for a sympathy meet up. You've clearly moved on.' Claire can feel her cheeks are flaming.

Why did I call him?

A montage rushes through her brain. Sebastian helping his dad upstairs in the farmhouse. Him doing up her seatbelt in his 4x4 after rescuing her. His strong legs and muscly bum hopping over the River Dove.

'I see you've maintained your quick temper,' he says in a teasing, singsong voice.

Now, a different collection of Baliston memories. His judgemental, smug face when she got lost. His complete and utter emotional shut down at the stables. Blaming hay fever for the tears in his eyes outside Bramble Cottage. Is he enjoying this? Enjoying humiliating her again? Fuck, this was a mistake. It's like being dumped all over again, with the new girlfriend as the audience. 'Ha ha, Sebastian, anyway, I was just ringing to say hi, so hi!'

'Hi, Claire,' he says in a deep, gravelly voice.

'Bye, Sebastian.' She hangs up the phone and puts her hands to her cheeks in a bid to cool them down. They're roasting, and her hands provide cool comfort.

I rang him, and his girlfriend answered!

Claire goes to the bar and orders another glass of wine before plonking herself back on the uncomfortable wooden chair. She sits for a few minutes, repeatedly sipping her wine, then crossing her arms and watching people walk by the pub window. She gets out her phone to text Saskia about what happened, the need to share her embarrassment overwhelming, she needs to unload some of it, give it to someone else, to try to get rid of it. But there's a text already waiting for her, so she opens it up first. It's from a number that isn't in her contacts and that she doesn't recognise.

CHRIS: Hi Claire, it's Chris, this is my new number. Was just thinking about you. I'm sorry about everything. Can we go for a drink?

A message from Chris. Her ex-boyfriend from last year, who broke her heart and let her down, he wants to meet up with her. When she bumped into him in the summer, he did seem really sorry about not coming to the hospital that night. Not so sorry about cheating, but she doesn't care about that anymore. So much has happened since. It was hard to see through the panic fog that night. It would be good to see him now that her head's clearer. Plus, she just tried to get back in touch with Sebastian, hoping to rekindle things and that's a dead end, but then Chris texts her, wanting to be back in her life. *Wow, it has to be a sign.* Claire texts him back.

Chapter Twenty-Six

Claire gets out of the taxi outside Hazel's house. A black cab treat from the train station rather than the bus, a little indulgence. Well, she's a full-time journalist at a London paper now. A trainee, but on the up, doing what she always talked about doing.

As the car pulls away, Claire takes in her surroundings. It's actually really lovely to be back in Baliston, it's only been two weeks since she left, but it feels like she's visiting home. London felt that way when she returned, though. *Can you have two homes? I suppose you can.* It's quite chilly and brown, red, and yellow leaves are blowing around, sweeping along the ground, making each step crunchy. Of course, Hazel's front garden is immaculate, not a leaf or blade of grass out of place. Claire knocks on the door. As she waits, she realises having a check and a snoop of Hazel's garden before she answers the door is one of her favourite things to do. A comforting habit.

'You're here. It's so fucking great to see you,' Hazel booms before bringing Claire in for a cuddle.

'You look fabulous. I'm so happy to see you too.' Claire cuddles her back before holding her at arm's length to have a good look at her. She's wearing a classic Hazel outfit, very 1950s. A smart red dress with a collar, cinched in at the waist with a belt and a full skirt, which, if she twirled, would fan out and spin with her. Both wrists are covered in bracelets to half way up her arms, and she has a single long necklace with a pendant dangling into her cleavage. It's the one Claire got her for her birthday. Her hair is the spitting image of Marilyn Monroe's, but grey, and her makeup and bright red lipstick finish off the outfit. She could be going on a big night out. 'You didn't have to dress up for me,' Claire says as she walks into the lounge, while inspecting her own outfit, feeling under dressed in her jeans – her best jeans, but still – and a fluffy, green jumper.

'But we're going for our Saturday afternoon walk. I would always get dressed up for the walks with Jack.'

'I see, and I suppose I've automatically put on the outfit I would have worn to the football with Dad.'

Hazel lowers her head slightly and gives Claire a small, knowing smile. 'I suppose you don't want to go straight away, having just done that journey. Are you hungry? I've got a nice prawn salad.'

'Oh, yes please,' Claire says while collapsing into her favourite velvety, green chair.

Hazel sets up the small table in the corner of the lounge for their lunch for two. As they start eating, she asks, 'So, how's it going?'

Claire puts her knife and fork down and leans on the table. 'The job? Yeah, I'm enjoying it. I've got loads to learn, and I feel nervous every day, but I'll get there.'

'Well done, keep going. It will only get easier.'

'How are you?'

'Fabulous, of course, darling. Andrew is making my life a breeze. He's on time, reliable, does what I ask.'

Claire pulls a face.

'That wasn't a dig. I think hiring you actually gave him a kick up the arse. He's putting more effort in. I don't think he would have tried this hard if I had just let him help in the first place.'

'I rang Sebastian,' Claire blurts out.

'Really? How come?'

'I just felt everything ended suddenly, and we had something special. I thought it was worth another try.'

'And?'

'His girlfriend answered.'

'Ouch.'

'Exactly. He suggested meeting up, but I don't need his sympathy—'

'He suggested meeting up? Well, maybe he wants to see you.'

Claire frowns. Sebastian did suggest getting together, but she was so embarrassed about ringing and Cassandra answering, she brushed it off. Surely, he was just being polite and was trying to save the situation? *I wonder how serious they are?* Anyway, it doesn't matter, he's moved on. It's definitely over. 'No, I think he was embarrassed for me and was being polite.'

'Or maybe he was genuinely happy to hear from you and despite him seeing someone else, he still wanted to meet up with you and invited you out in front of her. Sounds pretty keen to me.' Hazel stops eating, crosses her arms, and stares at Claire.

'Possibly… but I don't think so.' Claire almost buries her head in her salad. *Could Hazel be right?*

The two women go for their walk. They decide for their first one, to have a slow amble around the village and then maybe over one of the fields, but Hazel isn't really dressed for off-roading. They talk and they talk and they talk, while walking arm in arm. Claire keeps asking questions about Jack until Hazel speaks at length about him. Claire loves hearing her speak about her late husband. It's a joy to listen to. Their relationship sounds like it was full of fun, teasing, and pure love. They argued and disagreed, but they worked it out, usually with good humour. Hazel's face completely lights up when she speaks about him. The love in her eyes is clear. Claire longs to find that sort of love.

Maybe second time round will work with Chris, and he'll end up being "the one". She tells Hazel about meeting up with him for a quick lunch break coffee the other day. She enjoyed his company. They talked about their mutual friends and about what they've been up to over the last year. Claire and Chris kept it light and lively. They didn't talk about that phone call when he refused to help her. They also didn't go near Saskia's birthday when they bumped into each other. He's apologised. What's the point in re-hashing it, again? She'd forgotten how funny he is, always cracking a joke and not taking life too seriously. He's still handsome. Short dark hair, dark brown eyes, and quite tall. He's shorter than she remembers.

Can someone in their twenties shrink over time?

Surely not.

Maybe she's just comparing him to Sebastian.

Now, he's tall.

They're meeting for a proper date on Friday. Chris wants to go to this new bar he's been told about. He said he couldn't think of anyone else he'd rather go with. He always was a smooth talker. This is progress. Moving on. She's got her career, she's got Hazel, and now she's dating. Dad would be proud. Claire is proud. She's really pulling herself together recently, despite the anniversary of her dad's death approaching. Claire's reaching and striving for it all. She can have it all.

She doesn't need to think about a certain someone who just cast her aside all of a sudden. There will be no thinking about muscly arms and strawberry blonde hair, which repeatedly falls into crystal blue eyes. About soft lips, prickly stubble, or hands wandering to her waist, bum, and then all over, brushing by her breasts.

She tries to remember what kissing Chris was like, but draws a blank. Instead, a fond memory pops up; their weekend away in Newquay. During that break, Chris was at his best. He dropped the playboy act, and any pretension, and was himself. The class clown, who deep down, is sensitive and kind. They both had surfing lessons and failed spectacularly, and spent most of the time laughing at each other. *Did Sebastian really want to see me?*

Chapter Twenty-Seven

Claire taps her nails on the table, drumming a fast beat, similar to a galloping horse, before again scrutinising Sebastian's text.

SEBASTIAN: I can understand u being mad at me for the way I ended things. Hearing your voice made my day. Sure u don't want to meet up? How about a lunch break hang out?

He sent the message on Sunday, the day after Claire saw Hazel. She ended up pacing up and down her flat, not sure what to say or do. She eventually replied, suggesting a quick lunch at the café near the *Ealing Star* on Tuesday. Today. Claire didn't really think he would agree to it. It's a bit of a trek across London for him. But he said, "Yes!" Apparently, he's out and about for meetings anyway and it doesn't matter if he's out for a bit longer for lunch. She told him she'll only be able to meet for half an hour as she'll need to get back to work and still he said that was fine and he was looking forward to seeing her.

Sebastian strolls into the café and scans the room for Claire. Her first instinct is to wave to let him know where she is, but she stops herself, needing a moment to simply take him in. His whole work vibe is even better than she'd imagined. He's in a suit. It makes him appear taller and his shoulders broader.

There's no tie though, just a crisp white shirt… and open collar.

Fucking open collar.

Is he trying to kill me?

What's that?

Two buttons undone at the top.

The opening at the neck, hinting at what's below.

I can see the top of his chest.

Claire takes a deep breath. His hair is completely slicked back. *I wonder if it starts to fall into his eyes towards the end of the day?* During her comprehensive once-over, he spots her and heads over to the small, square table she's sitting at. Claire tries to re-arrange her face, conscious that she might actually be dribbling. She runs her fingers over her mouth. No, fine, she's not literally salivating over him.

She stands up as he reaches her. 'Hi,' Claire says with a diminutive smile.

'Hello.' Sebastian stretches out his arms, signalling he wants to greet her with a hug.

He reaches for her, and she has to stop herself nestling into him. She faces away and focuses her attention out of the window, watching people hurriedly walk past. Trying her best not to drink him in, smell him, and think about his closeness. To be in his arms again though, if she's honest, it's exactly where she wants to be. Despite her efforts, his aftershave dances into her nostrils. It's fresh and strong. As she pulls away from the cuddle, for a few seconds her mouth is centimetres away from his neck. Claire has to stop herself from kissing his soft skin. The proximity of Sebastian is messing with her head.

They sit down, look at each other, order coffees, and paninis, then look at each other again. He seems to be staring at her just as much as she's staring at him.

'I've never seen you in work gear before. You look awesome,' Sebastian says.

Claire glances down at her fitted red dress. It had taken her all evening, the night before, to choose it. It's quite the statement piece and a couple of people in the office had also complimented her this morning. 'Thank you. You look very smart as well.'

'I can't believe we're both back in London. You're different here, I'm not sure what it is?' Sebastian screws up his face and squints at her, like he's trying to work it out.

The waitress delivers their coffees. She's beautiful. All curves and flawless skin. Sebastian stays focused on Claire.

'Well, I'm a journalist now. I must have a new air of authority, or something,' Claire jokes, trying to lighten the mood. Sebastian is being quite intense. She doesn't want to be vulnerable with him. She knows how that goes.

'Well done on getting the job.' A huge smiles spreads across his face, but disappears just as fast. 'I am sorry about how I left things. I feel like I owe you more of an explanation. I know it was all a bit out of nowhere,' he mumbles into his coffee.

'It was. Does Cassandra know you're here?'

Sebastian frowns, confused by the change of subject. 'No, she doesn't. We're casual. We're not a "thing". Not like how we were.'

The sentence hits Claire, jolting her heart. He's admitting it. He felt it. They were something. There were real feelings. It was something special. 'I was starting to think I'd imagined the whole thing. I thought we had something good and then suddenly you bolted.' Claire can feel her emotions turning into perspiration. Why not tell him how she feels? There's nothing to lose now. She rubs her clammy palms on her red dress and braces herself.

'You were so angry when we first met. That worried me. It was hard to tell where the grief ended and you began. You were all over the place. The timing was off.'

Is he trying to put all the blame on me? 'A bit harsh, but true. I questioned starting something when I was such a mess. We had fun, though.'

'We did.'

'That can't be it. You pursued me, you kept asking me to do things despite... everything.'

'Well, no, it wasn't just that.' Sebastian hesitates. 'There was just so much going on. Dealing with my dad was enough to deal with. I really thought he was going to die. I mean, that's what happens when people get cancer, right? That's what happened to my mum. Dad was such a mess when she died. They were together for years and then suddenly she was gone. He didn't know what to do with himself. Anyway, and then the way the doctors were talking all changed, and they started talking about him being okay, and I couldn't believe it. Dad could go back to his life and I could go back to mine. And we seemed to be getting quite serious quite quickly... when I needed to just get myself back on track.' He takes a deep breath and stops studying the table. He gazes deep into Claire's eyes. There are tears in his, his beautiful blue eyes shiny with it all.

His mum also had cancer.

Claire's now seeing the whole picture, his moods and unpredictability, more understandable. She's never heard him speak this openly and honestly. Now he's choosing to be real, telling her exactly what was, and is, on his mind. Really talking. But now it feels too late. The explanation does make sense. She's really trying to see it from his point of view.

'Of course, you know I understand. I was unsure about starting things with you when I'd moved to Baliston to be alone and sort myself out. I suppose I chose to go with the flow, to see where it went.' Claire shrugs.

She takes a bite of her panini. The waitress brought it over a minute ago. The delivery of food hadn't really registered, she'd been immersed in Sebastian. His panini is untouched as well, but he starts eating when Claire does. They both quietly eat. She keeps thinking about what he's said and concludes he's scared to commit and actually have a relationship, scared of putting himself out there and then potentially losing someone he loves. She knows that feeling. She's felt it for so long. But she's ready now, ready to love, and be loved. She doesn't want to be alone anymore. Sebastian is obviously not ready. Maybe he never will be. Seeing his dad fall apart when he was ten years old, when his mum died, has scarred him. The time Claire and Sebastian spent together in the summer was amazing. The chemistry between them still crackles, but their timing's off. They can never quite get it together. It's probably a sign that it's simply not meant to be.

Maybe the timing is finally right for her and Chris? Well, she'll find out in a few days when they go on their date. Claire feels deflated. All the excitement of seeing Sebastian again has been translated into an empty tiredness.

'I'm loving seeing you happy and successful. You've come a long way since you first arrived in Baliston,' Sebastian says. He seems genuinely pleased and proud of her.

'Thank you. How are things with you being back here?'

'It's like I never left, straight back into the swing of things. Back to work, the gym, nights out with friends... just what I wanted,' Sebastian says. His smile doesn't reach his eyes, his face doesn't match what he's saying. 'Claire, I—'

Claire's mind is racing. *What's he going to say? Is he going to say he still has feelings for me? Surely not. Probably wishful thinking on my part.* He's still not ready for a relationship. Or maybe he wants to elaborate more on why he dumped her, to really explain the ins and outs as to why he doesn't want her. Either way, she doesn't want to hear it. Whether he still wants to be with her or not, it's clear to Claire that he's not ready for a relationship and to really let somebody into his life. So, she interrupts him, 'Well, guess what? I've got a hot date on Friday.'

Sebastian sits up straight and runs a hand through his hair, which loosens some of the wax and one strand falls into his eyes.

Claire starts choking on her food.

'Are you alright?' he asks, standing up, preparing himself to slap her on the back.

She coughs a few more times and then takes a slurp of coffee before regaining her composure. 'All fine, sorry about that.' How dare he be so bloody gorgeous and do the hair thing when she's trying to prove to him that she's doing okay since he dumped her, is managing to move on, and other men desire her?

'So, a hot date, you say?' Sebastian says then purses his lips.

'Mmm, it's someone I used to go out with. He got back in touch after he heard I was back in London. Should be fun.' Claire flicks her hair over her shoulders.

'That's something you don't object to then?'

'What?' She can hear the blood pumping through her body. The pulsing sound is loud.

'Getting back with an old flame?' Sebastian holds her gaze. He doesn't blink.

'No, not if it feels right.' Her eyes drop to his mouth, every kiss they've ever shared running through her mind.

'I've known Cassandra for a while actually, we were kind of dating a bit before I moved back home to look after dad.' Sebastian leans his elbow on the table and rests his chin on his hand as he narrows his eyes at Claire.

'Really? Oh, it's funny how things turn out, isn't it? You never know where life is going to take you.' Claire paints on a grin. She's had enough of this tit for tat now. This is a waste of time. A confusing, fantastic waste of time.

'Very deep, Claire.'

'Well, you know me, the deep thinker. It's been lovely to see you again, Sebastian, and thanks for texting after my phone call. It's been great to catch up, but I'm afraid I'm going to have to love you and leave you. I've got to get back to work.' *Fuck, I can't believe I said I'm going to have to love him and leave him. Shit.* In trying to appear light and breezy, she's somehow declared her love for him. It's a saying, it's not how she feels. Obviously.

'Yes, I need to get back to the office as well.' Sebastian glances at his silver watch, then stands up.

'You've not finished your panini,' Claire says.

'I'm not that hungry.'

They walk out together and hover on the pavement near the entrance.

'I'm that way.' She points behind her.

'And I'm that way.' He points behind him in the opposite direction.

Claire smiles at him, and Sebastian smiles at her. He's building up to say something, she's sure of it, he's deep in thought. Maybe she shouldn't have cut him off earlier. Maybe they could work, maybe he could get over his commitment fears. Maybe he is ready. Who's she to decide that he's not?

'Claire, I… I just… we had the best time together, didn't we?'

'We did.'

They hug again and say their goodbyes. Claire leaves wondering why there can't be more "best times". Bewilderment is the overriding feeling. She's not sure anymore how either of them feel or which one of them is stopping them being together. Claire knows one thing though, they're over. Well, they've been over for a while, but any flickers of hope have now been extinguished.

Chapter Twenty-Eight

It's 5.30pm on Friday and as Claire scans the office, she realises it's mostly empty. For the last hour she's been buried in a thick wedge of Council minutes. As the most junior member of staff in the newsroom, she's been given the weekly job of going through them all. It's so difficult because it's so boring, page after page of jargon-speak about littering and planning permissions, but there could always be a story buried within the dull and it's Claire's job to find it. The only problem is she keeps reading and not taking anything in. The words mean nothing, and she has to keep re-focusing and re-reading.

Steve wanders over to her desk. 'If you haven't found anything in there yet, there probably isn't anything to find.'

Claire looks up, her eyes bleary from staring at the lines and lines of words. 'Mmm, I was just double checking.'

'It's admirable that you don't want to miss anything, but you need to use your time wisely,' Steve says while adjusting his rucksack strap on his shoulder. 'Right, I'm off, and you should be as well.' He taps on the table to labour his point.

'Yes, I'm just about done.'

'Good, have a nice weekend.'

Claire is now the only one left in the office. She leans back on her chair and slaps shut the stapled together papers. There isn't a story in there, but she didn't trust her instincts, re-reading everything, and yep, there still isn't a story in there. She gets up and dumps the minutes in the shredding pile, which feels fantastic. Bloody waste of time. Claire checks her emails one more time and reads through her to-do-list in her diary. Yes, she's done everything she set out to do today, so why is she still here, faffing?

Could she be putting off going home and getting ready for her date with Chris?

Maybe.

She's not sure why she agreed to go.

What if she has another panic attack when she sees him? Those few months they'd spent together were great, but the way it ended was awful. Plus, she's not sure they've still got a spark, but there's only one way to find out. She needs to stop thinking about Sebastian. Their meet up was confusing and brought up her feelings again, but it's no use moping about him. She needs to move on.

What's the saying?

Get over one person by getting under the next?

Claire logs off her computer and puts her diary, notepad, and pens in her handbag.

The wind takes her by surprise, the cosy office is not replicated outside. It's chilly and gusty. Claire wraps her coat around her, holding it in place while crossing her arms.

It's nearly a year since Dad died and he's once again dominating her thoughts. Maybe that's why she can't really be arsed with this date. She keeps replaying her last conversation with her dad, brushing him off, choosing colleagues she doesn't even see anymore over him. Then ten days later, Christmas spent alone, opening the present he'd already bought and wrapped. A posh notepad and pen, a present intended with the best of intentions to give her a kick up the arse. She hugs her handbag close, the notepad inside. *If only he could see me now.* She looks back at the *Ealing Star* offices, and her mouth twitches into a hint of a smile.

An hour later, Claire is in front of the full-length mirror in her bedroom. Her flat is small but has everything she needs and is close to the office, which makes life easier. The lounge and small galley kitchen are completely open plan, meaning the two rooms are actually one big room. Then there's her bedroom and bathroom. It's in an old converted building, though, which means the ceilings are high, giving the illusion of space.

Claire takes in her appearance. She's wearing her new black skinny jeans and a tight-fitting sequinned top. As she moves it catches the light. Keeping Chris's height in mind, she chooses smaller heels. For a change, she's wearing her hair up in a high pony and she's done her makeup heavier than usual. She got a little carried away while trying to get herself in the mood for going out, trying to make up for her lack of enthusiasm. Satisfied, she turns away from the mirror and throws concealer, mascara, keys, money, a bank card, ID and her phone into a tiny, black handbag. She's meeting him at a new bar he wants to try out; she needs to get a couple of tubes to get there. She sighs, turns off the lights, and locks up.

Claire arrives before Chris, which pisses her off. *Now I look too keen.* She balances on a high stool at the bar while clutching the stem of a wine glass, her eyes flicking to the door every time it opens. The bar is very dark with funky bits of lighting hanging from the corners, lampshades made from non-lampshade items such as milk bottles, wine bottles, and teapots. The music is deafeningly loud, and every song has a deep, pulsating bass. A DJ in the far corner holds up one headphone to his ear and nods his head.

The barman keeps staring at her, in between making drinks.

'Bugger off,' Claire mutters under her breath.

There are a few dancing, but people are mostly sitting in booths and shouting at each other to make conversation. There's a cool vibe, even if it's trying too hard. She peeks at her watch. He's twenty minutes late, and she's drank half her wine. *He's got until I've finished the glass.*

'Claire.'

His voice makes her jump. She'd stopped watching the door. She swivels around, away from the bar, towards him. 'Hi.' She gives him a brief smile and checks him out. He's wearing dark blue jeans and a plain white shirt. He's cute and smells divine.

'Sorry I'm late. I couldn't find this place; I thought it was the next street. I'd heard good things, but I've never actually been,' Chris says at double-speed.

The nervous, fast talking transports her back to when he first asked her out, at a mutual friend's house party. It was endearing then, and it's endearing now.

'No worries, I've just been having a drink and relaxing,' Claire says, trying to sound breezy, which is hard when you have to shout to be heard.

She feels fine seeing him. No loud blood pumping through her veins, no speeding heart, no sweaty back of the neck. No panic.

'My mate said there's a quieter part, more away from the music,' Chris says while surveying the place. He orders a drink and leads the way through a door Claire hadn't spotted. Sure enough, there's a lounge area with large plush sofas. The music can still be heard, but it feels distant and more manageable for conversation. Chris plonks himself down on one of the sofas and Claire sits next to him, placing her wine on the low table in front of them.

They glance at each other and both take a sip of their drinks. 'Cool place,' she offers.

'Yeah, I like it in here.' Chris strokes the sofa arm. 'I got a promotion this week, so reason to celebrate.' He lifts up his glass and takes a large gulp.

'Wow, well done. What are you doing now then?'

'Before, I was the manager and now I'm the senior manager.'

'Great.' Over coffee, he'd told Claire all about his computer programming job. Recalling his enthusiasm for the subject, she smiles. She's not surprised he's been promoted.

'Have you had a good week?'

'Yeah, I'm getting settled into my job. I've not been there long,' she says.

Chris puts his arm across the back of the sofa, meaning it's also behind and around her. 'You look beautiful. What's it been, like a year since we dated? You haven't changed a bit, you know.'

Yes, I have. 'Thanks.'

'We're okay, aren't we? I regret that night.'

'Yes, fine. Let's forget it. Do you want to dance?' Claire asks.

'Go on then.'

They both neck their drinks and go back into the loud bar. There's a particularly bassy number thumping out of the speakers, and there are now lots of people on the dance floor. They weave their way through the sweat and armpits until they find a space. She remembers Chris loves a dance, the sillier the better. While flailing her arms around, she starts jumping up and down in time to the beat.

'I like your style,' Chris shouts. He joins in, copying Claire's moves, but adds spins and hip thrusts.

Claire laughs. He's absolutely ridiculous. She likes how he doesn't care what other people think and lets loose. She does "the robot" just to see his reaction. She's hopeless at it and she's sure she looks a fool, but it'll be worth it to see his face. As the current track comes to an end, Chris finishes his latest twirl, then stops dramatically on one knee in front of Claire, his arms outstretched, his eyes closed. Once satisfied with his over the top finale, he opens his eyes as the next song starts. She's still moving her arms in a stop-start abrupt fashion, doing an impression of a machine finding its rhythm.

Chris jumps up. 'Oh, it's like that, is it?' He drops to the floor and performs "the worm". A group of women behind him point and move out of the way. As his whole-body curves and flip-jumps backwards, coins begin to fly out of his pockets. The group cheers, then they all crouch down in their heels and short skirts, careful to put their knees to one side to keep their modesty, and collect up the cash. There must be at least ten people squatting on the dance floor, their boozy fingers picking at the floor, grabbing for any coppers, or if they're lucky, perhaps ten pence or fifty pence.

Claire's doubled over, clutching her belly, struggling to breathe. She can't stop laughing. Her muscles are clenching and aching, but the giggles keep coming. Once Chris is standing again, she signals to him about getting another drink and they go to the bar.

He orders a wine and a pint, plus four shots of Sambuca. 'I think I lost about a tenner then.' Chris grimaces while brushing dirt and glitter off his shirt.

'I'd forgotten what a wally you are,' she says as she slaps his shoulder and leaves her hand there.

'Anything for a laugh. You gotta let your hair down.'

'Indeed,' Claire says. They down both of their shots and take their drinks to the dance floor.

It feels freeing to let go and be silly. They get drunker and drunker and their dance moves become more and more wobbly and erratic. At one point, at seemingly the exact same moment, they both decide to try out a kiss. During a slower song, both their upper lips sweaty, Chris leans in and so does Claire. They have a bit of a snog. She closes her eyes but re-opens them when the room starts spinning. At one point he sways and seems to forget where her mouth is and he's goldfish like, opening and closing his mouth on her cheek. She grabs his head and their mouths find each other again. They press their bodies up against each other, their mouths wide and eager. It's an alright kiss, it's kind of sexy, but also like kissing a memory. It feels nostalgic, but she's not sure if she wants to do it again. Drunken nights out together, snogging, downing shots, then arguing and making up lurk in her subconscious.

As they pull away from each other, a banger of a tune comes on and they start leaping around again. As Claire bounces around, the taste of bitter beer in her mouth from Chris and the Sambuca sloshing around in her stomach, a drunken mirage of the last person she kissed appears. Sebastian is standing in the corner of the room, beckoning her to come to him. When she gets there, he disappears, and she leans her head against the wall before squinting and trying to focus on the dance floor, where Chris is head banging to a dance track. She giggles and wobbles back to him. She takes the scenic route, criss-crossing about, her legs bendy and stretchy.

While stuffing cheesy chips in her mouth at 3am, Claire feels very drunk but happy to have reconnected with Chris and have a new friend. A friend. As she watches him fold a pizza slice into his mouth, hot cheese dripping from his chin, she knows there's nothing romantic here. She's not attracted to him, she's not trying to impress him, she's not thinking about her appearance or how she seems in front of him, but they've had a right laugh. It's like any sexual chemistry they had has dissipated and they're left with a friendship. Earlier, Chris even apologised for cheating on her when they were together. His only excuse being he was young and horny. Claire had laughed, admiring his honesty, time having already healed any residual hurt. So much has happened, it just doesn't matter anymore.

Chris puts an arm around her neck, his hand dangling into her chest. 'You're wicked,' he slurs and pecks her on the cheek, tomato sauce from the pizza finding its way onto her face.

It's the most matey move and Claire is sure he's on the same page. You could probably file this under the most-fun-yet-friend-zoned date ever.

#

The next morning, she wakes up and immediately begins stressing whether Chris is actually thinking the same as her. What if he thinks they are now romantically involved? They did kiss, after all. *Shit, have I led him on?* The whole evening is a bit of a blur. Her phone bleeps and it's Chris. Oh no, this is going to be awkward.

CHRIS: Claire, I've just been sick everywhere, like literally all over my bedroom. It's carnage. Thanks for a great night. Let's do it again sometime. You're my new drinking buddy!

Claire lies back down in bed and releases the breath she's been holding onto. She chucks her phone on the floor and goes back to sleep. Hoping to sleep away the mother of all hangovers.

Chapter Twenty-Nine

Saturday 15th December 2007

Claire waits outside the gate to the cemetery. The entry point is black, spiky, and over-bearing, like something straight out of a horror film. She shivers and grips onto her phone. No missed calls or texts. Her watch confirms that Saskia is fifteen minutes late. She doesn't know why she's surprised. Surely, she could be on time today? Claire sighs and puts her mobile back in her handbag.

The street is busy with people doing their usual Saturday morning things; shopping, chatting, going for coffee. A woman who must be in her forties is struggling with several bags of food shopping. Claire watches her, noticing the plastic bags straining. One bag splits and fruit spills out and rolls down the road. A little boy giggles and points at four oranges making their escape. The woman stops, places her shopping on the ground, and glares at all the fruit splattered, or rolling free. She puts one hand on her hip and the other scrapes along her forehead. A man offers to help her. Smiling, they start gathering everything up. A teenage boy is walking and texting. He's nearly taken out three people and yet he carries on typing away. A couple are snogging, while leaning against a lamppost. His hands are wandering, searching, and then rest on her bum. They're in their own world, totally focused on each other, and unaware that they're surrounded by hundreds of people. Claire's staring at the hot and heavy couple and forces her eyes away. She thinks about going inside without Saskia. It's not like she can't do it on her own, but she decides to wait a few more minutes.

'Sorry I'm late.' Saskia almost bangs into Claire. She's travelling at such speed, panting and sweating.

'You're almost half an hour late.' Claire folds her arms.

'Sorry, I really didn't want to be late. I was really trying not to be. I don't know, it's just in my DNA or something. It doesn't matter how hard I try.' Saskia ruffles her hair and wipes sweat from the back of her neck.

Claire pouts. Saskia is right. It's who she is, and Claire is fully aware. She's probably spent days of her life waiting for Saskia. 'There should be some sort of science experiment to see if you can actually turn up on time, to see if it's genetically possible.'

'Ha ha,' Saskia says. 'So, are you ready? Is this the first time?'

'Yes and yes,' Claire says. Should she have come back before now? What's the point of visiting a grave? It's not like Dad will know she's here. She thinks about him all the time. She doesn't need to be in front of a piece of stone surrounded by other buried bodies. Lying in the ground, in rows, next to each other, some completely decomposed, others a collection of bones. It's a disturbing thought.

But today, she has to be here. A year since it happened.

A year since Dad got into Larry's car and never got out.

A year since Claire was supposed to have dinner with her dad and cancelled to go to the pub with her mates.

A year of guilt and grief. Half of that year spent in Baliston meeting the wonderful Hazel… and of course, Sebastian. At least she still has Hazel.

'Are you coming then?' Saskia asks.

Claire is still standing by the gate; the graveyard is visible. A lawnmower is rumbling and groaning inside. Headstones line the grass. Which one is Dad's? She can't even remember; the funeral is a complete blur. Claire hasn't even seen the headstone. It wasn't ready for the service. They were going to put it in a few weeks after. She doesn't even know what it says on it. She couldn't find the words. Uncle Arthur, Dad's brother, sorted it. What if she doesn't like what he wrote? What if she can feel Dad's presence when she's near where he's buried? *Don't be ridiculous.* She doesn't believe in ghosts, or the after life or heaven. The image of worms weaving their way through a skeleton flashes through her mind. Claire believes in life and then death. There's nothing after death, just nothing. The thought absolutely terrifies her. She doesn't usually let herself think about it.

'Claire? We don't have to do this,' Saskia says, looking intently at her. She puts her arm around Claire.

'I want to, I think.' But instead of going into the cemetery grounds, she sits on a bench to the right of the gate. 'I'll go in, in a minute.'

'Okay.' Saskia sits down next to her and rubs her hands. It's icy cold. Saskia tries to fill the silence with stories of wild nights out, wild sex with Stuart, and gossip from the modelling industry. Half an hour passes. Saskia lets out a long, cloudy breath. 'I'm all for taking your time, but it's fucking freezing.' She chatters her teeth together to labour the point.

'Well, you should have dressed for the weather.' Claire looks down at Saskia's mini-skirt, thin black tights, and short fluffy jacket. No hat, no scarf, and no gloves. 'Sorry, you're right, we need to get moving.' Claire pats Saskia on the leg, then frantically rubs Saskia's arms to try to create friction and warmth. They hold hands as they walk through the gate into the graveyard. 'I think it's at the top left.' Claire points while scanning the uniform rows of remembrance.

'No, it's on the right.' Saskia offers a small smile.

'Really?'

'Yeah, I made a mental note at the funeral.'

Claire wells up and squeezes Saskia's hand as they walk to the far-right corner.

'Here we are,' Saskia says quietly.

Claire Morris is Completely Lost

In loving memory of
ALEX MORRIS

13/10/1954 – 15/12/2006

A loving father, son and brother
We love you, always

It's perfect. Claire sobs into a tissue, and Saskia wraps an arm around her. Uncle Art found the right words. She promises herself she will ring and thank him. Claire hasn't really spoken to him since the funeral. They're not close. Maybe she should make more of an effort.

'I bought these.' Saskia pulls out a bunch of daffodils from her humongous designer handbag. There's a stunning assortment of white and yellow petals with beautiful ferns and green foliage.

'Oh, thank you, I didn't think to bring anything. You're the best,' Claire says before hugging her best friend. She takes the bouquet out of Saskia's arms and places it in front of the grave. Claire brushes the stone as she lets go of the flowers. The smooth coldness surprises her, and she jerks her arm back. 'I didn't think you could get daffodils at this time of year,' Claire says while taking in her friend's thoughtful offering.

'Mmm, I wasn't sure, but you can, and the florist told me they're actually one of the birth flowers of December. Who knew?!' Saskia shrugs and then says more quietly, 'I remember him saying he used to always get daffodils for his mum on Mother's Day. He said he chose daffodils because they look strange, with their little trumpets in the middle.' She chuckles, while clearly studying Claire's reaction.

'Yeah, he did say that, god, your memory is impressive.' Claire can see him now, holding a bunch of daffodils as they walk up Grandma's front garden path. She must have been five or six, him pretending to play the daffodil-trumpet, holding a flower to his mouth and tooting away.

'When it comes to you, it is.'

'Thank you for being here.' Claire tries to swallow, but her throat feels blocked.

'Thank you for asking me to be here. There's been so many times I've wanted to be here for you, but you've been wanting to do it alone. Thanks for finally leaning on me.'

Claire smiles. Saskia is more switched on than she's ever given her credit for. Claire reads the words again and finds solace in them. *Maybe this is why people visit graves?*

'I'll give you some time alone. I'll go and get us some coffees.' Saskia rubs her hands together again and does a little jig, her breath visible and floating.

'That would be great, thanks,' Claire whispers. She watches Saskia speed walk to the high street, while marvelling at her friend's ability to know exactly what she needs. A waft of greasy chips hits Claire as she observes the rectangular stone in front of her. The nearby chip shop must be preparing for lunch. Seaside trips and Saturdays at Enfield hang in the air.

'Sorry, Dad. I shouldn't have cancelled that night. Maybe if I hadn't, things would have turned out differently, or maybe we could have had a lovely final night together. I miss you every single day.' She lets the tears flow. She can feel her makeup dripping into her eyes, so she wipes and dabs her face with a tissue. 'Want some chips, Dad? Go on, I bet you do.' Claire chuckles as her tummy rumbles. Then she simply stands in silence, standing vigil, paying her respects, and marking a year since her dad's death.

Her feet feel like blocks of ice, so she stomps and jumps up and down. She twirls around to look at the gate to see if Saskia is back yet with the coffees. Claire could really do with a lovely warm drink right now. Her friend is nowhere to be seen, though. Instead, in her line of vision is a woman in a massive sleeping-bag-like coat, walking up the path towards her. *I wish I had that coat on.* Claire smiles at the woman and takes a step forward onto the frosty grass to let her pass by. Claire continues to stare at the gate longingly, willing Saskia to come back with two steaming hot cups.

'Hello,' the woman says quietly.

Claire flinches. The woman didn't carry on walking, she's standing right next to her. What? Surely, you don't disturb someone in a cemetery, doesn't standing by a grave… scream, "private time, leave me alone". 'Good morning,' Claire gives her a straight-line twitch of the mouth.

The woman stays still and continues to stay close. The woman is taller than her, slim with curly blonde hair, and probably in her fifties. A floral aroma fills the air and Claire's old paddling pool springs to mind. Pictures of fish swimming around the sides. She glares at the woman. *Go away, weirdo.*

'I was hoping you would be here today, Claire.' The woman's eyes are glassy as she lifts her head to make eye contact.

Claire frowns at her. *What the fuck?*

'Here we are, two cappuccinos. The queue was massive,' Saskia announces. Claire turns around and takes the coffee from Saskia while gesturing with her eyes to the woman behind her. Claire automatically takes a sip, seeking comfort, but it's bitter and already lukewarm.

'Oh hello, I didn't see you there,' Saskia says to the woman, and sensing Claire's discomfort says loudly, 'are you ready to get going?'

'Yeah, just one sec,' Claire says to Saskia. 'Who are you?' Claire asks the woman.

'I'm Laura, your mum.'

Claire drops her coffee. The brown liquid splashes up their legs, making everyone take a step back. Claire drinks in the woman. The curly hair, the shape of her eyes, the dimples in her cheeks. *She looks like me.* 'Why are you here, now? I haven't seen you since I was three,' twenty-five-year-old Claire's voice wobbles on the word "three". She feels transported to their brown lounge, watching Mummy walk in and out of the house, her dad's voice, loud.

'Sorry, it must be a shock. I heard about Alex and I just wanted to see how you're doing,' Laura says, almost in a whisper.

Claire blinks at Saskia and then at Laura. 'What the..? This is the moment you choose to show up. This is the moment you fancy being a mum? What about the past twenty-bloody-years?' Anger pulsates through every inch of her body, her head throbbing, the noise of her emotions, unbearable.

'I know. I've missed a lot. Can we talk? I'd like to try to be here for you now.' Laura takes a step forward.

Claire takes a step back and bumps into Saskia. 'But you left—' she can't think of anything else to say.

'I convinced myself you'd be better off without me. I can see I was wrong. I can explain,' Laura says so fast that her words tumble together. She rubs away her falling tears, dragging her hands across her face, smearing black mascara stripes under her eyes.

What's that supposed to mean? Who's better off without their mum? 'I can't do this.' Claire storms away, leaving Laura and Saskia behind. She wants to kick something, hit something, and shout until she loses her voice. How fucking dare she?

She thinks this is the moment to swoop in and save me now?

What about when he died?

What about when I got my first period?

When I wanted boy advice?

What about any time in the last two decades?

Claire starts running, tears streaming down her face. She doesn't know where she's going, she just knows she needs to be away from here and the older reflection of herself standing next to where her dad is buried. Her legs give way and she falls to the ground, scraping her hands as she tries to save herself. Claire sits and leans against a wall to inspect her wounds.

Seconds later, Saskia arrives. 'Bloody hell, you're fast,' she says as she sits next to Claire. 'Why are you sitting on the floor? It's freezing. Oh,' she says when she sees Claire's scraped and bleeding hands.

'Did she follow you?' Claire says, her eyes darting about.

'No. I've never been so speechless in all my life. I didn't know what to say. You got your feelings across pretty well, though.' Saskia smiles.

'Yeah, I suppose.'

'She gave me this.' Saskia passes a note to Claire, which she unfolds. It simply says "Mum" and a mobile number. 'She said whenever you're ready, give her a call.'

Claire scrunches up the paper and stuffs it into her bag. 'She ruins everything,' Claire cries. Her whole body is shaking. The blood on her injured hands is making her stomach churn even more. She can't stand the sight of it. She feels like she's going to vomit, but the sickness doesn't come, there's no relief.

'You don't have to speak to her, but don't you want some answers?' Saskia pushes a loose strand of hair out of Claire's face.

'Maybe, I don't know. I just wanted to visit my dad. I want him, not her.'

'I know. Come on, let's get you home.' Saskia drags Claire to her feet and gives her a cuddle.

Claire nestles into her friend's fluffy jacket and leans on her shoulder, letting Saskia take her weight for a few seconds. Claire gets the strongest urge to speak to Sebastian. He'd suggested finding her mum. What would he think to this situation? He'd tell her not to run, do the right thing, be the better person, and hear her out. She wishes he was here now. Claire wants to hear his calm, soothing voice. She pulls away and rummages around in her bag. 'I'm going to call her now. We need to talk.'

Saskia frowns, her head twisting to one side. 'Really? Are you sure?'

'Yeah, I'm tired of running. I need to hear what she's got to say.' Claire glances at her phone in her hand and then starts searching for the piece of scrunched up paper.

'Wow. I think you're doing the right thing.' Saskia nods her head and puts her hands on her hips.

Claire dials the number. 'Hi, it's Claire. Can we meet now?'

Chapter Thirty

The conversation on the phone is short and to the point. Claire and her mum arrange to meet at a café close to the cemetery. This is it, time to get answers, answers to questions that have always lingered.

Saskia and Claire are still standing where Claire fell over, not far from the graveyard.

'Do you want me to come with you?' Saskia asks.

'No, I think I need to do this on my own.' Claire appreciates the offer. She knows she's not doing her usual self-preservation thing and pushing Saskia away to only rely on herself. This is something which she really needs to do alone.

'Okay, how about I walk with you to the café, then I'll go home?' Saskia suggests.

'I'd like that.'

As they get nearer, Claire takes smaller steps, almost dawdling. Thick, grey clouds hang in the sky, making the capital's streets even more concrete-esque than usual. They reach their destination. You can't miss it. The exterior is covered in orange wooden panelling, which pops amongst the drab, almost glistening in the winter sunshine. Through the large windows, people scoff and yak away. Claire and Saskia stop a few steps away from the door.

'Call me when you're done. I hope it goes well. Try to stay calm.' Saskia smiles.

'Mmm, I'll try.' Claire smirks, knowing her friend's heart is in the right place and she should focus on keeping her temper in check.

'Good luck.' Saskia pats her on the arm, then leaves.

Claire watches her march down the street. Saskia turns around just as she's about to go out of view, round a corner. When she sees Claire still standing outside, she gestures, her arms flailing. Claire waves and moves towards the glass door, ready to go inside.

This is it, time to meet her mum, for the first time. Well, of course she knew her when she was little, and she'd briefly met her in the cemetery, but that's their relationship to date. She's not sure if this is something she wants to do or indeed if it's something she can handle. Claire loudly inhales through her nose and then gushes air out through her mouth as she exhales. She catches her reflection in the door as she walks in. Her plain black dress is serious and sombre, while her thick winter coat is warm and comforting. Her curly hair is pulled back into a bun; it was completely untameable this morning and she simply lacked the patience.

Claire's hit by the smell of bacon. They must still be serving breakfast. Is it still the morning? Surely not, so much has happened. Scanning the room, she realises she's the first to arrive and takes a seat close to the window. Typical. The place is pretty busy and noisy, full of people having their weekend treat of a full English. At least if there's raised voices, no one will notice. They'll blend into the crowd. Fiddling with the menu, she stares out of the window and then back at the menu.

'Hello, Claire,' Laura says. She's standing next to the small, square table, clutching her handbag to her hip. It's a large leather bag, dark brown, and well-used. Her eyes are small and bloodshot and her skin is blotchy. Laura's blonde curls are wild after being blown about outside. She unzips her massive sleeping-bag-style coat. Underneath, her black skirt is sensible and to the knee. Her flowery blouse has a mumsy look, which somehow infuriates Claire.

'Hello,' Claire says as she forces a smile and points to the seat in front of her, encouraging Laura to sit down. 'You're here.'

'Yes, thank you for calling and deciding you'd like to meet so quickly.' Laura rests both elbows on the table and then changes her mind and clasps her hands on her lap.

'Sorry I ran. I do want to hear what you've got to say.' Claire looks her mum straight in the eye. 'I think.'

'I appreciate you taking the time.' A single tear drops and Laura quickly wipes it away and shakes her head. 'First, shall we order some brunch?' She forces a happier expression.

They both order coffees and toast and find themselves in silence. Where to start? How do you catch up on twenty-odd years of relationship? Claire has many questions. But how do you ask a complete stranger about your inner most thoughts and worries, which have been bubbling inside you since you can remember? Claire rubs her forehead, then straightens her eyebrows with her fingers before dragging a hand over her lips. She leaves her hand over her mouth, pushing her top lip to one side, her elbow resting on the table.

'You said in the cemetery you thought I would be better off without you. Why?' Claire can no longer hold the words in, she needs at the very least the answer to this question.

'I didn't know at the time, but after you were born, I had post-natal depression and I stayed depressed for a long time. I never really bonded properly with you and your dad was such a natural straight away. I envied him.' Laura's eyes are wide, and she keeps tucking her hair behind her ears, but it keeps springing forward.

'Where are you living now?' Claire needs to speak about something more day-to-day and mundane to give her time to digest. Laura had post-natal depression. Of all the possible scenarios that Claire had gone through in her head, that hadn't been one of them. But people have post-natal depression and stay with their children. They work through it.

'Reading. I'm still with Dave, the man I left your dad for.'

Claire swallows. At least she left for lasting love.

'I know now I shouldn't have left you. I don't think your dad and me would have worked out, but I still could have been in your life. But I only know that after years of therapy. At the time, I was utterly convinced your life would be better without me. I was very low and Dave was very kind. I thought it was best if we all started over.' Laura can no longer hold back her emotions. They're flooding her face. She picks up a paper napkin and dabs her cheeks.

Claire's surprised that she can understand what Laura's saying. She can understand the logic and maybe how Laura was feeling at the time, even if the logic is flawed. Running and starting over, she can identify with. There was no death all those years ago though, only the loss of a mum, which her mum chose and made happen. It feels odd to have more information, filling in the gaps about what went on. Claire had conjured up so many different stories over the years. The truth, well, she assumes it's the truth, is so different. It's startling. It's as though she's had the outline of a drawing, ready to be coloured in all her life, and now someone is chucking paint at it. She doesn't know what to say. It's not like she can say, *oh don't worry about it, we all make mistakes.* Claire stays close-mouthed.

Laura takes the quiet as permission to carry on with her story. 'I always knew you were okay, I still had friends in the area who would let me know when they saw you about.'

'Why didn't you contact me before now, if you were so interested?' Claire re-finds her voice, the words tumbling out, a familiar feeling returning. The beginnings of rage pumping through her veins, as it often does when she thinks about her mum.

'It took me years to sort myself out and then so much time had gone by. I didn't want to disrupt your life again. I felt like I had made my decision, and I should stick with it. But then Alex died, and you were all alone. But it took me until the first anniversary of his death to build up the courage to seek you out. I'm sorry, I'm selfish and weak, but every day I'm trying to be a better person.' Laura puts her head in her hands and scratches her fingers through the front of her hair before lifting her head.

Desperation and melancholy drip from her.

Claire absorbs the speech but says nothing. There's a rehearsed feel to it. A waitress brings over their food and drinks and Claire takes a bite of toast but the cooked bread sticks in her throat and she puts it down, while wiping her mouth. Her mind is racing. An apology is welcome, but it's just words and there's a mountain of new knowledge to take in.

'It's good to have an explanation,' Claire finally says while nodding her head, her eyes fixed on the table.

'I am sorry, and I would like to keep seeing you.' Laura tries to catch Claire's eye.

'That, I don't know about.' Claire gazes out of the window and then at her watch, the urge to sprint, strong. She shuffles in her seat, uncomfortable in every way.

'I don't want to take up too much of your time. I understand if you need to get going. But please think about what I've said. There could still be time for us.' Laura's eyes are pleading.

Claire searches her mum's face, exploring its unfamiliar yet familiar features. She seems genuine, this feels genuine, but she can't shake this uneasy feeling. 'Yes, I suppose,' Claire says slowly. 'I just never expected to see you again. It's been so many years.' *I nearly came looking for you.* She can't quite believe her mum came looking for her. Mum sought her out. Finally.

'I have two daughters with Dave. They're twenty and eighteen,' Laura blurts out.

Sisters, I have sisters?! A whole hidden family. 'Shit.'

Laura lets out a forced chuckle. 'Well, yeah. Sorry, I didn't know how to say it so I just came out and said it. I finally told them about a month ago that you exist. They're absolutely fuming with me and Dave and they're barely talking to us. I think they're just trying to get their heads around it.'

She only just told her daughters about me? I'm some sort of dirty secret. I bet they're feeling some of what I'm feeling. So much hurt caused by one woman. 'Did Dad know?'

'About Ruby and Joanne?' Laura asks.

Claire visibly flinches at the sound of their names and nods.

'No, he didn't know. We had no real contact after I left. He didn't know where I went.'

Ruby and Joanne. Claire raises her eyebrows in way of reply and then starts eating her toast again, this time munching it furiously. She's not an only child, not alone, she has two sisters. Family. They haven't done anything to her, they've not abandoned her, maybe they could be friends, maybe they could be family. One day. Claire sips her coffee and feels sick. The mixture of anger, excitement, and general high emotion isn't doing her insides any good.

'Can I meet them? Ruby and Joanne?' Claire struggles to say their names. It feels odd, surreal even.

'I hope so. I don't think they're ready yet. I'll ask them, soon. Can we meet up again?' Laura holds onto the edge of the table.

'Maybe, I don't know. Maybe we can meet here again… and take it from there?'

All Laura's birthdays and Christmases have come at once. 'I'd like that,' she says as she bites into her toast, appearing suddenly ravenous.

They say their awkward goodbyes and agree to meet again, here, soon. Claire says she'll be in touch. She doesn't want to agree on a date and time now, it's too much. She has so many more questions, but she only has enough energy to ask a couple at a time. She needs to process what Laura has told her today, and then she'll have space for more information. She vows to write down some questions for their next meet up, whenever that might be. That's what Dad would advise her to do. She bows her head, taking a moment to think of him, imagining his face and reaction to today's news.

If only he had come back today.

Chapter Thirty-One

They meet again a week later, a few days before Christmas, at the same café near the cemetery. This time Laura arrives first and is sitting waiting. Clutching her notepad, Claire sits down.

'Merry Christmas, Claire,' Laura says.

Claire recoils. At twenty-five, she shouldn't be hearing her mum say that for the first time. Well, she probably heard it at one, two, and three years old, but those memories are wiped, nowhere to be found. 'Hello.' Claire shuffles in her seat, straightening her pencil skirt, and re-tucking her white blouse. She's come straight from work, and it's been a long day. She's a bag of nerves.

It went okay the last time they met up. It was illuminating; she got some answers, but she's not sure how to go forward, how to build a relationship. Anger and hope pulsate through her. Claire doesn't know how to navigate this. There's no guidebook, no "how to". She doesn't know this woman, and there's no natural closeness. In her daydreams she'd thought maybe, if they did ever meet, that there would be this instant bond, genetics linking them easily, and some semblance of a mother-daughter connection would be evident. The reality is a stranger, who she has so many mixed feelings about, that she has to work to get to know.

This place has a different vibe in the evening. It's now more restaurant than café. The lighting is low, sultry blues-jazz-type music is playing in the background, and the laminated menu has been replaced with a leather-bound one.

'I'm so happy we can meet again before Christmas,' Laura

says. She's wearing a Christmas jumper, featuring lots of sleighs carrying Santa, his reindeer galloping through the air. Laura's more put together this time. Her blonde curls are behaving themselves, her makeup is fresh, and her eyes aren't blood-shot and teary. She's pretty and normal looking. You would never know she abandoned her child; her appearance holds no clue.

'Yes,' is Claire's response. 'Shall we order some teas?' *She could do with something stronger, but tea is the sensible option.*

Laura nods, and Claire gets the waiter's attention. They then sit in silence for a while, taking each other in, sizing up the situation.

'I would like to find out more about you. I feel like we talked about me a lot last time and I didn't get to learn about you,' Laura says.

You don't get that privilege. You lost that when you left for over twenty years. 'We can get to that but first—'

'Two teas,' the waiter – a small man, with long, grey hair in a ponytail – says as he plonks two mugs on the table. Hot, brown liquid sloshes onto the surface. He ignores it, spins around in a dramatic flourish, and heads back to the kitchen.

Laura cleans up with a serviette. 'What were you saying?'

Claire watches her mum wipe the table. Sweeping and absorbing the tea with the paper tissue. It's a very mum-like move. How she'd imagined her mum might act. To see this live and in front of her, touchable, her floral scent wafting Claire's way as she moves, is somehow disturbing. It feels unreal, like she's hallucinating.

'How did you know where Dad's buried? And why didn't you come to the funeral?' Claire blurts out and glances down at her notepad. The first two questions on her list, asked. She takes off her already unzipped coat.

Laura clears her throat. 'I thought you might ask about me turning up at the cemetery. I asked your Uncle Art. I've called him a few times over the years to check in on you and your dad.'

'Did Dad know?'

'I don't think so, no.'

A snake in the grass. 'Surely, Uncle Arthur's loyalty should have been with Dad, not you?' Claire's cheeks flame. Heat spreads and flushes through her entire body. She rubs her clammy hands together and then wipes her upper lip.

'He wasn't happy about telling me, but I pleaded and we were friends once.' Laura shrugs, her shoulders only making a slight movement upwards. Her eyes dart around the café.

Claire follows her gaze. It's busy again. Lots of people have obviously come straight from the office, still in their smart clothes, grabbing some food with colleagues, friends, or significant others. There's laughing, loud voices, and expressive hands, a collective festive feel. Everyone's ready for Christmas, for a break from the norm, for family time, for making memories.

Claire sighs. 'And the funeral?'

'I thought about coming and I nearly did. But I thought that would be too dramatic, in front of so many people.'

'I agree with that,' Claire says and sips her tea.

Laura mirrors her and sips from her cup as well. 'Oh, I nearly forgot, I've brought you a present. You can open it now or wait until Christmas Day, whatever.' Laura places a small box, wrapped in gold paper, in the centre of the table.

'Thank you,' Claire says automatically. She picks up the gift as if handling a bomb. It's unexpected and unwanted, like an explosive device. It hadn't occurred to her to bring a present. She's never had to buy a present for her mum before. Why start now? And now Laura decides to give her a present. After Christmas after Christmas and birthday after birthday went by with nothing, absolutely nothing. A gift would have meant more when she was a child. Now it feels dirty and wrong. A trinket encased in deceit, lies, and regret. There is no way she's going to open this up in front of her. Claire slides the present into her bag.

'Actually, what are you doing for Christmas?' Laura asks.

'I'm not sure.' Claire holds her breath. Is Laura about to invite her? Surely not. *Her daughters, my sisters, aren't even speaking to her at the moment.* It would be too much. She wouldn't invite Claire into their home yet. 'Dad and I would usually keep it pretty low key. Present opening, monopoly, dinner, telly. That sort of thing.'

'Your first Christmas without him.'

'No, that was last year, like a week after his death,' Claire shoots back, not missing a beat. She has no idea. No fucking idea. *If I can handle being alone last Christmas, I can handle being alone this Christmas.* 'I might go to my friend's house.'

Saskia has invited her round to her parents' house.

Well, practically begged her.

Claire hasn't yet decided if she's going. She should probably let Saskia know what she's doing once she knows. Christmas at the Jansens would be totally over the top and very different to what she's used to, which might actually be perfect. Finn and Cheryl – Saskia's parents – are so kind and lovely, and the champagne will be flowing. And her brother, Aart, will most likely be there and fun follows him wherever he goes. The more Claire thinks about it, the more she wants to go. She'll text Saskia later.

'Sorry. I'm an idiot.' Laura wells up.

Claire doesn't correct her. 'What are you doing for Christmas?' Keep it moving.

'Just me, Dave, and the girls this year.'

The girls. Will I ever be included in the girls?

'They've been through a lot recently, so we thought we should have a quiet...' Laura trails off, realising who she's speaking to.

Yeah, your girls have been through a lot. Make sure you protect them and look after them. 'Lovely,' Claire says quietly. Laura hasn't been thinking about her. That's becoming apparent. The norm is not thinking about her. Taking Claire into consideration seems completely foreign to Laura, which means inconsideration keeps falling from her mouth.

'Sorry, again. God, I'm awkward. It's like I've lost all social skills.' Laura takes a big gulp of tea.

'It's a weird situation. Made weirder by you having a family and me having no one.' Claire plunges the figurative knife into her mother's heart. She deserves it for the years of neglect and for clumsiness and carelessness now.

Laura's face is terrified and forlorn.

I need to get my anger under control. There's no use in emotionally beating her up. I've pined for a mum and now she's here. 'I won't say anything like that again. I'll be nice, otherwise there's no point in being here.'

'I deserved it. But yes, let's move on.' They both finish their teas. Laura orders a couple more. 'Is that okay? Can you stay for a bit longer?' Laura looks at Claire out of the corner of her eye and then at the floor.

'Yes, let's chat more.' Claire smiles.

Laura's face lights up. 'I'd like that.' She sweeps her hair away from her face and asks, 'So what's your job? What are your interests?'

'Well, I've been working as a trainee journalist at a local paper for a few months. That's what I did at uni: Journalism. Before that, I was in admin. I lived in a village in the Peak District for a while after Dad died,' Claire swallows, saying those words is still a struggle. 'But it's great being back in London again.'

'You moved away on your own? Do you have family… friends there?'

'No. I didn't know anyone, but I made friends.' Sebastian's crystal blue eyes spring to mind and Hazel giving her 80th birthday banner the finger. 'I just wanted to get away and be alone, which didn't quite work out as planned, but moving away definitely helped.'

'Sorry, Claire. I should have come to see you sooner. It had just been so long, it became harder and harder. I should have come to you as soon as I heard about your dad. I'll try my best to make it up to you.'

There's so much, Laura can't possibly make it all up, but she wants to try. Claire's eyes fill up and she surveys the ceiling to try to stop them from spilling. It's dusty and could do with a clean. *Mum is here, and she wants to work on us and be in my life.* Claire stops looking at the dirt and aims a smile at Laura and the tears drop, anyway. Laura is crying too.

Claire dabs under her eyes, trying to mop up any smudged black mascara. 'So, tell me, what's your job and what do you do with your time?'

'I was a school secretary for years. I got made redundant a while back. I'm now a TV extra and cleaning lady and I also make pottery, which I sometimes sell.'

Claire tries to take it all in. Her mum is an extra on telly? She might have seen her in a programme and not known it. The thought sends a shiver down Claire's spine. 'You're busy,' she finally says.

'Yes, I like to keep busy. The telly stuff, the cleaning, and pottery is all part-time though. I'm not too far from retirement. I want to start slowing down.' Laura looks deep in thought before taking a sip of the new cup of tea, which the ponytailed waiter left a few minutes ago.

'Being an extra must be interesting.'

'Yes, you get to work on all sorts of different things. I've been drinking – well, pretend drinking – in The Queen Vic in *Eastenders*. I've been in the background loads in *Hollyoaks*.'

In her mind, Claire's back at Sebastian's farm, engrossed in *Hollyoaks* with Robert, nibbling bits of chicken salad. Had she watched her mum, sat there with Sebastian's dad in the summer? 'I watch *Hollyoaks*.'

'It's a small world.'

'When you had more babies – daughters – and you were coping and doing well, why didn't you look me up then?' There's no point in beating around the bush.

'I thought about it and almost did many times. But the reports I was getting back said you seemed happy with your dad. I didn't want to turn your world upside down. I'd made my choice, and I thought I should stick to it. I regret it now. I should have given you the choice. You could have turned me away if you didn't want me around. The thought of that scared me as well, though. You might have rejected me and you would be fully within your rights to do just that, then and now. It's a mess. There's no excuse. I should have been there, and I wasn't and I'm truly sorry.'

'I hear what you're saying. Thank you. Hopefully, we can be in each other's lives now. Like, properly.' *I want to meet my sisters. I even want to meet Dave.*

'That's what I want too.' Laura reaches for Claire's hand, but hesitates and withdraws.

Claire slides her tongue across the front of her teeth, and without raising her eyes from the table, reaches for her mum's hand and clings on once she has it.

Laura squeezes Claire's hand.

'And you and Dad never spoke again. You had no contact since you left?'

Laura removes her hand from Claire's. 'No, well… we spoke on the phone a couple of times around when we got divorced. He suggested I visit you. He wanted me to be in your life, but I was deep into thinking you would be better off without me at that point.' Laura wipes her hands up and down her trousers. 'Shall we order some food? I haven't eaten, and I only had a small lunch.'

Claire glances at her watch: 6.35pm. 'Yeah, I haven't eaten for ages either. Let's eat and then I need to get going.' *It's going okay, let's not push our luck.* A lump forms in Claire's throat. Dad tried to get Mum to see her. *God, I wish he was here now.*

Laura nods and they both read their posh evening menus.

The waiter returns to the table and looks expectantly at the two women. 'Are we ready, ladies?' His hands held behind his back.

How do they remember orders without writing them down? It baffles Claire. 'After you,' Claire says, gesturing to Laura.

'No, after you,' is her reply.

'I insist…'

Both women frown, glance at their menus again, and at the same time say, 'Spaghetti bolognese, please.' They laugh, an almost identical laugh, low and loud. *We've got the same laugh.*

'Is that everything?' the waiter asks.

'Yes, but are there any mushrooms in the spaghetti bolognese? I'm allergic to them,' Claire says.

'I'll check.' He scuttles away.

'You've got food allergies?' Laura asks.

'No, I just hate mushrooms.'

'Me too,' Laura whispers, her blue yet grey eyes sparkling.

'Really? Maybe it's genetic.' Claire giggles. She's starting to loosen up and have fun.

'I've never thought to check if they're in spag bol, though.'

'Sometimes they're in, sometimes they're not. Always best to check if they've sneaked in.' Claire winks and gives her mum a little grin.

'Thanks for the tip.'

#

They eat their meals – without mushrooms – and chat about lighter things such as Claire's work, what sports they like, how best to manage curly hair, and celebrity gossip from TV sets Laura has been on. It's pleasant, and the conversation has a flow to it. There are more difficult questions to ask, but they can be asked another time. Outside the café, they agree to meet again in the New Year. They both want to meet regularly but at the same time want to take things slow. Laura hugs Claire goodbye. It's quick and fleeting, a brief leaving cuddle, but it stuns Claire and as she treads away, she feels in a daze.

Her mum just hugged her.

She just had a nice time with her mum.

As she makes her way home, Claire re-runs the evening like a film in her head, analysing every word, while she floats through the streets of London.

Chapter Thirty-Two

Four months later…

Friday 18th April 2008

'Mum… Hazel has had a fall,' Andrew stumbles over his words. He sounds choked up.

Claire grips the phone tighter and walks away from her desk. She pushes the door of the Ladies toilets, hard. 'What? What happened?' She holds onto the side of the sink and takes in her reflection; all the colour has drained from her face.

'She was doing some gardening… and I think she tripped on the back step as she was coming back into the house. She's okay. She called me, and I called an ambulance. They took her to hospital to be on the safe side. I can't believe she didn't break anything. You should see the bruises, though.'

Claire takes a deep breath. *She's fine, she's fine.* Her heart is racing, and her hands are clammy. It's taking all her strength not to run straight to the train station. 'Is she home now?'

'Yes, she's gone for a lie down. She asked me to call you and let you know.'

'Thank you. I'm so glad she's okay,' Claire's voice wobbles and tears threaten to fall.

'Claire, she is. I'm not just saying it. Are you still planning on visiting tomorrow?'

'Why? Do you think I should come up tonight?'

Andrew chuckles. 'No, there's no need to rush up, just come

up for your normal Saturday visit.'

Claire chews on the inside of her bottom lip. 'Okay, I feel like I should come today.'

'There's really no need. She's resting now and then Sarah and Elizabeth are coming later.'

Oh yeah, Hazel's daughters. Hazel has people. 'Okay, it does sound like tomorrow is best. Give her my love.'

'I will. You're a good friend,' Andrew says before hanging up.

Claire stares at her open mobile, the kind words lingering in her ear, twirling and tickling, as she tries to comprehend them. Andrew just gave her a compliment? He must be in shock. She slowly closes her flip phone and rests it on her mouth as her fingers tap on the sink. How is she going to work the rest of the afternoon now?

'Claire?' Katie pops her head in the door. 'Steve wants a word.' Katie turns to leave, then stops herself. 'Are you okay?'

'Yeah, fine. A friend had to be rushed to hospital, but she's fine. I'm going to see her tomorrow.' Claire frowns. 'What does Steve want?'

'Oh no, I hope your friend is okay, and I have no idea.' Katie lifts up both of her arms in an overemphasised shrug before scooting off back to her desk.

Claire walks across the open plan office towards Steve's desk.

'Ahh,' he says when he sees Claire. 'Let's grab one of the meeting rooms.' He strides off, and she follows.

It must be serious for us to need privacy. I can't take any more bad news.

Steve sits down and motions for Claire to sit in the chair across from him. He's clutching onto some papers. 'You've been doing really well, and as you've been here roughly six months, I thought we should have a catch up.'

Claire nods and smiles. *Roughly six months? Typical Steve, he doesn't actually know how long I've been here.* Has it really been almost half a year, though? Wow, that's gone fast.

'I would like to offer you a full-time journalist position. I know you're due to be a trainee for a year, but I think you're ready.'

Claire's mouth drops open before a smile spreads across her face. She's no longer going to be a trainee? 'Wow, that's brilliant, thank you.'

'You deserve it. Of course, it's more money.' He shuffles his papers. 'Don't get too excited. I'll send the details over to you. We're just finalising everything.'

Claire thanks Steve, and then once again heads in the direction of the toilets. Once inside a cubicle, she cries, letting all the emotion out. It's all too much, too much news. Bad followed by good.

#

As soon as Claire sees the "BALISTON" signs from the taxi window, her jaw loosens. She'd been clenching and hadn't realised now her teeth hurt. She ignores the pain. She's here. Claire rests her forehead on the glass, enjoying the vibrations, as she takes in the village. The pub, the shop, and the chippy. The place looks different. She's never been here in April, having moved up in May last year. Almost a year since she ran away to Derbyshire, it feels like a lifetime ago. Pink blossom lines the main road, squawking geese fly overhead, and a peloton of cyclists wizz by, deep voices bellowing in conversation.

Claire's eyes widen as she notes the state of Hazel's tiny front garden. It's not a mess by any stretch of the imagination, but it's also not up to her usual standards. The grass is longer than usual and some fallen leaves are in the borders. It's the first indication that all is not well with Hazel. Well, she's not going to be gardening after having a fall. Gardening got her into this sorry mess. Maybe she's been struggling more than she's let on before this? Claire starts removing brown leaves from the soil and is bent over when someone opens the front door.

'Hello?' a woman's voice questions.

'Hi,' Claire says as she straightens up. It's Hazel's daughter, Elizabeth, answering the door.

'Claire! Mum will be pleased that you're here.'

'How is she doing?' Claire asks as she steps inside.

'She's healing well from a physical point of view, but she's not coping very well with keeping still and resting.' Elizabeth tenses her neck as she makes a face. 'Would you like a drink? Andrew's just boiled the kettle.'

'No, thanks. Is she in bed?'

'Yeah, go straight up if you like.'

Claire nods. She gradually makes her way up the stairs. As she ascends, Hazel and Jack over the years, travelling through time, smile at her. Claire desperately wants to see her friend, but now she's here and is about to, she's taking baby steps to her room. What will she look like? Andrew said she's just bruised, there's no broken bones or anything.

Her dad in the hospital bed wheedles its way into her mind. Claire tries to dismiss the thought. She wants to forget that image and only remember the happy, lovely memories. It's vivid, though. She can smell the hand sanitiser and the peach floor cleaner in his curtained room. The sound of the plastic runners as hospital staff opened and closed the material surrounding him is imprinted into her being. Claire imagines a black hole in her mind, empty and painless. She opens her eyes after a few seconds and knocks on Hazel's bedroom door.

'Hazel?' she says as she opens the wooden door.

'Claire, thank fucking god you're here, I'm so bastard bored.'

Claire laughs. She's never been so pleased to hear "fucking" and "bastard". She raises her eyebrows when she sees her elderly friend, and then quickly rearranges her expression. She absorbs what's in front of her. The woman lying in bed is her dear friend, and she looks well, considering. But there's no getting away from the fact that Hazel is in bed with black and green bruises down her arms. For the first time since Claire has known her, Hazel looks her age. She's wearing a pink nightie; her hair appears to have been brushed but not styled, and there isn't a scrap of makeup on her face except her lips are smothered in bright red lipstick.

'You look crazy wearing lipstick without any eye makeup,' Claire says as she perches on the edge of the bed.

'I know. I just needed to put something on to cheer myself up. I felt facially naked.' Hazel adjusts her pillows and sits more upright. 'The doctor said I need to rest and take time to heal, so now the kids have insisted on bed rest for a week, a week! Can you believe it?' Hazel throws her hands in the air and winces.

'Those bruises do look nasty.'

'Yeah, they're not fun,' Hazel says as she runs a hand over her left arm, which is particularly blackberry coloured.

'What were you doing?'

'Just gardening, no cartwheels, or anything.' Hazel fiddles with her hair and pats the tips, feeling for her Marilyn Monroe do which is decidedly pensioner at the moment. 'I misjudged the back step, that's all.'

'Easily done,' Claire says, while stroking the rose print on Hazel's bed spread.

'At least I haven't started my Silversmithing course yet. I'm still going to do it. You know, Andrew's talking about getting a carer in twice a week, on top of him helping out.' Hazel shakes her head and picks up a photo frame from her bedside table. It's a picture of her in hospital clutching a newborn baby. Her smile is wide and her eyes tired. The baby is screaming.

'Who's that?'

'Andrew.' Hazel puts the frame back in its place. 'Getting old is shit.'

'But a privilege.'

Hazel tips her head back before glaring at Claire. 'Well, you're annoying today.'

'No, you're annoyed at the idea of having carers.'

'Fair assessment.' Hazel stops glaring and twists her head towards the window. The morning sunshine streams in and lights up her face. She closes her eyes to bask in the warmth. After a few seconds, she turns to Claire again. 'Tell me about you, I'd much rather hear about a twenty-five-year-old's life.'

'I'll be twenty-six next week. Anyway, I think your life is far more interesting. The most exciting thing that's happened is I'm no longer a trainee journalist. I'm a journalist,' as she says the words, a lump forms in Claire's throat, which surprises her. She can't quite believe what she's saying. *I hope he knows, I hope Dad knows.*

'Well done. I never doubted it.' Hazel pats Claire's hand.

Claire can't help but study the bruises on Hazel's arms.

'It looks worse than it feels,' the eighty-year-old says, while touching the largest black splodge.

'There's nothing wrong with accepting help. You taught me that. You can't do it all alone. You also taught me that.'

'Gosh, I really am very wise. I know. I know. Thank you.' Hazel straightens the duvet and fidgets against the pillows. 'Talking of not being alone. Have you seen your mum again?'

'Yeah, we've met five times now. It's okay. It just feels really strange. We're strangers. I was expecting to feel a closeness that just isn't there. I suppose we need to build it.' Claire shrugs.

The whole not-being-close-immediately thing is incredibly frustrating, Claire has wanted a mum her whole life, and now she's here, she's in her life, but she's not her mum, she's some woman. She wishes she could click her fingers and instantly have a proper mother-daughter relationship. Claire knows they just need to keep seeing each other and it will grow. They'll be in each other's lives, and it will become real. In fact, the promotion will be something to talk about next time they see each other.

Laura talks about Dave a lot, which makes Claire feel uncomfortable, like she's betraying Dad. Each time they meet, it's at the same café near the cemetery, and each time Claire visits her dad's grave afterwards to tell him all about it. It's strangely soothing to have a one-way conversation with a slab of stone. When will they do something real? When will they really be in each other's lives? Go to each other's homes? Claire wants to take things slow while also wanting to rush, but their relationship can't be fast-tracked. She really hopes they get there.

Hazel is watching her. 'It will take time. You've got to get to know each other. And the sisters?'

'I've been messaging the older one, Ruby. I think we might all meet up, eventually. It seems to be going that way, anyway.'

'Now that is big news. That should have been the headline. Call yourself a journalist?!' Hazel tries to give Claire a playful nudge, but stops when moving her arms proves too painful.

'Alright, alright, cheeky. Shall we chill out for a bit and watch some crappy telly?' Claire suggests. The colour has drained from Hazel's face.

'Yeah, that sounds good. I don't think I'll be up to our walk today.'

'I figured as much,' Claire says. She scoots up next to Hazel and balances the spare pillows into an upright position before resting her back against them. Claire grabs the remote and flicks through the channels. 'Ahh, perfect.' *The Real Housewives of Orange County* blares out of Hazel's small black box of a TV. One of the housewives, Vicki, is shouting about her love tank not being full.

'What is this rhubarb?' Hazel asks.

'Have you not seen it? It's *The Real Housewives of Orange County*. It's a reality show about a group of rich women. It's a window into their lives. They meet up, go for lunch, go shopping, and go on holiday together and get drunk and argue, basically. It's brilliant.'

Hazel chuckles, but her eyes are already glued to the screen. Claire smiles to herself, pleased that the reality-drama-crap is pulling her in. She just knew Hazel would like it. There's just enough story to keep you interested, but it's not too taxing.

The episode finishes, there's a few minutes of adverts, and then another one starts.

'Yes,' Claire whispers, but Hazel's fallen asleep. Claire tiptoes over to the telly and switches it off before leaving the room.

Andrew is downstairs, washing the dishes. He's humming to himself, but stops and turns round when Claire enters the kitchen. The water in the sink is really bubbly, and he's covered up to his elbows.

'Looks like you're having fun.'

'Well, yeah, as much fun as you can have washing up. Is she okay?'

'Yes, we were watching some TV, and she fell asleep.'

'Oh good, she needs some more rest.' Andrew dries his hands on a tea towel. 'Did she mention about the carers?'

'Yes,' Claire says gently.

'I think it might be time. She gave me an earful though.'

'I think she's coming round to the idea. She's not impressed, but I think she will accept the help, eventually. She's just got to get her head round it.'

Andrew nods. 'I promised my dad I would look after her. It's a big responsibility, knowing what's for the best.'

'You're here and you're trying. That's all you can do.'

'Thanks.' Andrew blushes and starts drying a plate with the tea towel.

'I think I'm going to head out for a walk. I'll be back in a bit. Hopefully, she'll be awake later, before I go home.'

Outside Hazel's green front door, Claire takes a deep breath of country air, ready to enjoy the freshness, but it smells like shit. 'Typical,' she says under her breath before giggling.

Chapter Thirty-Three

While coughing on the cow-shitty farm smell, Claire meanders through the village towards the woods. She's missing her usual Saturday afternoon walking companion. It feels odd, but she knows Hazel will be back to it soon. It's a bright yet chilly April day. Claire zips up her coat and gets her sunglasses out of her handbag. Wearing the shades in the cool sunshine makes her feel like somewhat of a celebrity and her stroll takes on something of a swagger until she passes Simon's house. He's at the front window of his bungalow, sitting in his lounge when he spots Claire and waves. Simon is genuinely pleased to see her, but then his smile quickly disappears and a darkness crosses his face. He's looking at something. Claire follows his line of sight. Simon is staring at his replacement gnome. Shit, his first thought when he sees her is to protect the gnome! Claire straightens her glasses, gives him a little wave, and scuttles away, any trace of swagger gone.

She takes a slight detour, so she can have a nosy at her former cottage. As she passes by, she tries to subtly take in her old home. Of course, it's only been months, and it's basically the same. Apart from there are flowers and ornaments in the window. Someone else is living there. Claire misses the place and Baliston, but it feels right to be back in London. Visiting Baliston, every fortnight, is usually a highlight, and it feels strange that this time it isn't. The colour of next door's privet hedge reminds her of Hazel's dark green bruises. A strimmer is buzzing nearby, like a huge bee invading her mind. Claire quickens her step and heads for the woods. As soon as she's at the edge of the trees, she slows down.

Claire enters the sea of trunks and takes a moment. She stands still and tips her head up to the sky, listening to the birds tweeting and the leaves swishing. There's such a calming atmosphere here, which is like no other place. This is what she misses in her day to day life. She wishes she could bottle this feeling and take it home with her. Then she shakes her head at the thought. She would still need to come back to Baliston. Hazel is here. She's her Saturday afternoon partner.

They had taken to telling stories about their former Saturday partners. During their last walk, Hazel had told her about how Jack would always do the kids' bedtime stories. She would be at home with them all day, and by the time he came home from work, she'd be strung out, after caring for four little ones on her own and her husband knew this. Despite he himself having had a busy day at work, he would take over. Jack was keen to see the children. He'd missed them all day and his favourite thing was to read to them before they went to sleep. Or on occasion, he would make up stories from his head. He'd ask each child what they would like to be in the story and they would each choose something, an item, an idea or even an emotion, and he would incorporate it into his made-up story. Hazel would hear parts and be amazed at his imagination and enthusiasm. Sometimes she would sneak a peek and he would have all four children's attention, listening intently to the tales he would come up with. Sometimes Jack would get too carried away. He would make the stories too scary or too exciting then the kids couldn't sleep, and Hazel would have to settle them down, which would irritate her, but she still appreciated the effort he made when he walked through the door.

Last time, Claire spoke about her dad's stammer. He grappled with it as a child, as he grew up, it faded away. However, at times of stress or high emotion, it would reappear, which infuriated him. Claire was thankful for the stammer, though. It was like a sounding alarm to indicate to her that she needed to calm down, or she needed to stop shouting or that her dad needed help. As a child, she found it immensely helpful. Dad tripping over his words was a signal for her. It let her know when he was struggling, without it she probably wouldn't have known. This was at its most useful when she was a teenager, when they had constant arguments about what she was allowed to do. Dad would be fine for weeks, but she would push it too far, upping his stress levels too much and his broken speech would appear. She would then know she needed to back off a bit. Maybe it's something she can ask Laura about; does she remember his stammer too? Were they together when it started to improve? Claire makes a mental note to add it to her physical list of questions for her mum. There's so much to find out, so much time to catch up on. Claire often thinks about the little things from the past and what her mum's take is on them.

Claire beams as she returns to thinking about her dad and Jack, a man she never met, but feels like she knows through Hazel's stories. The ground is wet from rain over the last couple of days, and she starts submerging and sliding. Claire sighs as the squelchy mud sinks into her white trainers. She didn't think to wear more suitable shoes, usually when she's with Hazel, they don't venture this far or this much off-road. Claire grabs a dock leaf and uses it as a cloth to wipe off the mud, but it smears and spreads the brown stink across the leather.

She hears footsteps behind her. 'Sorry,' she mumbles as she steps aside into the grass, letting the person walk past her on the path, making sure she's out of the way.

'You would have been better off in wellies,' says a familiar voice.

Claire peers up to see Sebastian scratching his head and smiling down at her.

Shit! She stands up straight and drops the dock leaf.

Her heart is pounding. *What the fuck is he doing here?* 'Hello,' is all she manages to say.

He's wearing a green jacket and blue jeans with wellies. His hair is shorter, but still satisfyingly floppy and able to fall into his eyes. *His eyes! Are they bluer?* Her gaze automatically shifts to his upper arms, but the stupid jacket is hiding them.

They stand a metre apart, taking each other in. 'You look like you've seen a ghost,' Sebastian says. A chocolate Lab then comes bounding towards them. It's wet and covered in mud and is charging right for them.

'Argh,' Claire says as she jumps backwards. 'Why don't people keep dogs on leads?' She shakes her head.

Sebastian delves into his back pocket, pulls out a lead, and clips it onto the dog's collar. The animal is panting manically, and its tail is causing a breeze. 'This is Bailey.' Sebastian beams.

'Sorry, I didn't realise he was yours.' Claire gingerly pats Bailey's head while trying not to touch patches of mud and saliva.

'He's my dad's. He got him about a month ago. Last thing he needs really, he's got enough to do, but this woman he knows said she couldn't look after him anymore and was going to take him to the RSPCA. So, dad said he would have him. Bailey loves all the space on the farm. Don't you, boy?' Sebastian changes his voice to soft and singsongy when he speaks to the dog, similar to how people talk to babies.

Claire holds onto a snigger, which is fighting to burst out. It's kinda cute but also kinda funny. She flicks her hair out from behind her ear and tries to remember if she put on eyeshadow this morning. 'It's good to see you,' she says quietly.

'You too. I've been thinking about you.'

Claire twitches, her eyes searching his. 'Really?'

'Yeah, especially since we met up for lunch. That messed with my head.' Sebastian runs a hand through his hair and then rubs the end of his nose.

'Mmm,' Claire doesn't know what to say. 'How's Cassandra?' *He shouldn't be saying he's been thinking about me if he's got a girlfriend.*

'Cassandra?' Confusion floods his face. 'Oh yeah, she answered the phone when you rang, didn't she? Yeah, we were seeing each other for a bit, nothing serious.'

'She's not your girlfriend?'

'No, never was.' Sebastian shakes his head. 'How's Chris?'

Now, it's Claire's turn to be confused. 'Oh yeah, I told you about our date, didn't I? We just had that one date. We're mates.'

'So, we're both single, both living in London, and both currently standing in the woods in Baliston.' Sebastian looks Claire straight in the eye. 'I've missed you.'

'You dumped me.'

Bailey tugs on his lead, and Sebastian lets him off again. The dog charges off, disappearing between the trees. 'I know, we just seemed to get so serious so quickly... it was a bit much... and then I was heading back—' Sebastian shrugs his shoulders.

'Afraid of commitment? How original.' Claire puts her hair back behind her ears and folds her arms. She can feel a headache approaching.

'I suppose. I explained over lunch. It was just all so full on, with my dad and your...' Sebastian's voice trails off.

'Mmm, grief can be inconvenient.' *Get lost.*

'Don't start getting nasty, you don't mean that. I get it, I hurt you. I'm sorry.' Sebastian reaches out for Claire, stroking his hand down her arm.

Fuck, why did he have to touch me? She finds her anger melting away, dissipating into the grass. Claire knows she's mad because she's hurt, and despite herself, she still cares. The love that was building inside her for this man never went. It's still there and one touch from him and it's flowing again. 'Thank you,' is all she says. The wind blows her hair across her face, and he brushes it out of her eyes, the back of his hand stroking down the side of her cheek. 'My mum got in touch,' Claire blurts out, then frowns. He's the first person she thought of when her mum turned up. After all, he was adamant that she should try to find her. Sebastian popped into her head as soon as Saskia passed her that piece of paper with her mum's number on it. In that moment, she wanted to ask his opinion. She wanted to talk it through with him and have his help in making a decision. 'Sorry, that was a little random.'

'Don't apologise. Have you met up with her?'

'Yeah. It's awkward.'

'You should definitely keep working on your...' Sebastian stops himself and then smiles. 'I'm not going to put my foot in it again. I'm saying nothing!' He puts his hands up in surrender.

Claire laughs. 'No, I want to hear what you've got to say.'

'I was just going to say you should definitely keep working on your relationship. Keep putting the effort in. It will be worth it.' Sebastian strokes and squeezes her arm again.

Claire nods and focuses in on his lips. She coughs and says, 'Why are you here, anyway?'

'Um, my dad lives here. I'm visiting him.' Sebastian laughs. 'What about you?'

'Hazel. She had a fall.'

'Yes, I heard. How is she?'

Claire chuckles, of course Sebastian already knows. Good old Baliston. 'She's bruised but okay.' She tries to focus on the conversation, but she's struggling. He's standing close to her. He stepped in to stroke her arm and move her hair and he hasn't stepped back. He smells outdoorsy, with a hint of fresh aftershave. She wants to feel those arms around her again.

'I'm glad she's okay,' Sebastian says, briefly meeting her eye. 'I was hoping I'd see you,' his voice is small, almost a gruff whisper, 'I was either going to visit this weekend or next. Then Dad mentioned Hazel's accident on the phone. I thought you might be here. So, decision made.' He shrugs his shoulders; his expression is sheepish. 'I was falling for you, you know. I just got scared.' Sebastian is finding the ground very interesting while muttering these potentially life-altering words.

He was falling for her?

Oh my god, what have they been messing about at?

They both feel the same?

They both feel the same.

She takes his head in her hands, gazes into his gorgeous eyes, and then reaches her lips to his. His mouth is soft and his stubble spiky. They explore each other, enjoying their tongues being back inside each other. It's a kiss to end all kisses. The want is clear. They pull away, their breathing heavier, and they both giggle.

'Well, that was unexpected.' Sebastian winks.

The comment takes her back to the picnic day. Now, she's sure they're both thinking about sex. She playfully shoves him. *He wants me to think about that day, the sneaky, sexy idiot.*

'You want to come back to the farm?'

Claire goes to say yes, then stops herself, hesitating. She wants him, my god she wants him, but can she do this again, go with the flow, thinking he's into her, just for him to drop her and run away? She's not sure.

'Claire?' Sebastian steps back and tries to catch her eye, but she's studying some sticks on the ground. 'Claire?' He gently lifts up her chin, so their eyes connect. 'I love you. I knew it then and I know it now. I just wasn't ready. There was too much going on. It's scary letting someone in and getting close. It means you can get hurt. I didn't know what to do with all these feelings. I've never felt like this before,' Sebastian babbles, held in emotions suddenly spilling out. 'I was stupid ending things. I really have missed you. I really want to be with you. I'm realising love is a risk but a risk worth taking for the right person.'

Claire searches his blue eyes with her brown. He means it. She can feel it. She can see it. He's sorted his head out since last summer. 'I love you too.'

'You want to come back to the farm?'

'Oh, yes.'

Epilogue

Claire nestles in, finding the perfect nook between Sebastian's chest and shoulder to cradle her face. She watches his chest rise and fall as he continues to sleep. She's been awake for ages, her mind too busy to rest, but Sebastian's definitely not having any problems with getting some shut eye.

He's been staying at her flat more and more over the last few months, leaving a toothbrush in the bathroom, clothes in the wardrobe, and his smelly gym trainers near the front door. For a man who was scared of commitment and being vulnerable, this time round, he's fully committed. There's no messing about, no games, and Claire loves it. She loves him.

She strokes his freckly, stubbly face and kisses his cheek. 'We've got to get up soon. It's nearly 9 o'clock,' she whispers.

'Hmm,' he says as he stretches, which ruins Claire's carefully curated resting place.

'I'm going to have a shower,' she tells him before leaving the bed.

Claire stands facing the falling water and lets it hit her straight in the face. Her eyes squeezed shut while she runs her fingers through her hair. She opens her mouth, letting the water pool around her teeth before dribbling it out. Claire then turns around, so the force hits her shoulders, giving her a gentle massage, while she mentally prepares for the day ahead and tries to wash away the worry and doubt.

'Morning, I'm certainly awake now,' Sebastian says as he pokes his head through the shower curtain. His gaze lingers on her body.

Claire leans out of the flow of the water, and they share a

deep, wet kiss.

'An exciting day?' Sebastian asks.

'Yeah, I just hope it goes okay.' Claire bites her lip as she starts shampooing her hair. She can hear the sound of Sebastian's electric shaver.

'I can hang around if you want?'

'No, it's fine. I want you to come and say hi, but that's it,' Claire shouts above the noise of the water.

It's the day she's been waiting for, the day she gets to meet her two half sisters, Ruby and Joanne. She's been messaging Ruby for a while and now it's agreed everyone's ready to meet. Claire goes over the plan in her head. They're meeting at Acton Park at 11 o'clock. They're going to have – hopefully – a lovely summery walk around and then, if things go well, they'll possibly get lunch together somewhere nearby.

It's so weird.

Ruby's at university in London, at Imperial College London. They could have rubbed shoulders in the street and never known their connection. Joanne is still living at home in Reading and is about to finish her A Levels. She's been struggling the most with having a secret older sister from her mum's previous marriage, which she didn't know had happened or existed. From what Claire can gather, they're both now speaking to Laura again, but there's been some massive arguments about the huge secrets their mother has held onto. It's been difficult for everyone involved. A huge adjustment in all their lives. Claire continues to meet Laura, usually short visits out for a drink or lunch. They're taking things slow, which feels right. She still can't quite bring herself to call her mum. It feels foreign and odd. Maybe she'll always just be Laura, and that's okay.

Claire puts on a short yellow dress covered in daisy patterns. The colourful friendship bracelet her mum gave her for Christmas dangles on her wrist, she tugs it into place and caresses the bumps and patterns, while deciding to leave her hair down and not wear any makeup. She grabs her sunglasses as they head out of the door. Sebastian is in his usual jeans and T-shirt combo, not really caring what he looks like. She admires him as they make their way down the communal stairs. The muscly arms, the hair falling into his blue eyes, and the freckles on his nose and cheeks, adding a hint of cuteness to the manly gorgeousness. He catches her staring at him, smiles and pulls her in for a kiss.

'Woah, I'm not sure I can kiss and walk down the stairs at the same time!' Claire laughs against his mouth.

'Was worth trying out.' He smiles.

They reach the agreed meeting place, the bench near the main entrance to the park, but instead of sitting on it to wait, they hover nearby, cuddling under an enormous mature tree. The trunk is wide and the branches long. It must have been in the background of many meetings, many conversations over hundreds of years. Claire shivers in the shade.

'You cold?' Sebastian asks.

'I don't think so.'

She then notices three women walking towards them. One of them is her mum. Claire frowns. She didn't know she was coming as well. She thought this was a sister meeting. The fizzing in her stomach becomes a sinking instead. No one told her about a change of plan. Things are improving between Claire and her mum. They're gradually getting to know each other and are becoming closer, which makes this unknown and uninformed change of plan even more surprising.

Another secret, another betrayal.

No, it's fine, plans can change. *It doesn't mean she set out to keep something from me.*

Claire tries her best to keep control of her emotions and to stop her automatic response of anger. She takes a deep breath and drags her eyes away from her mum and instead stares at the two young women with her. One is slim and petite, like Claire, and the other is really quite tall. She must be almost six-foot. They both have brown hair, but theirs is straight and tame, not curly and bouncy. They're both dressed casually. The tall one is wearing a denim mini-skirt with a pink top and the smaller one is wearing a green, strappy dress. Claire clears her throat.

'It's fine. They'll love you. You're easy to love,' Sebastian whispers, his arm around her waist giving her a comforting stroke.

'Fucking hell, I hope so,' Claire mumbles quietly as the trio reach them.

'Good morning.' Laura smiles at Claire and Sebastian and then takes a long drag on a cigarette.

Claire knows she smokes, but this is the first time she's actually seen it. It's odd, there's too much newness going on. Laura notices Claire frowning at her fag, coughs, and then throws it on the floor and stamps it out.

'Hi,' Claire says loudly. 'I'm Claire, and this is Sebastian.' She shivers again despite not being remotely cold.

'I'm Ruby and this is Joanne,' the tall one says quietly.

Everyone then stands looking at each other. No one speaks. It's excruciating.

Laura starts talking first, 'I just thought I would come along for the introductions, make sure you all found each other, but I'll now make myself scarce so you can get to know each other. I just want to say, it's so lovely to see all my children together. I never thought I would see the day.' Laura folds her lips together and adjusts her sunglasses, before dabbing a tissue behind them.

Oh, I get it now.

'Yes, I'll be going as well,' Sebastian says. 'Lovely to meet you,' he says to Ruby and Joanne. 'And you, of course, Laura. Do you fancy getting a cup of tea?'

What? He doesn't have to do that. Sebastian is going to go for a cup of tea with her long-lost mum, just them alone. Gosh, really? Claire's not sure about this plan. *Shall I insist there's no need?* No, that would be weird and kind of rude, and what he's offering to do is incredibly sweet. He's giving Claire, Ruby, and Joanne some space while making sure Laura is okay.

'It'll be fine,' Sebastian says to Claire softly, before kissing her on the forehead. 'Have fun, just be you. The nice you, not the angry version.' He smiles.

'Ha ha, what a comedian,' she says to him out of the side of her mouth.

'Laura, shall we?' Sebastian offers his arm.

'We shall,' Laura says and takes his arm.

Claire watches them leave in utter amazement. A sight she never thought she would see.

'So, is that THE Sebastian then, your boyfriend?' Joanne asks.

'It sure is,' Claire says, realising just how much she's talked about him in her messages, which Ruby must have shared with Joanne.

'He's a bit of alright!' Ruby says, a cheeky grin on her face.

They all look at each other, eyes wide, lips tightly pressed shut, and then at the same time, the three sisters burst out into fits of laughter. The awkwardness broken, sharing a moment of silliness, hopefully the first of many to come.

THE END

Acknowledgements

My thank yous go to... My husband, Rich who is so supportive and has listened to hours of writing chat/angst. You're ace.

Max and Jude – my two boys – who try their best to show an interest in Mum's writing, but don't really understand why every part of the process takes forever!

Mum, for always being there and introducing me to the world of women's fiction and romantic stories.

My mother-in-law, Ann for her encouragement and providing Nanna days out.

Alice, a great friend, who has been cheering me on, every step of the way.

Northodox Press for publishing my debut novel, *Claire Morris is Completely Lost*. Thank you James, Ted, and Amy for believing in me and the book.

Amanda, Isobel, and Craig at Retreat West. I wrote the first draft of *Claire Morris is Completely Lost* on Retreat West's 'The Novel Creator' course. It was an insightful and inspiring year.

My writing buddy on the course, Alison, for being an excellent sounding board.

The Romantic Novelists' Association's New Writers' Scheme for its helpful and encouraging feedback.

My GCSE English Teacher, Mr Taylor for igniting my passion for books. Shout out to Balby Carr School in Doncaster circa 1999!

SUBMISSIONS

CONTEMPORARY
CRIME & THRILLER
FANTASY
LGBTQ+
ROMANCE
YOUNG ADULT
SCI-FI & HORROR
HISTORICAL
LITERARY

SUBMISSIONS@NORTHODOX.CO.UK

NORTHODOX PRESS

SUBMISSIONS

Q *Northodox.co.uk*

CALLING ALL
NORTHERN AUTHORS!

DO YOU LIVE IN OR COME FROM NORTHERN ENGLAND?

DO YOU HAVE AN INTERESTING STORY TO TELL?

Email submissions@northodox.co.uk

☐ The first 3 chapters OR 5,000 words

☐ *1 page synopsis*

☐ *Author bio (tell us where you're based)*

* No non-fiction, poetry, or memoirs

SUBMISSIONS@NORTHODOX.CO.UK

NORTHODOX PRESS

FIND US ON SOCIAL MEDIA

www.northodox.co.uk

@northodoxpress

@northodoxpressofficial

@northodoxpress

@northodoxpress

www.northodox.co.uk

Printed in Great Britain
by Amazon

45192718R00172